WHITE CRANE

A Nathan Hawk Mystery

COPYRIGHT

© Douglas Watkinson 2021

The moral right of the author has been asserted

All rights reserved. No part of this publication may be reproduced, stored in a retrieval system, or transmitted in any form or by any means, without the prior permission in writing of the publisher.

www.douglaswatkinson.com

~ Other titles in the Nathan Hawk series ~

HAGGARD HAWK

EASY PREY

SCATTERED REMAINS

EVIL TURN

JERICHO ROAD

Dear Reader,

I was reluctant to get caught up in the search for Suyin Qu, a young Chinese woman, and I persuaded myself that it was because she didn't want to be found. Her prerogative. The real reason, and I'm ashamed to admit it, was that her disappearance didn't involve any blood and guts, so why would I be interested?

Then two men broke into my son Jaikie's house looking for Suyin and made the mistake of giving him a black eye, a gash down the inside of his cheek and a bruised face and ego. Nothing valuable was stolen, the place wasn't trashed and the only thing taken was a 150-year-old bonsai tree, which had been standing on the kitchen drainer.

The tree bugged me, but the crime was hardly one of the big three: murder, rape, kidnapping. It was small-scale breaking and entering, burglary and ABH, and the police were only passingly interested.

That all changed, however, when I stumbled across a body. The murder was brutal and callous, and the only person the police wanted to interview about it was Suyin Qu. And she was nowhere to be found…

Hawk

Before

Jaikie Hawk had always needed to be woken gently, especially at five in the morning. He stared up at the ceiling and wondered if the hammering on his front door had been real or the tail-end of a bad dream. Seconds later the hammer struck again, five blows in quick succession, this time accompanied by a female voice calling for the door to be opened. Normally he would have waited for Jodie to sigh and then slip on a dressing gown while he pretended to still be asleep. But Jodie wasn't there. She was in Edinburgh, defending a client.

He swung his legs round and reached for yesterday's clothes: jeans and a T-shirt. Jesus, they were knocking on the door again! He looked at his phone. 5.13. He groaned his way towards the landing.

From the stairs he could see life forms through the coloured glass in the front door, and only now did he question what the purpose of those beyond it might be. To warn of a fire in a neighbouring house? A gas explosion? Or had he misread a filming schedule and it was Delphine, his driver, in a panic?

"I'm coming, I'm coming!" he called.

He switched off the alarm, slid back the safety chain and the door was barged open from the other side. A woman in uniform held up an identity card that said something unreadable. The heads behind her ducked down as if forming a rugby scrum and their combined bodyweight propelled them into the hallway. Jaikie staggered backwards until he was flat against the wall. The hall was suddenly heaving with blue serge uniforms, handcuffs, radios and the smell of cheap deodorant.

"What the hell is…?"

"Try to keep calm, sir."

"Who are you?"

"Immigration, alright?" said one of the men, in a London accent.

"Does a Miss Suyin Qu live here?" a tall man in a turban asked.

"Why d'you want to…?"

"I asked you not to be aggressive, sir," the woman said.

"You asked me to be calm. I was. I'm not now. Christ, how many are you? Middle of the bloody night."

"Does a Miss Suyin Qu live here?"

Jaikie looked at her. The adrenalin surge had woken him and he was beginning to think coherently. He reached into his pocket and took out his mobile. Two of the intruders, a middle-aged Pakistani and a short, balding Caucasian, had gone through to the kitchen.

"Where are they going? Stop 'em. And you, put that down."

He was addressing the Londoner, who was flicking through mail on the hall table. Finding nothing that took his fancy, he replaced it. Jaikie homed in on the woman, who tried to turn away as he filmed her.

"Camera-shy," he said to his phone. "It's five-fifteen in the morning, Monday 7th September, and six immigration officers have just burst into my house looking for Suyin Qu."

"You know her then," the woman said. "Is she here?"

He swivelled round, adjusting the phone. "Another one is now searching the living room. Come out of there! They have not asked my permission. They have not shown me any kind of warrant."

"We don't need one, buddy," the Londoner said.

Jaikie turned back to the woman. "I take it you're in charge. What's your name?"

She flashed her ID badge again. It was no more readable now than it had been when they first entered.

The commotion had woken Suyin, who came down the stairs, pulling a silk dressing gown around herself. She was wearing glasses, which made her seem oddly fragile and older than her years. Her eyes were darting from face to face.

"Jaikie, what is this, please?"

"Miss, can you confirm your name for us?" asked the tall Indian.

His voice came from behind her and made her flinch. She turned to him.

"Your name?" he repeated.

"Suyin Qu."

"You have ID? A passport? Visa?"

"Both with Home Office," she said.

"Can we have a private word with you?"

They swarmed around her. Most of them, including the woman in charge, twice her size. The Indian tried to steer her away to the kitchen.

"Su, stay right where you are!" said Jaikie. "Geezer, step away from her. You are making a big mistake."

The woman snapped her fingers at him. "Address your remarks to me."

"You are making an even bigger one. Get these bastards out of her face. Miss Qu's lawyer is waiting for the Home Office to get off its arse and deal with her application."

"That application isn't on our system," said one of the men.

"Then it should be! You come in here mob-handed, and blame your system?"

The possibility of an administrative foul-up made the team leader pause. She turned away into a corner and prodded a number into her phone. Above her one-sided conversation, the middle-aged Pakistani recited more lines from the prepared script about the purpose of their visit, their rights under the law, Suyin's obligations to co-operate. He tried to smile as he spoke, but a gold incisor made it come across as a sneer. He finished with the inevitable, "We are just doing our job…"

"You think people don't know why you do it this early?" said Jaikie. "Because most are bollock naked and half asleep."

"Sir, there is nothing personal in this. If we find things in order, then we…"

"One girl against six of you? You're the ones out of order! I've just told you, she's applied."

The man smiled. "That does not mean she will be allowed to stay here. Is nice, this house. And big."

Jaikie frowned. "So?"

His smile became a laugh. "So it's nice. And big."

"Sir." The woman had finished her call. "Thank you for your help. Everything's fine."

"No, it isn't! Why didn't you check on your 'system' before you came here?"

"Calm down, sir."

Jaikie raised a fighting finger. "If one of you says that to me again…"

"Please don't threaten us."

Jaikie laughed and pretended to count the number of people he'd be ranged against if he tried to carry out any threat. At a summons from their boss they all returned from the rooms or alcoves they had drifted into. When assembled, the woman pointed to the front door and they began to leave.

"We're leaving, Suyin," said the Indian. "This is us going. Goodbye."

The Londoner hung back. "Could I have your autograph, Mr Hawk?"

As a rule Jaikie was delighted to be recognised, but not this morning, not by this particular fan. "You what?"

"Your autograph?"

The man was offering him a notepad and biro.

"No," said Jaikie. "But if you bend over, I'll ram that pen up your arse."

The man shrugged and followed his colleagues out of the house, closing the front door behind him. Jaikie went to it, opened it a few inches and slammed it as hard as he could, then slumped against it and allowed himself a few tears. Stanislavsky came to mind as he considered how to recall this moment if ever required to act out tears of anger. He took a few deep breaths.

Suyin had slumped down on the bottom stair, curling herself into as much of a ball as she could manage. Her head was bowed, her hands covering her face.

"Jaikie, why you think they come?"

"You tell me." She stared at him with a no-speak-English expression on her face. "Bastards! You apply for an extension, a week later they come knocking on your door?"

"We apply two months ago."

He laughed. "Okay, so they took their time. *Lazy* bastards. You want some coffee?"

"That nice coffee?"

"Come on, I'll make some."

-1-

I'm still not sure why things didn't work out between me and Laura Peterson, but the camel's-back moment occurred in a Waitrose car park. I've asked myself since if it was Waitrose's famously high prices that triggered my relapse, or if it was just another opportunity to have a go. Anyway, Laura was about to reverse into a space when a mock Range Rover swung into it ahead of her. I walked over to the car and banged on the roof. The driver got out, at which point I discovered he was twice my size and a good fifteen years younger.

"Problem?" he said.

I gestured back at Laura who was glaring at me as she approached. "My friend was signalling to go in here."

"Sorry, I didn't see."

He smiled at his wife, who was already climbing down from the passenger side. The world narrowed until all I could see was his head, just begging to be grabbed by the greying perm and brought down on the roof of his car.

"You stole our parking space," I said.

The man frowned in disbelief that such a thing bothered me. Laura, having recognised the signs, prodded me on the shoulder.

"Map, Map, Map," she said.

The Map she was referring to was an imaginary map of the world, which an old career criminal had given me just before he died. At a potential flashpoint, Roy Pullman would take it out of his pocket, unfold it with elaborate care and spread it on a nearby surface. He would then raise a finger and set it down on what he called 'a far more agreeable place'. For me that was usually where one of my children had gone to live – Nepal, New York, Hawaii. I hadn't heard from Fee and Ellie in weeks. None of us had heard from Con in six months.

The man in the 4 x 4 watched uncertainly as I spread The Map on the roof of his car, but when I raised my forefinger nothing happened. I screwed it up, tore it into eight non-existent pieces and scattered them. Then I hit the driver. It was like punching the wall in a padded cell. He grabbed me, turned me round and had me face down on the tarmac in five seconds.

It was shock as much as anything that deflected my attention away from him and towards Laura.

"Get back in the car, Nathan!" she said.

The padded cell gradually released his grip and looked at Laura, amazement on his features. "Does he often do this? I mean… it's a parking space."

A queue of cars had built up behind us and one or two drivers began honking. Laura took a step towards them and said in exasperation, "And I'd be awfully grateful if you lot would pipe down!"

They did. There is something about a person who doesn't lose their rag that commands immediate respect. Whenever I remember that, it's invariably too late. We abandoned the shopping trip and drove back to Beech Tree.

We didn't hold a post-mortem on the incident. There was no real need. And when she moved out of Beech Tree, back into Chestnut Cottage, I'm sure it provided our neighbours with hours of gossip. The doctor and the ex-copper splitting up? Many of them were still wondering why we'd got together in the first place.

One good thing came of us having been an item, however. My children gained another sympathetic ear to bend: a defender, an admirer, an unconditional care package. They blame me for what they call 'the breakup'. It wasn't a breakup, I insist, it was the end of an experiment that didn't work.

Six weeks and two days later, on the evening of the dawn raid on Jaikie's house, Laura phoned me. I'd nodded off over a biography of Ferdinand Magellan. Four hundred years ago, aged forty, the man had travelled to most of the places that were on my bucket list. His journey hadn't been without problems, and at the point where my chin fell onto my chest and the Kindle dropped to the floor his fleet of six ships had hit the doldrums in the mid-Atlantic.

"Nathan, are you up to speed with this early-morning raid on Jaikie's house?"

I winced and massaged my neck back to life. "This what?"

"The ten o'clock news has just trailed an interview with him. Turn it on and call me back afterwards."

I tried to turn on the television with the phone handset. It never works. The controls were hiding under the dog, the only member of my family who was pleased that Laura had left. Under her regime, Dogge had been banned from the sofa.

Whatever Jaikie had been up to wasn't top of the news. He was preceded by Hurricane Jago, which had flattened an island in the Caribbean. Then came the shooting of five men in a bar in Munich. Fair enough. But Jaikie would not have been pleased that a possible rise in UK interest rates was considered more newsworthy than him.

Early morning raid? Who by? By whom, Laura would have corrected. Police, narcotics, vice? Nah! The boy thought too much of himself to get into that sort of bind. His brother Con would have been a different matter. And as I briefly considered other possibilities, Jaikie appeared on screen. He didn't look as if he'd been raided. He gave the appearance of having just come off stage after a round of applause. Smart, smooth and pleased with himself.

His anger was forced. I could always tell with Jaikie. Peas in a pod. If our rage is genuine we don't look anyone in the eye. Although to be accurate, we do, of course: we just don't see them. A female interviewer was asking questions and Jaikie was rolling out well-rehearsed replies. Immigration Enforcement had raided his Chiswick home at five o'clock in the morning, he said with polite umbrage. They were looking for his and his wife's Chinese house guest, Suyin Qu, and no doubt would have carted her off to West Drayton immigration centre if he hadn't been there to stop them. He summed them up with the rule of three: they were abusive, intimidating and aggressive.

I was sure they hadn't been a model of good manners, but I also knew the account of their visit had gained brass knobs in the retelling. There was no mention of Jodie not having been in the house. There was no glimpse of Suyin herself. Just Jaikie with his actor's voice, which was slower than his day-to-day one. He once told me that when you think you're speaking too slowly, you're going at exactly the right speed. Your audience will be able to hear and appreciate what you're saying. The last person I tried it on was a traffic warden in Oxford. He was writing out a ticket for the Land Rover and listened intently, appreciating every word I said. Then he slapped the ticket on my windscreen. I digress…

Jaikie had nearly finished. He had been interviewed by *The Guardian* newspaper, he told us, and they were doing a full investigation into the bully boy tactics of Immigration and the allied shortcomings of Home Office visa policy. I doubted if that would be front-page news either. He smiled and thanked the interviewer, and the news turned to tomorrow's weather.

The phone rang almost immediately. It was Jodie's father, Martin Falconer, a local farmer and a longstanding friend.

"Did you see it, Nathan?" he asked, affronted.

"Yes, as a matter of fact…"

"Raiding their house at sparrow-fart, for God's sake! What are we going to do?"

I tried calming him down with a groan. "You sound like Laura. You both ask me questions assuming I've got the answers."

He chuckled. "Do you hear yourself? Any conversation I have with you these days, the first chance you get you mention Laura." I could sense him shaking his head wearily. "You should never have split up. You were perfect for each other."

"We haven't split up, Martin. We just live in different houses."

He went back to being affronted. "Anyway, what are we going to do?"

"Nothing. Jaikie handled it."

"How do you know?"

"Suyin is still at the house, the immigration officers cleared off and *The Guardian* has waded in."

His voice tensed up a little. "Is that good? I mean, have you read *The Guardian* lately?"

"Not since Laura left."

"There you go again!" he said and finished the call.

The phone rang a beat later.

"You were on the phone," said Laura, accusingly.

"Yes, I know…"

"What did you think? And what are we going to do about it?"

I laughed. "You sound like Martin Falconer."

"I beg your pardon?"

"Laura, Jaikie's a big boy. He would have asked for my help if he'd needed it."

"I think that's rather casual of you."

I took a deep breath. "I'll phone him tomorrow."

"Good." She relaxed a little. "How are you?"

"Great," I said.

She paused. "Nathan, I want to put something to you. And I'm about to use a word that I know you loathe. Have you ever considered one of the talking therapies?"

"That's two words."

"I have a friend who's a counsellor…"

"Three."

"Oh, do stop being smart and listen. Her name is Drusilla Ford and she helped me after my house was vandalised. I'm sure she could make a few suggestions about the… anger thing. Shall I text you her number?"

"Goodnight."

"Is that yes or no?"

"It's goodnight."

A few moments later my phone pinged with a text giving me Drusilla Ford's contact details.

As I returned from a long walk with Dogge, it struck me that Beech Tree Cottage was looking pretty sorry for itself. When I bought the place, the thatch had just been renewed and held on to its shredded-wheat appearance for two years thereafter. Then it started to mellow, which is to say it turned grey and developed patches of moss rooted in the straw. The jackdaws had started picking at the ridge and the top line was becoming ragged. The straw *commedia dell'arte* masks, happy and sad, had lost their mouths and eyebrows to high winds, leaving them blank-faced. The outside walls had been hammered by the weather and a crack had opened up in the rendering on the south side. It was a result of the wychert still settling, even after 350 years, a local builder told me. He then waited for me to ask for a quote to do whatever was needed. For all I know he's still waiting.

Laura's bike was propped against the massive tree that gives the house its name, and as I approached she appeared round the side, garden gloves on her hands and carrying a pair of secateurs.

"Those roses should've been deadheaded two months ago," she said, reproachfully. "I did mention it."

"Often."

"Any chance you're about to make coffee? I'd have made some earlier but the spare key isn't under the birdbath."

"Jenny's probably got it."

Jenny Tindall is a friend in the village. I refuse to call her a cleaner, or rather my father's voice in my head won't allow it. People who don't clean their own houses should be shot, was his extreme view. Not that he ever did any cleaning, and my mother wasn't exactly house-proud, either. Anyway, Jenny pops in once a week to 'straighten the place up'.

Laura wandered over to her bike and took a folded newspaper from the front basket.

"*The Guardian*," she said.

"Oh, good," I muttered.

***

When the brewing coffee gave its final hiss I nodded at *The Guardian*. "So?"

She opened it at the centre pages and spread it flat on the table. On one side of the two-page article was a large photo of Jaikie and Suyin, both gazing past the camera in a south-easterly direction as if waiting for the future to arrive. I recognised my son, of course, but every time I see a photo of him I expect a reluctant schoolboy to be scowling back at me with rebellion in his eyes. Instead there's a man twice that age, good-looking to the point of envy.

The photo of Suyin was also interesting, but for different reasons. She was beautiful, no doubt about that, but in this photo she was leaning into Jaikie, almost trying to tuck herself behind him. I would have said she didn't want to be there.

Laura sighed. "I'm not sure it's a very effective piece."

"Is that because it doesn't praise Mr Wonderful for being handsome, courageous and a brilliant actor?"

She smiled. "Silly. Yes, they criticise Immigration and the Home Office, in fact every Tom, Dick and Harry involved, but you come away asking if it'll do any good."

I sat down beside her at the table and we touched shoulders. I shifted away a little.

"What did you want the article to say? That we shouldn't question anyone who might be here illegally?"

"I know we shouldn't haul them out of bed at five in the morning."

"I used to do it all the time."

"Yes, to catch murderers and rapists, not mere visa dodgers." She turned back to the photo. "Beautiful girl. Not quite as Chinese as most Chinese people. That'll be the Russian in her, I suppose."

She pointed to a paragraph about Suyin's heritage.

"Chinese? Part Russian?" I said. "Fate sure threw the book at her. You sure there's no North Korean in there as well?"

She smiled. "Somewhere that's bound to be a racist remark. Anyway, what are you going to do about it?"

I shrugged. "The answer is still nothing."

Laura stayed at Beech Tree for the rest of the day, deadheading everything in sight. I made dinner for us, occasionally glancing over my shoulder to fend off any criticism, not that much can go wrong with grilled salmon.

As I put the meal on the table she took an open bottle of white from the fridge and filled two glasses. After dinner we watched an old film, one that Laura had seen only once before. I think I'd seen it three times, and all but sang along with it. Then we went to bed.

***

My phone rang and woke us both.

"Jaikie, Jaikie, hallo mate," I managed to say.

"Dad, I don't want you to worry…"

Tell someone you don't want them to worry and the first thing they do is worry. I struggled to sit up in bed.

"What's happened? It's seven o'clock."

"The house was broken into last night."

"Hold on, hold on." I pressed speaker so that Laura could hear. "Your house?"

"Of course my house. Two blokes. I took 'em on and, well, the face is a bit swollen, lip's cut and…"

Laura rocked herself out of bed, a slave to the Hippocratic oath and any medical emergency that presented itself.

"I must see him!" she said.

"Dad, is that Laura? I thought you two had decided to call it a day."

"Jaikie."

"Sorry, none of my business who you sleep…"

"You're on speaker."

"Oh, hi, Laura!"

"You called the police?" I asked.

"They were a bit hesitant at first, till I told them who I was."

Even at moments of crisis his sense of his own importance was breathtaking. It used to be endearing. As he passed thirty it became ever so slightly obnoxious, but still made me smile.

"And once they learned who you were, they came running?"

"Not exactly, and they did bugger all once they got here. Poked around a bit, but…"

"Jaikie, I'll drive in. Give me an hour."

"I hoped you'd say that, Dad. See yer."

I got out of bed and the blood rushed to my head, or drained away from it… whatever it does when you move too quickly. I spent the next five minutes convincing Laura not to drive into London with me, that any damage to Jaikie will have been superficial. In the end I reminded her that it was Wednesday, which meant she had a surgery starting at eight. She was surprised.

"You remember my schedule. Odd how those things stick in the mind."

I drove to Chiswick in the Land Rover, which had long ceased to be a pleasurable experience. The bodywork had begun to rattle at anything over thirty miles an hour and it had developed a strange smell that I had yet to identify.

Jaikie and Jodie had bought a large Edwardian end-of-terrace in treelined Elwyn Road. Red brick and square bay windows, with a rounded portico over the front door. I forget how much they paid for it, but I remember thinking it was outrageous.

He was there at the front door, and before I had chance to look at his injuries he gave me a hug. Since when did he have to stoop in order to embrace me? I can trace the first occasion back to his sixteenth birthday, but it still takes me by surprise. I looked him over. He'd been thumped just above the left eye. It was bulging. The right cheek was also swollen and the top lip on that side had been cut inside his mouth. Traces of dried blood were smeared down his chin.

"Purple," I said of his eye. "My favourite colour."

He smiled. "Welcome, friend. I'll put some coffee on."

He led the way through to the kitchen, where he told Alexa to open the curtains, turn on some background music and switch on the light over the work surface.

"How's the series going?" I asked as he ground some beans. "Can they do without you for a bit?"

I was referring to *Warrington*, the story of an eighteenth-century adventurer, owner of a triple-masted sailing ship, who had made his pile in Argentina out of beef and silver. With the proceeds he bought up half of

Mayfair and two thousand acres in Surrey. Enter Jaikie's character, Claude Darley, who set about relieving the said adventurer of all of it.

"They can shoot round me. They're delighted with my contribution, by the way. In fact, Claude Darley's been fleshed out, so when there's a second series I'll be virtually carrying the show." He paused. "You've gone quiet."

"You were talking," I said. "About yourself."

"You must bring Laura here, Dad. Jodie'll make dinner. She loves cooking and now that Laura's back in…" He looked away. "Is she?"

I reached out and took his hand. "They hurt you?"

He laughed. "Only my pride. Trouble is, you never know what people are carrying. Knife. Gun. Acid." He went quiet for a moment and looked at me. "I'm not saying I wasn't afraid, because I was. Needed to see the man who makes stuff like that go away." He lowered his voice. "That would be you, Dad."

He set down mugs on the kitchen unit, then reached into a cupboard for a tin of Coffee Mate. I settled at the table and he perched on a spindly barstool, legs akimbo, his hands helping him to tell the story.

"I came home about ten o'clock. I'd been to a friend's house for dinner. Jonathan Blakely. You know him? Great actor. He was in that series where three blokes get…"

"Jaikie."

"You can see the attic window, Suyin's room, from the street and there was a beam of light hovering. I thought maybe a bulb had gone, she'd found a torch and was looking… I don't know. I walked up the path and the porch light triggered. The guys in the attic must've seen it, so when I opened the door I heard feet hurrying down the stairs. There we were, in the hallway, face to face."

"What did they look like?"

He shook his head. "Ski masks, overalls. 'What the hell are you doing?' I said. The taller one replied, 'Out the way, motherfucker, and no one gets hurt. Come at me, I'll kill you.'"

"Accent?"

"South London."

I smiled. "And in spite of his advice you went for him."

"I got one punch in, a bit girlie, to be honest. I think his mate was more of a brawler. Pop, pop, and down I went. They legged it out the front door. I heard a car screech to a halt, doors slam and away."

"A third person, then."

He turned to fill the mugs and placed them on the table. He pushed a tin of biscuits towards me.

"Cops had most of those last night." He chuckled. "The bloke in charge said I was a tosser for leaving the downstairs bathroom window open. I said, hang on, mate, my Dad used to be a DCI. He said his dad used to be a brickie."

I dug around for a bourbon and took a sip of the coffee. It was different. You could almost taste the price. "Did these jokers take anything?"

"Not from us. I mean, the first thing I would have nicked, price-wise, is the Dransfields, but now…"

"What are the Dransfields?"

"Paintings. Come through, I'll show you."

He led the way across to the living room, where he introduced me to his latest acquisitions. They were four oils on canvas, each the size of a tea tray, a series that a junior officer called Marion Dransfield had painted in the trenches between 1916 and 1918. Sinister but beautiful, full of foreboding and terrified faces.

"Lucky to get them. Suyin arranged it a couple of months ago with an art-dealer friend."

"Very nice."

I was anxious to get away from the battlefield and headed back to the kitchen.

"Did Suyin have anything stolen?"

"I need her to check. Haven't seen her since we spoke to *The Guardian*. Tuesday." He paused. "Oh, hang on, they *did* nick something. A tree from off the kitchen drainer."

"You grow trees in the kitchen?"

"Bonsai, Dad. I've sort of… taken it up. This was a juniper, present from Suyin. Usually lives outside."

"Why nick that?"

"Trees of its age can be pricey."

I nodded. "So, her room's top of the house and they didn't go anywhere else? Just the kitchen?"

He shrugged. "They must have heard me and called it a day."

Don't ask me why, but a platoon of spiders had started crawling up my neck. What had set them off on their journey? The tree? The attic room? Or simply embarrassment that the police were right? Jaikie had been a fool for not locking his windows and he'd nearly paid the price.

"You haven't seen Suyin since Tuesday. Have you called her?"

"Goes to message. Always does."

"Show me her room."

Jaikie led the way up the stairs. The house still smelled of fresh paint and there wasn't a scuff mark or chip on any of the walls or doors. When we reached the attic I stood in the doorway and looked round. It had been left exactly as the police had found it. The wardrobe and a chest of drawers had been rifled through in a television cop show way. The drawers were open and clothes were drooling out of them. In the wardrobe a couple of dresses were still hanging on a rail, but had been roughly moved aside. They were of red silk with elaborate embroidery – dawn redwoods and black swans, pagodas with scalloped roofs.

A small metal rubbish bin stood beside the bed and I crouched down to it. It contained the usual stuff. An apple core, tissues, dental floss, screwed-up wrappers, all scattered with a handful of polystyrene beans. Around the room there was the usual array of soft toys that most young people collect, mainly pandas, which didn't surprise me. There was also a long-necked bird propped in a corner, its bendy legs splayed out in front of it – a crane.

I went over to him. He was three feet tall, but short on personality. I'd homed in on him because his feathers were ruffled, as though he'd been handled recently. I picked him up and read his label. Yunnan Wildlife Park, in English and Chinese symbols. I turned him round in my hands and felt under his feathers.

"Shall I leave you two alone?" Jaikie asked.

Running down the crane's back was a strip of Velcro, concealed by plumage. When I pulled it apart, a handful of polystyrene beans fell out and bounced on the carpet. I reached into the crane and felt around, touched a small roll of paper. I removed it carefully. Banknotes. There must have been two dozen fifty-pound notes. Two and a half thousand pounds.

I nodded to a Harrods carrier bag hanging on a hook beside the door. Jaikie brought it over and I tipped the contents of the crane into it. Its body flopped but its head and neck stayed the same.

"Should we be doing this?" Jaikie asked.

There were seventeen more rolls of notes, fifties and hundreds. I reckoned we were looking at close on ninety thousand pounds. Jaikie was shaking his head in amazement, whispering reasons why it might be there.

"Drug money, a robbery, blackmail… I mean, why does she have all…?"

"Where was she living before?"

"Er, Muswell Hill, I think Jodie said."

"Does she work?"

He hesitated. "Well, occasionally she buys and sells stuff."

"Why do I get the feeling you're holding back? What stuff?"

"Dad, she's more Jodie's friend than mine. Stuff to China." He recognised the end-of-tether look I gave him. "European art. High value."

"Have you ever seen her passport? Visa?"

"They went off to the Home Office with her application."

"In other words a woman you know nothing about is living under your roof. She could be anything from a spy to a serial killer." I opened the crane. "Help me fill him up again. He's coming home with me."

That really worried him. "Dad…"

"The police didn't want him. Why shouldn't I have him?"

We started to refill the crane, money and all, until it regained its original shape. We crawled on the carpet for beans, which seemed to jump every time we got near them. Eventually I pressed the Velcro together.

"I'll take the laptop as well."

"Dad, if the cops.…"

I laughed. "Jaikie, your break-in is history. I just hope Suyin isn't."

He exploded. "What the fuck does that…?"

I patted him on the shoulder and led the way downstairs.

In the kitchen, I took another swig of the coffee, which was now lukewarm.

"This is really nice," I said. "What is it?"

"It's, er… Indonesian. Kopi Iuwat. It's a civet coffee."

I laughed. "As in sieve?"

He smiled back. "No."

"You're holding back again. Did you nick it from Harrods or something?"

He took a breath before explaining. "The beans are first eaten by a weasel, then… well, collected once they've passed through."

I put the coffee down and looked at it. "You mean I've just drunk a mug of weasel shit?"

"In a manner of speaking."

I paused. "Have you got any more interviews lined up?"

"One with LBC. Tomorrow."

"Cancel it. Who else knows she's here, by the way? Apart from the entire readership of *The Guardian*?"

"No idea."

I put my jacket back on, tucked the laptop under my arm and picked up the crane.

"You kept the tape of the dawn raid?"

Jaikie nodded.

"Email it to me. When Jodie gets back, tell her I'd like a word."

***

Whenever I drive into London I always return feeling that a layer of grime needs peeling off me. Back at Beech Tree I went straight up to the bathroom, showered and put on some fresh clothes before going across to the log cabin.

I hadn't been in there for a few days and must have left the heater on last time. The place was like an oven and the ficus was wilting. I used a dirty mug to scoop out water from the rain barrel beside the door and tipped it into the plant pot, then settled at the desk, conscious of the faint smell of stagnant water. I switched on my laptop and saw that Jaikie had sent me the tape. I'd also received a WhatsApp message on the family group from Fee in New York.

"Jaikie, your injuries. Just how bad are they? Are you in hospital?"

Via the miracle of the instant communication she had heard about his ordeal and made sure that her siblings were in the loop. They would now blow it out of all proportion if I didn't step in.

"Guys, his injuries are superficial. Dad x"

Fee pounced on that immediately.

"Then why is he in Guys? Honestly, Dad, you still treat us like kids."

Ellie came to the rescue, all the way from Nepal. "He meant Guys as in 'you guys'. Not the hospital! Right, Dad? That said, how serious is it?"

I wished I'd taken a photo of Jaikie to prove how relatively unscathed he was. I messaged back, "Jaikie has a cut on the inside of his mouth, one black eye and two small bruises on his cheek. None of this will harm him as an actor or as a human being, the two being very different animals! PS Nice to hear from you. Con, are you there, by the way? Haven't heard from you in the last six months? x."

That didn't really do it for Fee and after ten minutes thinking about it she messaged back.

"Why does Dad mention it not harming your career, J? Is there a problem?"

"How many times do I have to say it?" I replied. "No, no, no, no, there isn't a problem. Anyone heard from Con?"

She texted back after what I suspected was careful thought. "No whisper from Con."

"Are you sure?" I asked her by return. "You're not hiding something from me, I hope. Dengue fever? Prison?"

She was straight in there with, "What makes you think that? God, Dad, sometimes you can…"

"Gotcha! Now you know how it feels."

In spite of the match having swung in my favour, she won the day with her final dig. "How's Laura, Dad? Jaikie says the other morning he phoned you and guess who was…"

I quit WhatsApp and opened the dawn raid file, which began to play of its own accord.

As Jaikie had said, the immigration officers were aggressive, not so much physically as in their tone and manner. They crowded round their target, but from the outset it was clear they weren't going to get much trouble, neither from the self-regarding thespian nor the wispy girl from China. They should have let the team leader do the talking. Instead, they split up and started roaming the house.

The tape was clear and steady. It didn't suddenly flash from a face up to the ceiling then down to the floor like most home movies. Jaikie had captured all six of them full on at some stage.

I finished watching and ran it back again on the grounds that you always see something extra on a second viewing. I reached the point where the Indian guy wanted Suyin's ID, her passport. He gestured towards the kitchen, asking if he could have a quiet word, but whatever he had in mind was scotched by Jaikie telling her to stay put. I paused the tape. Ran it back a few seconds, played it again. I stopped it.

That platoon of spiders was crawling up my neck again.

***

"I've been calling you all day," Laura said, as she opened the door to me at Chestnut Cottage. "How is he? Why are you carrying a stuffed bird?"

"I need your help."

"With Jaikie? What's wrong?"

I headed for the couch and sat down. It helps to make the place look bigger.

"I air-dropped you the video he made of the dawn raid," I said. "Will you look at it for me?"

She settled beside me and opened the file on her laptop. Five seconds into the tape she muttered, "I can tell you straightaway that the middle-aged Englishman has a skin condition. Psoriasis, probably."

When she'd watched the whole tape she turned to me with an apologetic frown. "I'm meant to be seeing something important, aren't I?"

"There's no meant to be about it, it's just there!" I said, rattily. "I'm sorry ... sorry."

I leaned over and replayed the video. When it reached Suyin's first appearance I paused it.

"The expression on her face. Let it sink in." I moved the video on. "See how the Indian's voice takes her by surprise? She looks at him, mouth opens as if she's going to cry out. Camera goes to him. He asks her for ID, then her passport. His gaze settles on her. He's got an open face, eyes wide, brows arched. He's almost telling her not to worry, things will be fine…"

She ran that section again. "Yes, I see what you mean."

"Now he's trying to get her away from the others and into the kitchen. She's about to go with him… look at her. Jaikie stops her." I fast-forwarded to the team's departure. "'We're leaving, Suyin,' he says. He calls her by her first name. And look! He raises a hand and almost smiles, stops himself, glances at his colleagues to see if they've noticed."

She turned to me. "I'm with you. And I think you're right."

I nodded. "He knows her! And she knows him back."

She took off her glasses and began to fiddle with them, something she does when playing devil's advocate. "Is that… significant?"

"On its own, maybe not, but I also found my friend here in Suyin's room." I reached out for the crane. "He's got a bad case of indigestion, having swallowed ninety thousand quid without chewing it properly."

"Good grief! What on earth is a young woman doing with that amount of money?"

"I don't know, but I think the boys who broke into Elwyn Road were looking for her. Question: why leave behind cash, jewellery, iPad, laptop, Kindle… but make off with a small tree?"

-5-

My appointment was for ten o'clock in the morning. Driller, as Laura referred to Drusilla Ford, had a Scrabble board of qualifications and worked out of a Quaker meeting house. It was a barebones kind of place, set among dripping beech trees, with winding stairs leading to floorboarded offices. Her own part of it contained two Swedish armchairs, a round table and a satsuma vase in the fireplace, billowing with dried grasses. Every surface had a fine layer of dust.

"How can I help you?" Driller asked.

"The shortened version of your name. Driller. Is it because you… drill down into people's psyches?"

"No, but please think of it that way if it helps."

Having had so many people try to con me down the years, I wondered about the all-seeing, all-knowing persona she projected. True or false? She was wearing a grey jumper over jeans and, rather strangely, Doc Martins on her feet. A reminder of a misspent youth, perhaps? She didn't use makeup and her hair was shoulder-length light brown, falling round a freckled face.

"I'm having trouble with my temper," I said. "I used to be able to handle it."

I explained briefly about the imaginary Map bequeathed to me by Roy Pullman.

"Interesting," she said when I'd finished.

"Map doesn't work anymore."

She waited, burning up the hundred quid she charges at one pound sixty-six per minute. Plus petrol.

"People have a habit of leaving me, drifting away…"

"Well, which is it? Drifting is unintentional, leaving is deliberate."

I nodded. "People ditch me. Kids, wife, recent partner. My wife didn't leave, actually. Cancer." I paused. "I can hear my father, on behalf of a whole generation, telling me to pull myself together."

"Suggest to him that he minds his own business."

"He's not that easy to get rid of."

"I understand. Ask him to wait outside. I mean, actually say the words."

I glanced over my shoulder. "You heard the lady."

"Shame about The Map," she said, eventually. "But I think I can help. You've heard of the 'four effs'? Fight, flight, freeze and fawn. I doubt you ever fawn, freeze or flee. So next time your equilibrium is challenged and the urge to blow up sweeps over you, why not bring something beautiful to mind instead?"

I'd expected a daft suggestion or two from her, but nothing quite so homespun.

"It doesn't sound like much of a cure."

"You'll be surprised. Personally, I think of a favourite flower…"

My father was beckoning me from the door. I reached into my pocket, took out five twenty-pound notes and fanned them out on the table. I turned and left the room.

"See you again?" she called out after me.

When Jaikie and Jodie arrived at Beech Tree the next morning, I was in the garden pretending that it was still summery enough to have breakfast at the big table. I say breakfast as if I mean a fry-up with all the trimmings. I mean black coffee.

I'd wanted a private *tête-à-tête* with Jaikie and Jodie, but obviously I hadn't made that clear. They had brought a third party with them. The newcomer stepped out of Jaikie's car and looked across at Beech Tree with the mixture of envy and wonder that attaches to thatched houses. Dogge went haring towards him, kicking up a cloud of fallen leaves, and the new face stooped to make a fuss of her. When somebody shows affection towards dogs they win me over, until I remember that Adolf Hitler was a dog lover.

I got up from the table and embraced Jodie. She was looking tired, thanks to Edinburgh, and anxious, thanks to Suyin, the dawn raid and subsequent break-in.

"How'd it go north of Hadrian's Wall?"

"Success, in that my client didn't wind up in prison. They fined him a hundred and fifty thousand pounds instead." I winced. "That's the price you pay for importing dodgy food. I'll explain some other time…"

"Dad, this is Suyin's lawyer, he's been handling her visa application."

The new face was what my mother would have called "a fine specimen". He leaned forward and stretched out a hand.

"Great to meet you, Mr Hawk. Alessandro Scutari."

Italian name, London accent. His hand was big, like the rest of him, and the tattoos on his forearms told the story of a battle between mythical creatures. He smiled a great deal, revealing a portcullis of perfect teeth. In his left earlobe he wore a diamond stud that he fiddled with occasionally, as if to check that it was still there.

"You've had breakfast, I take it? Sit and watch me drink mine."

They swept away the autumn leaves from the bench seats and settled.

"I really appreciate you offering to help find her, Mr Hawk," said Alessandro.

"I didn't know I had."

He glanced at Jaikie. "I thought Jaikie said you…"

"I can imagine what Jaikie said."

"Dad, Jodie's been worried sick. Nobody's seen or heard from Suyin…"

"I understand how you feel, but my main interest is to save you two idiots from yourselves."

Jodie stared at me. It was the first time I'd ever voiced a criticism of her.

"I take it you'll elaborate on that," she said, icily.

"A woman you know nothing about moves in with you. In my opinion, and in Alessandro's, I imagine, because he knows the type, she's an overstayer at best. Remember the Sikh immigration officer? I think he and Suyin knew each other."

Jaikie frowned. "She never said…"

"I'm sure she didn't. How d'you meet her, Jodie?"

"Through a lawyer friend, a year ago." She shrugged with her eyebrows. "We just hit it off."

"I need more than that. Sudden friendships are all well and good."

"You think she might have been using me? I disagree. We have things in common. For a start, her family came from Yunnan, way back. I spent my gap year there. It really is the most beautiful part…"

"You never thought to ask if she was here legally?"

"I'm a barrister for ten hours a day, not twenty-four."

"Don't go making that mistake, Jodie. You're a barrister, full stop. Why'd she leave China? Anyone know?"

Alessandro half raised a hand. "She won a nursing scholarship to St. George's, London. That's the address I had for her."

"So the course was three, four years?"

He nodded.

"How come she wound up staying at Elwyn Road?"

Jodie shifted, defensively. "Six weeks ago she rang and asked if we could put her up for a bit. I said of course. She moved in two days later."

"In a hurry, by the sound of it. And you still didn't ask questions?"

"She's a friend, Nathan, not a witness to a crime!"

"When did you last hear from her?"

"Ten days ago," said Alessandro, checking the diamond. "I should have kept a closer eye…"

"It wouldn't have made much difference. She either doesn't want to be found, or she's dead."

"Dad, for God's sake…!"

"Why else would she leave ninety thousand pounds in a stuffed bird in her room?"

Alessandro had one of those faces that starts to twitch when it hears bad news. It went into overdrive.

"Ninety grand?" he said. "Where does a nurse get that kind of money?"

I turned to Jodie, who was clearly upset that her friend might be in peril. Before I could stop myself, the words were out.

"I'll find her for you, Jodie."

There was a pause followed by a collective sigh of relief, after which Alessandro offered to meet my usual fee and any expenses I incurred.

I began looking for Suyin that same evening. I settled her laptop on the kitchen table, only to discover that it was playing hard to get and kept asking me if I'd forgotten the password. If so, would I like a new one? Using my own laptop, I trawled the web for assistance. There were a hundred answers to my question, nearly all of which set my teeth on edge with their patronising tone.

"It's easily done," said the page I'd landed on. "You forget your Windows password and didn't create a password hint. Ooops!"

Ooops is one of many computer words that I would kill to be rid of. I began drumming my fingers until they hurt.

"Here's a few things you can try in order to log in without the password," the page went on. "Obviously we provide these tips on the basis you're going to use them on your own computer and not for accessing someone else's. Clearly, we do not condone that… etc."

Two A4 pages later, the guy broke into the private lingo that only techies understand. I reached out to grab his voice and caught sight of my hands approaching the screen. I paused. Had I reached the stage where soundtracks and pixels were as real to me as human beings? Would I have grabbed nothing and slammed it down on the kitchen table? I'd been threatening to put my fist through the telly for years, but the nearest I'd ever got was to launch the contents of a packet of crisps at it.

I made a cup of tea and decided to put my problem to The Others on WhatsApp.

"Hi, all, it's Dad. Anyone know anything about hacking into a computer you don't have the password for?"

Fee was first out of the blocks.

"Two things, Dad. One: you don't have to tell us it's you every time. We can see that on screen. Two: I do have a few ideas about the laptop, but may I ask whose it is first? xx."

I smiled. Suspicious, as always. Ellie was close behind her. "Dad, is it Laura's laptop? And if so, why?"

"If that's the case, it's outrageous," said Fee. "I mean I'm trusting you that it isn't, but why don't you just say whose laptop it is."

Because you haven't given me the bloody chance, my love. It was typical of all our online communications. It had got out of hand in a matter of three, four sentences and I was now suspected of spying on Laura.

"Get off his bloody back, you lot," messaged Jaikie. "Any ideas about hacking? None. I've tried it myself, nearly drove me mad. Find yourself a dodgy pro. You're an ex-cop, you must know someone, tee-hee. How's Laura?"

I responded. "Laura is well. It is not her laptop. It belongs to a girl called Suyin Qu who has gone missing. So, if anyone's got any ideas, please share. xx."

It was half an hour later when Fee messaged me privately.

"D'you remember Harry Blythe? That friend of Ellie's in Longwick? When he was eight he could've hacked in to the Bank of England. Ring his mum. You never know. Love you. Still. xx"

"I am not about to ask an eight-year-old to commit a crime!" I said.

"He isn't eight. He's sixteen. But very telling that you think everyone's still a kid. xx"

I phoned Sharon Blythe early the next day and she tried to have a chat with me. I made it a short one and asked to speak to Harry. He was still in bed, she said, and yelled up the stairs, "'Arry, it's Mr 'Awk from Winchendon!"

Harry came to the phone, bleary as custard by the sound of it, and I said I had a job for him. He should be on my doorstep in half an hour, or the deal was off.

The bike ride must have cleared his head and he crouched down to stroke Dogge.

"How are you, Harry?"

"Okay," he muttered.

"What've you been up to? Anything interesting?"

"No."

He was not only six feet tall these days, but had grown into a good-looking teenager, albeit with a computer stoop and over-developed thumbs. Behind the monosyllabic arras there lurked a high IQ. I just hoped there was personality to match and he wouldn't commit himself to a lifetime of binary codes.

I explained my problem, telling him that Suyin's laptop was an old one of Jaikie's that I was thinking of selling. I sat him at the kitchen table and within five minutes he said, "Write this down on the whiteboard, Mr Hawk. Hawksville17. Capital aitch. It's the new password."

I did as he'd instructed.

"Thanks, Harry."

His hands lingered over the keyboard, all set to sabotage his work if I didn't pay up. "That'll be ten quid."

"Ten quid!" I protested.

"It's Sunday."

He had a point. I fetched a ten-pound note from my jacket and handed it over. He made a farewell fuss of Dogge and left.

***

Naively, I'd expected Suyin's life story to come tumbling out of her laptop, but no such luck. It didn't help that most of the content was in Mandarin. Her nursing coursework was in English, but the last entry to that folder had been made a year previously. The search engine had no history and no bookmarks. The contacts file contained less than thirty names, most of them Chinese. Her emails had been deleted recently and she wasn't on Facebook, Twitter or Instagram. Suyin Qu was apparently a highly unsociable young woman.

But she had made one mistake. There was a photo folder containing just under a hundred pictures, and presumably they'd all been taken by Suyin, since she didn't appear in any of them. The dozen or so that caught my eye were of a barbecue in a suburban garden, back in early summer. The man holding the metal spatula aloft, a friendly smile on his face and looking straight into the lens, was none other than the Sikh immigration officer. I slapped the table in triumph. It had not been self-deception or wishful thinking on my part. He and Suyin knew each other.

Jaikie had mentioned Muswell Hill as the place where Suyin had lived before moving to Elwyn Road. Muswell Hill is a populous place and I suddenly had a picture of myself traipsing from street to street, accosting anyone wearing a turban, looking for a Sikh immigration officer. As suddenly as my spirits plummeted, they rose again as I studied one of the photos more closely. It showed the man's wife and family, friends and neighbours at the same barbecue, but in the background was a relic from the Second World War. It was nothing so romantic as a restored field gun, a Churchill tank or a Spitfire. It was a brick-built, flat-roofed air-raid shelter, recognisable to me as such because there'd been one in my grandfather's back yard.

It took me an hour and forty minutes and I've rarely felt a sense of achievement quite like it. I used Google Earth Pro, which up until then I had only played with. It's an application which gives a 3D street map, and on that morning I got my money's worth from it.

I had divided Muswell Hill into squares and hovered over each one. I have to say that most back gardens look the same and large areas of them are blurred green for privacy. However, since the shelter was a building, I eventually found it. A grey slab in a garden, its roof twenty feet by twelve. And as I moved the cursor to the street itself and descended to walk the pavement I identified the house. Number 26 Ventnor Road.

Late the next day, I borrowed Laura's car to drive into London. It played Classic FM at me the whole way. Its soporific sameness gave me a sense that all was right with the world. Nothing could have been further from the truth.

It was almost dark as the satnav told me that my destination was up ahead. I drove past the turning for half a mile, parked and walked back to this respectably dead corner of North London. Maybe it was the advance of autumn that had cleared the streets of people, anxious to avoid the chill which had dropped out of nowhere. It wasn't cold enough for breath to hang from my face, but enough to make me shrug into my jacket and pull up the collar.

I turned into Ventnor Road, a street of small semis typical of the shove-'em-up style of the 1950s. Number 26 was in complete darkness, no vehicle parked on the driveway, but as I approached the front door I triggered a porch light. When that happens, I always feel I've been caught in some felonious act. I looked round to check if anyone had seen me.

As I went to press the bell I noticed that the door was slightly ajar. I pushed it with my toe and it whined open. The adrenalin kicked in a beat later. I've asked myself several times since if, in that moment, I knew what I was about to find, or if the *déjà-vu* nature of hindsight is responsible. Whatever the case, it didn't make the man lying face down in the hallway any less dead.

At a rough guess he had walked into the house, headed towards the kitchen and met his killer, who had struck him with a single blow from something like a meat cleaver. It had perfectly divided his skull. The turban had unravelled and the long hair was treacly with blood, now congealing. The inevitable blowflies had found their way in and were humming with delight.

I closed the front door behind me, again with my foot, then slipped off my shoes and left them on the mat. The porch light switched itself off and I pressed the flashlight on my phone.

This was my forty-first murdered body, and as I stood over it the previous forty flashed before me in precise date order. It's odd how proprietorial I've always felt towards my victims, not that this particular body was mine. It wasn't anyone's yet. I made my way past it, to the kitchen.

The fridge door stood open, telling its own story. Whoever had broken into the house had been peckish. On the top shelf there was a six-pack of small pies, one of which had been removed. Half of it was on the floor. When the victim arrived home the snacker had dropped it, rushed to the hall and killed him.

The fridge light filled the room and I noticed on the wall, almost as if it had been installed for my convenience, a dispenser filled with plastic gloves, the kind used in surgery or preparing food. I took out a pair, put them on and began my search in the room adjacent to the kitchen.

I'd had a Sikh friend in my early days in the job, so I recognised the gurdwara, a home temple, in what most people would use as a dining room. I immediately felt that I was treading on sacred ground. A religious man, then, our immigration officer, who had spent time and money on his faith. The room was draped with sumptuous fabrics, gold and silver thread running through most of them. The furniture was heavy teak and the scriptures were arranged dead centre of the room on a *takhat*, a raised plinth. Ornaments and vases were placed around them. They were mainly of silver and still there, which meant the motive of the killer had not been robbery.

I moved on to the front room, a quite ordinary lounge with a sofa, armchairs, television and low tables. I could see by the streetlight shining in through unclosed curtains that the room had been untouched by the murderer.

Nothing broken, nothing fallen, nothing moved aside. It was as neat and perfect as the lady of the house had left it.

There were photos of her on the wall, standing beside her husband, taken on their wedding day, I imagined. Opinder and Shirina, one said. Another showed two girls, one in medical scrubs, the other in school uniform. And in pride of place was a black-and-white photo of a young Sikh, a lance corporal in Indian army uniform. A brass plate on the bottom of the frame bore the name Inderveer Pandeshi and the date, 1941. Opinder's father, I imagined. I left the room and went upstairs.

The bathroom was as ordinary as you please, neat with his and hers coloured towels over a heated rail. Flannels were perfectly stretched out beside them. An array of vitamins in plastic tubs stood on a shelf in a dead straight line. Electric toothbrushes were plugged into a socket. Toothpaste, two tubes with caps screwed back on.

There was one anomaly in this fastidious room. The lavatory seat was up. I shone the torch into the bowl. Someone had peed in it recently. Could it possibly have been the killer? If the good order of the rest of the house was anything to go by, I doubted if any member of the family would have left the room without flushing the toilet. I had half a mind to scoop out some of the urine, but it has never been a good source of DNA. I left it.

The room at the front, the master bedroom, was untouched, but the back bedroom was a different story. There hadn't been much to find, but someone had recently searched it. In the wardrobe, there were hangers but no clothes. Likewise a chest of drawers. Empty. The bed had no linen, no pillows on it, but the bare mattress had been shifted as if someone had looked underneath it. There were no ornaments, no personal effects, no sign that someone was sleeping here. However, on the wall straight ahead of me was a poster depicting two tall birds, necks entwined. In bold letters with a Chinese flourish to them were the English words White Crane. The back of my neck told me that I'd been right. Again. Suyin not only knew this Indian family, she had lived in their house.

I went back down the stairs and over to the clockwork phone on the hall table. Placing the hem of my T-shirt over the mouthpiece, I dialled 999 and gave the responder the address and a single word – murder. He tried to get to know me better, asking my name, but I replaced the receiver. I opened the front door a few inches, leaving it just as I had found it, and picked up my shoes. I left the house via the kitchen, pausing just for a second to pay my respects to the dead man. I slipped on my shoes, unlocked the back door and hurried across the garden.

Seeing the air-raid shelter in the flesh triggered memories of my grandfather, who would spin a dark romance in which bombs rained down on London and neighbours came running from nearby houses to take shelter, creating a world of huddle, hair curlers and tartan dressing gowns. The faces were ghostly white, especially those of the children, squeezed between loving parents for extra safety. When the 'all clear' was sounded, they became flesh and blood again, lit untipped cigarettes and began to talk about bastard Gerries, narrow escapes and work tomorrow.

Like my grandfather's shelter, the one here had been smartened up into a garden store, with a window and a wooden door, a trellis with a rose clinging to it. I climbed up onto the roof via a water butt and crouched there for a moment looking across at the houses backing on to Ventnor Road. The one directly behind number 26 was alive with evening bustle. I eased myself down into the garden and headed for the side gate. As I passed by the kitchen window I could hear the closing music of *Coronation Street* and smell dinner being cooked. I sank deeper into my jacket and walked out into the street.

As I made my way along the pavement I heard the scream of approaching sirens and saw the flicker of blue lights against the orange halogen of the London sky. By the time I reached Laura's car the world had gone quiet again.

It wasn't until I pulled into a petrol station on the North Circular that I took a real breath and allowed the adrenalin to subside. Then I stoked it up again with coffee and a sandwich and began to relive the horror of what I'd just seen.

***

When I reached home, I bagged up any trace of me having been at 26 Ventnor Road. On the bottom of one of my socks was a stark reminder of the evening, a patch of blood the size of a bottle top. It had soaked through to my skin. I balled up the socks and binned them, along with the plastic gloves and my shoes.

I spent one of those clock-watching nights where endless possibilities get played out, none with a satisfactory conclusion. Opinder Pandeshi had been killed in his own home. Who by? Could his murder, the image of which was etched into my mind forever, have been committed by the shy, demure Suyin? In which case, was she really that shy and demure? Or were the same two men, the tree thieves who had broken into Jaikie's house, responsible? Would they return to Elwyn Road, especially after his bleating to *The Guardian* about unfair treatment by immigration?

I was in two dozen minds about whether to call Martin Falconer and tell him about the murder. To what end, I wondered? To watch him vortex himself into the ground with impotent anger, then decamp to Elwyn Road and sit in the porch with a loaded shotgun between his knees as he waited…?

It was a tempting thought, but I decided against phoning him. Next morning, I phoned Bill Grogan instead.

"Bill, it's Nathan Hawk."

"I know. Says on the phone."

"How are you keeping?"

"Fine."

There was a hiatus.

"Bill, this is where you ask me how I am."

"You sound fine."

I took a breath. "Well, I'm not. I want to come and see you."

"Place is a bit of a mess."

"Oh, for fuck's sake, Bill! I'll be there in an hour."

I put the phone down and had a sudden vision of him in apron and headscarf, working at double speed to clean up ahead of my visit.

***

Bill Grogan was an ex-copper, a detective sergeant who I'd started out by not liking much only to wind up believing he was one of the wisest men I'd ever met. He wasn't good on the phone, admittedly, and not much better face to face. In spite of that, his clear-up rate was impressive, probably due to him being a watcher and listener, as opposed to a talker like me.

He lived in Summertown, Oxford, with his partner, a psychiatric nurse who worked at the John Radcliffe. An odd couple indeed. Bill the lumbering giant, Viv the svelte officer type who might have stepped out of a 1960s war film. They had met over their mutual passion for cacti, and in the last three years had travelled the world to attend 'cactus events'. That included the one-night flowering of *Hylocereus indatus*. For a month afterwards he spoke of little else but the moment when the Honolulu queen bloomed, dispensed her exquisite fragrance, then curled up and died.

I pulled up outside the terraced house. He must have been curtain-twitching – the door opened as I closed the front gate behind me. I stepped forward to embrace him. He held his breath, then finally patted me on the shoulder.

"Hi, Bill. How you doing?"

"I said earlier. Fine."

He ushered me into the main room of the house with its *fleur-de-lys* wallpaper and solid walnut gramophone, relics from another era. He had grown up in the place and in truth it was too small for such a large man, let alone his partner as well, but to have sold it and moved on would have felt disloyal to his parents.

The conservatory was rather more spacious than the living room, having been added by Bill just 20 years previously, and that's where he steered me. It was home to a collection of passive-aggressive cacti, some still in flower, others standing ready to fend off attack.

"You want tea?" he asked.

"Yeah, thanks."

"Or coffee? You can have coffee."

"Tea'll be fine."

"Only we've got proper coffee…"

I knew from past experience that it would take him about ten minutes to relax.

"Tea," I said, and he went back into the kitchen to fill the kettle.

"How's Viv?" I called to him.

"Fine."

I'd often wanted to point out that there were other words to express well-being besides 'fine'. "I thought you said he was retiring?"

"Next year. That'll be two of us wondering what to do with the rest of our lives. How's Doctor Peterson?"

"We've gone our separate ways, Bill."

He thought about that for a moment. "Pity. Kids alright?"

"Sort of."

He came into the conservatory with two mugs of tea and a biscuit tin with a picture of Lord Kitchener on the lid pointing the finger. The chocolate digestives inside it were more recent. He settled beside a ball of daggers the size of a deep-sea mine.

"Bill, I've got a favour to ask."

Without adding too much drama, I filled him in on the events of the last few weeks, everything from the dawn raid to finding Opinder Pandeshi murdered in his front hallway. He listened without a murmur, to the point where I wondered if he'd gone into some kind of trance. When I'd finished, I shrugged.

"We've both seen nasty stuff, Bill, but this poor bastard with his head split like a melon, straight down the middle…"

"Those diagrams you get of a brain scan, slice by slice. And this Suyin, she's the common denominator? Could she have done it?"

I shrugged. "Given that he tried to get her sent back to China, yes. In which case, who are the two blokes who broke into Elwyn Road? And will they return?"

"If you think I can be of any help…"

"Couple of weeks, mate. Will Viv mind?"

He shook his head. "We like to get out of each other's way occasionally." He started on a biscuit and batted the crumbs from his cardigan. "Know what I'd do first? I'd make Suyin Jaikie's friend, not Jodie's."

"Why?"

"Actors don't get struck off for failing to report an overstayer. Barristers probably do."

"Good thinking. One other thing… tiny, tiny. D'you know anything about bonsai trees?"

He pursed his lips. "Viv'd be your man for that. There's a club at the hospital. Why?"

"The only thing taken from Elwyn Road was a bonsai tree, a juniper, two feet tall. Jaikie's into it, evidently. Worries me. It's that business of wanting to reduce things to a size you can control. Like model railways."

"Time to worry is when he buys himself a dolls' house."

On my way back through Thame I got a phone call from Laura, which I pulled on to the verge to answer. She was controlling her annoyance with a strangled whisper.

"Nathan, two police officers have turned up on my doorstep and want to interview me! My car was spotted yesterday close to the scene of a murder in North London!"

"Laura, don't try and talk your way out of it, just 'fess up and…"

"Will you stop that and say something sensible!"

It wouldn't have happened if I'd taken the Land Rover. The number plates on it were so muddied nobody could have read them.

"Take 'em round to Beech Tree, make them coffee."

"Oh, certainly," she said, huffily. "Provided I can find the key!"

"I'll be twenty minutes."

***

I parked beside a black Audi, polished to a gleam with a blue flasher unit and a couple of stab-proof gilets on the back seat. For all its attempt at anonymity it screamed unmarked police car.

When I entered the kitchen my two visitors stood up and the elder man stretched out a hand, setting off Dogge. The younger bloke looked at her warily.

"She doesn't like me," he said.

I love it when outwardly hard men quiver at the prospect of my aged canine friend attacking them, when all she wants to do is lick them to death.

"If you're frightened of her," I said, "I'll put her in the utility."

"Wouldn't mind."

Once I'd settled Dogge we started again. The younger man spoke in a grammar-school voice. No dropped aitches or -ings pronounced -inks.

"I'm DCI James Parfitt, SIO of a Major Incident Team. This is DS Gadsden. I gather Doctor Peterson lent you her car yesterday. Is that right?"

I looked at Laura, who was rinsing the dust out of mugs she'd taken down from hooks on one of the beams.

"You found the key, then, found the coffee?"

"Yes, thank you, and yes, you borrowed my car."

I gestured to the table. "Sit down, gents. I was going to come and see you anyway…"

"Really?" said Parfitt. "When Doctor Peterson mentioned your name it rang a bell. Didn't you break your guvnor's jaw and were asked to put in your papers?" He smiled, crooked teeth, wine-stained. "No violence today, I hope."

It was hard to tell if he was serious or joking. I made it equally difficult for him.

"Can't guarantee it."

"How d'you keep your pension after a thing like that?"

I smiled. "Too many people were cheering me on for having thumped him. Are you here to discuss my chequered career or to listen and maybe learn?"

He glared at me. "Get this straight from the off. I'm not here for the benefit of your wisdom. What were you doing in Ventnor Road two nights ago?"

"Passing by."

He screwed his face up, trying to keep it together. "Listen, I don't think you realise…"

Anyone who begins a sentence with the word 'listen' really means "Listen, dickhead, you're so stupid you need this spelling out for you…"

"…the position you're in."

"Sorry, wasn't listening."

"You were the first person to see Opinder Pandeshi dead, which could also make you the last person to see him alive."

"I don't normally walk around with a meat cleaver under my jacket."

"It was there, ready and waiting, part of a set of knives in the Pandeshis' kitchen. We haven't found it. Any ideas?"

For the second time that day I recounted the full story of my search for Suyin Qu. Gadsden made notes. When I got to the discovery of Opinder's body lying dead in his hallway Laura stared at me in horror, no doubt concerned about Jaikie's future safety. Parfitt growled at me,

"You've made me uneasy, Mr Hawk. I mean the very fact that you were there…"

I turned to Gadsden. He was old-school, approaching retirement, and reminded me of an excellent teacher I once had, all nose and no chin. Like Gadsden, Mr Dury's hair was thin, his skin pasty, and he somehow gave the impression of being dressed in someone else's clothes.

"Suyin Qu's been living with my son and his wife for the last six weeks. Before that she lived with your victim."

"We know," said Parfitt. "Top back bedroom. Left six weeks ago, according to Mrs Pandeshi. Anything else to share?"

"Only this. Of the two people most qualified to tell you what's going on, one of them's dead, the other's missing. If you take my advice…"

Parfitt slapped the table, making Dogge bark from the utility room. "Why can't blokes like you forget the job? Buy yourself a set of golf clubs and move on?"

"I think Pandeshi wanted Suyin sent back to China," I said.

Parfitt shrugged as if I'd stated the obvious. "He was an immigration officer. That was his job."

"I don't think he gave a toss about her being an overstayer. He was more concerned for her safety."

"That's a nice, cuddly point of view, but it doesn't mean she didn't kill him."

Gadsden intervened. "We'll need to speak with your son, Mr Hawk."

"I'll get him to ring you. He reckons there was a third person. A driver. Someone else you should talk to is Suyin's lawyer. He was meant to be getting her a visa."

"Name?"

"Alessandro Scutari."

"How are you spelling that?" asked Gadsden.

"I'm not."

Gadsden smiled, a one-sided smile, the corner of his mouth reaching to his left ear. He wrote down an approximation of Scutari's name. Parfitt rose from the table, came close and looked down his nose at me.

"Your style of doing things might be a legend in… where was it?"

"Hamford."

"It might have had people swooning there, but I prefer real evidence."

"Fair enough, see what you make of this…"

I fetched Suyin's laptop from the dresser and set it down in front of him. He looked at it as if it had just flown in from Mars.

"Suyin's," I said. "Password is Hawksville17. It's not the only thing I removed."

He flared. "Evidence from the scene? What is wrong with…?"

"From her room at my son's house. A stuffed bird. A crane. Very Chinese. Laura, would you mind? He's on the sofa in the living room."

When she returned with the crane Gadsden laughed. "Do they talk, do you know?"

"What do you think he'd say?" I asked.

"How about Suyin Qu has got away with murder?" said Parfitt. "See, trouble with people like you is you want life to tangle up a bit, give you something to think about in retirement. The rest of us look for straight lines. Opinder tries to send her back to China. She doesn't want to leave. She has a barney with him and it turns nasty."

I winced. "So she picks up the meat cleaver, buries it in his head? How did she manage that? She's five-foot nothing, he's over six foot."

He gave me his sardonic best. "She jumped. Thanks for the coffee, doc. And remember what I said, Mr Hawk. Keep your nose out of my business."

He nodded at Gadsden to bring Suyin's laptop and the crane.

"Have you got a couple of…?" Gadsden asked.

I took two bin bags from the roll under the kitchen sink and handed them to him. He shook them open and bagged the evidence. Parfitt couldn't resist a parting shot.

"And if it turns out that your son or daughter-in-law had a hand in getting her out of the country, then ton of bricks. Capiche?"

He suddenly became the only thing in the room. His hair was short, like a lavatory brush, but his ears were prominent enough to grab and the head just begged to be slammed down on the kitchen table. Laura must have sensed the free radicals in the air and stepped in front of me, forefinger two inches from my nose. I felt in my inside pocket for The Map. It wasn't there. It was lying in pieces in Waitrose's car park. I turned back to Parfitt's ears but he and his sidekick had left the building. A minute later we heard their car speed off down Morton Lane, out of our lives. Temporarily.

When I'd calmed down a little Laura asked how things had gone with Drusilla Ford. I said they'd gone quickly. She sighed and began clearing away the coffee debris.

"I do hope those two yobs who broke into Elwyn don't return," she muttered.

"We can safely say they're more than yobs, Laura, but if they do show up the first thing they'll meet is Bill Grogan. Can you imagine that? Dead of night? Full moon? Wolves howling in the distance…?"

"Is that where you've been today?" I nodded. "How is he?"

"The same as ever, I'm pleased to say. He's become the only constant in my life."

She ignored the oblique dig at her and glanced round as if to check that we were alone. "Nathan, I know you gave Parfitt the crane, but shouldn't you have told him what was inside? I mean suppose they burn it or…"

"The ninety grand, you mean? Who said it was still inside him?"

***

The night-time trip to Thame was a strange experience, both unsettling and reassuring, the former because of the play-acting involved, the latter because the outcome would provide me with a safety net. I had slept on the sofa, fully clothed, and my alarm went off at two in the morning. I made a cup of tea to clear my head and then drove the four miles to Waitrose.

Busy and aggressive car parks are surreal places when completely empty, and the tall lights shining at half strength onto the tarmac gave my mission an otherworldly glow. I pulled up by the locked barrier and walked across to where I'd had the spat with the driver of the mock Range Rover. I looked round for the pieces of The Map. As I picked up the eight imaginary fragments from where they had come to rest I couldn't help but bring to mind, with affection, Roy Pullman. He had pushed The Map across my desk, saying words to the effect that he wouldn't be needing it anymore and would it be of use to me, a fellow volcano? To have ripped it up in a hissy fit, over something so trivial, had been a betrayal of our mutual respect.

Back at Beech Tree I laid the eight pieces out on the kitchen table, drew imaginary sellotape from the air and stuck them together. Once whole again, I folded The Map and returned it to my inside pocket.

***

I contacted Jaikie the next morning on Zoom, which he loves, because it's a camera, and I loathe because it makes me look twenty years older than I think I am.

"Nice," I said of his skin tone. "More lilac than purple now. Remember Bill Grogan?"

"I do."

I tried to be jolly about it. "He's coming to live with you for a bit. If those two buggers who broke in make a return visit…"

He clearly wasn't delirious about the idea and didn't think Jodie would be either.

"You want me to speak to her?" I offered.

"No, no. Are you sure it's necessary? I mean, don't think I'm not grateful for…"

"That Sikh immigration officer."

"What about him?"

"He's dead. Murdered."

His mouth guppied before he managed to say, "Are you sure?"

"Don't be so bloody silly! I found his body! I think Suyin used to live with him and his family."

He dropped out of sight as he slumped down into one of the kitchen chairs. "Jesus!"

"Alexa, get the smelling salts," I called out.

He realigned his laptop and came back into view. "You think she's responsible, gone to ground, gone back to China?"

He was catching on to the possible angles. "I plan to visit this poor man's widow once the police are clear of the house. And by the way, tell Jodie to box up anything delicate. Bill Grogan tends to lumber."

A couple of days later I drove to Muswell Hill and hit the bad-tempered swirl of evening traffic. The streets of North London seemed ablaze with light: shops, streets, houses, all distorted in the rain running down the Land Rover's windscreen.

I parked round the corner from the Pandeshis' and walked the few hundred yards to number 26. From the outside, it didn't seem like a house in mourning, though I'm not sure what I mean by that. Maybe I'd expected cones of wilting flowers to be crowding the pavement and to sense that inexplicable pall of sadness which drops on a house where tragedy has occurred.

However, in keeping with Sikh belief that life and death are on a continuum that cannot be interrupted, a young woman was in the driveway removing bags of shopping from a grey Peugeot, the kind that's always two feet behind my car, driven by mothers hurrying their children to school. I took this girl to be Opinder's daughter, even though she appeared to have abandoned the conventions her faith might have imposed. She was in her early twenties, wearing clingy leggings and a fleecy jacket. I hovered until she spotted me and removed the eternal earphones of her generation.

"Can I help you?" she asked, in a curt North London accent.

"My name is Nathan Hawk," I said. "I'm a retired police officer and I'd like a word. I'm guessing you're Opinder's daughter?"

"I'm Maya Pandeshi, yes."

We paused to size each other up.

"Well?" she said.

"I'm the person who found your father the night he died. I'm the one who phoned the police."

Her face came alive with indignation and she asked the same question I would've done.

"What were you doing here?"

Her mother had appeared at the front door and beckoned us both in out of the rain. I guessed her eyes had always had a mournful look to them, but the drawn face spoke of more than inbuilt reservations about life. I walked over and shook her hand.

"I am so sorry about your husband, Mrs Pandeshi."

She was dressed more traditionally than her daughter, wearing what Google informs me are a salwar and kameez, which sound far more elegant than the loose top over baggy pants that, in plain English, they were. A flow of black and grey hair was pinned back away from her face. She nodded and apparently decided that she quite liked me.

"You must come in, Mr…?"

"Hawk. Thank you."

The carpet in the hall and on the stairs had been removed and was no doubt sitting in some evidence locker. The blood spatters on the walls had been cleaned off. Mrs Pandeshi led me towards the kitchen and I heard the Peugeot tailgate slam as Maya took out the last of the shopping and brought it indoors.

"You must forgive the state of the house. We have been at my sister's for a few days."

I waved her concern aside. "When is the funeral?"

"Tomorrow. A special dispensation from the coroner."

"Then I won't keep you long."

As Mrs Pandeshi and her daughter put the shopping away, I told them I knew Suyin had lived here and that when she left she took a room in my son's house, which had recently been broken into. I believed the intruders were after the same thing they hoped to find here in Ventnor Road. Suyin herself. Or at least some information about her.

"You're a policeman?" Mrs Pandeshi asked.

"Was. Is there a… reason Suyin left your house?"

"Why do you want to know?" Maya asked.

"Because I plan to find her. She was my son's friend and he's concerned. In finding her I hope to discover who killed your husband."

"The police will…"

"The police will try, certainly. I will succeed."

Christ, I suddenly thought, did Jaikie inherit the braggadocio from me or did I catch it from him?

"Perhaps you would like some tea? Maya, would you…?"

Maya filled the kettle, irritably. Spray from the cold tap hit her in the face and she cursed under her breath. I had the mother onside apparently, but the daughter needed time to draw level.

"I told the police I cannot think of any enemies he had," said Mrs Pandeshi. "A peace-loving man. A kind and gentle man."

"And Suyin?"

"She was a paying guest, but a welcome one who was here for over a year. She and my husband, house on fire. He treated her like a third daughter."

I turned to Maya and smiled. "Ah! You have a sister?"

"Jasnam," said Maya. "She's still with my aunt."

"Did you like Suyin?"

She nodded. Her mother perched on one of the stools at the kitchen counter and folded her hands in front of her. A picture of serenity and, perhaps, a hidden secret or two.

"Opinder raised his voice at her only once. Three months ago."

"Why was that?"

"He said she must return to China."

"So he knew she was here illegally?"

She chuckled. "That would not have troubled him. Her safety, on the other hand…"

It was a while since I'd drunk tea from a cup and saucer. Maya placed them on the counter as she made her first voluntary contribution to the conversation.

"She'd applied for an extension to her visa."

"For how long?"

"She wanted to stay here forever. Sugar?"

"No, thanks. Had she met someone?" She shrugged. "Were you close enough that she would have told you?"

Her mother smiled. "She had a boyfriend to begin with, but he wasn't right for her. My husband certainly didn't think so."

I smiled with paternal sympathy. "I've known a few of those myself. Is that why the boy's out of the picture now?"

"She discovered he was crazy about Chinese girls," said Maya. "He had quite a collection. He was a prick."

Her mother pounced on her. "Maya, will you use such language to your patients?"

"If necessary…"

"You're a doctor?" I said.

"Medical school. Barts."

"Oh, my… ex-partner studied there. She's a GP." Martin Falconer was right. At the slightest excuse I brought Laura Peterson into the conversation. "What was the boyfriend's name?"

"Charles Beaumont. They met online. A site called The Loving Cup." Maya smiled. "Perhaps you know it?"

I smiled back in kind. "Oh, intimately. Did she ever… replace Charles Beaumont, do you know?"

"I've no idea," said Maya.

"Well, is there anything you *do* know that might help me?"

"Not much. Suyin is very good at extracting information from others, but unwilling to share much about herself."

"It's called modesty," said her mother.

"It's called being secretive, Mata. It's the Chinese way."

"I would speak to DCI Parfitt if you want to know more," said Mrs Pandeshi. "James, such a caring and courteous man."

"Yes, I've met him. A real charmer."

"Don't let your tea get cold," said Maya, stiffly.

It was her way of saying drink up and get out of our lives.

***

I thought it only fair to update Martin Falconer on the situation at Elwyn Road, though I wasn't looking forward to the conversation. How do you tell a man that a pair of homicidal maniacs might well break into his daughter's house, but he shouldn't worry because I'd installed an old friend as guard dog? I thought it best to give him the news face to face at our regular Friday night moan and groan at The Crown. A few beers would take the edge off it.

Some would call it telepathy. Martin would be one of them. Ten minutes after I'd made the decision to brief him he phoned, wanting to know if we could meet at the Hen and Chickens in Ashendon tomorrow 'for a bit of a change'. Under no circumstances, I said. Ashendon was five miles away, whereas I could see The Crown from my bedroom window. Martin groused a little, then rang off.

I arrived early at the pub to find the usual crowd already there. They sat in their appointed places, Easter Island statues who apparently hadn't budged since the same time last week. Was it my imagination, or did the place fall silent when I walked in these days? Did my neighbours regard me with a degree of pity, verging on disdain?

Annie McKinnon, the licensee, was pregnant again, which may have explained her motherly descent on me. She poured me a double scotch with ice to the brim and leaned in for a heart to heart.

"How are you keeping, Nathan?" she asked, as if I'd been seriously ill.

"To be honest, I'm feeling a bit, you know…" I screwed my nose up by way of elaboration.

"Do you want to talk?"

"What about?"

"Well… things."

'Things' was an oblique reference to Laura having moved out of my house, of course, but I pretended not to know that.

"Okay, Annie. I'll start."

I nodded down at the bump in front of her and she clutched it with both hands.

"Me? Us? Three weeks left. It's a girl, by the way." She stopped being polite and her accent became Glasgow stroppy. "Why the hell did you two call it a day?"

I back-footed her. "Thank you for that, Annie. You're the first person to imply that it was Laura's decision as much as mine."

"Of course it's mainly your fault, you knob. I was being polite."

"But you're not now."

"Shepherd's pie?"

Martin arrived a few minutes later, bringing with him the reason he'd wanted us to meet at the Hen and Chickens rather than here at the Crown. She was a head-turner, to be sure, but not for the right reasons. For a start, she was on the downhill side of forty, which is fine but not if you dress like a twenty-year-old on the make. She also had red hair. Not romantic red, like Titian or auburn, but the kind you paint on a garden shed to preserve it.

"Nathan, this is Elaine Merrill. Elaine, Nathan Hawk."

"Martin's told me so much about you," she said, with a smile that was a bit too-ready for my liking.

She perched on the stool next to me and the hem on her skirt rose six inches up her thigh. Martin had a look on his face that begged to know what Annie and I thought of his new friend. I can't speak for Annie, but I tried to say, face only, that he was a good-looking bloke with all his hair intact and, more to the point, a one-thousand-acre farm worth millions. I'm not sure that he heard.

"I guess the dawn raid business has fizzled out," he said, fishing for the answer I gave him.

"Yeah, bound to have done."

And then he uttered words that I never believed would cross his lips.

"We're going to a quiz night, next Saturday. We wondered if you and, well, Laura would care to join us."

"Martin says she's a doctor," said Elaine. "She'll know tons of stuff. Much more than I do."

No doubt about that, I thought. "I've never been to a quiz night."

"They're such fun and they keep the old grey matter in working order."

"Where is it?"

She smiled. "So you are interested?"

"No. I just wondered where it was."

"The Bell, in Aylesbury."

I was even less interested. "Where do you live, Elaine?"

"Wendover. Do you know it?"

I smiled. "Yes, it's just five miles away. You work there?"

"No, London. Train every day. I mean, when I first moved out here I used to drive in, but honestly, the A418 is just murder. You were a police officer, Martin tells me."

"Mmm."

"Tell me all about it."

"All of it?" I had one more stab at being friendly. "Where did you two meet?"

"Online, a site called The Loving Cup," she said, loud enough for Martin to cringe. She turned to him. "Honestly, darling, some of my best friends met each other on dating sites."

"The Loving Cup?" I said.

"Yes, it's not just for kids, it's for young, old, in-betweeners." She dropped her voice to a giggly whisper. "I'm sure Martin lied about his age, but so did I…"

I'd stopped listening and was toying with various options. I could suddenly feel sick, clutch at my stomach and exit. I could answer a non-existent phone call, requiring my immediate attention. I could suddenly remember that I'd promised to call one of my children in exactly ten minutes. I certainly couldn't tell Elaine that she had just pointed the way forward for me.

"I'm sorry, guys, I've got to go. Nice to meet you, Elaine."

I walked out of The Crown, leaving half a glass of whisky and a barely touched portion of shepherd's pie.

***

Back at Beech Tree I dived straight in. I cranked up my laptop and went to The Loving Cup, where I began to create a profile. Given that Maya Pandeshi had said Charles Beaumont was 'crazy about Chinese girls', I invented a young woman by the name of Sandy Zhang. She was a recent pharmacology graduate whose visa didn't run out until next May. Between now and then she planned on seeing the sights and making friends. She was 25 years old, born in Xian and her interests were conservation, traditional cookery and travel. On a far-off web page I found a picture of a Chinese twenty-something standing on a rock beside a river. I copied it, reduced it to a headshot and primped it with a fancy photo app.

I sat back, pleased with the hour's work until I went to pay. My credit card said, unsurprisingly, Nathan Hawk, not Sandy Zhang. If some bright algorithm at The Loving Cup looked up my name they would be mad to allow Sandy Zhang's membership. I phoned Jodie.

"Can you talk?" I asked her.

"I'm a barrister, Nathan. I can talk for England. Except, apparently, to our new house guest, Bill Grogan, who moved in this afternoon. He seems very sweet but isn't what you'd call a chatterbox…"

"Did Jaikie explain what he's doing there?"

"Oh, yes."

She was ever so slightly up on her high horse and I decided to leave her there.

"Jodie, I'm phoning about Suyin. I've discovered that she had a boyfriend by the name of Charles Beaumont. They broke it off a year ago. Did you know him?"

"No."

"They met online. Given that neither you nor your husband knows much about Suyin, I'm hoping Charles Beaumont can tell me more. I plan to seduce him in the guise of a 25-year-old Chinese woman…"

There was a pause. "Erm… you are sure about that? I mean, for a start he might not still be on the site."

"Trouble is, I need a credit card to pay the joining fee. A fifty-plus male trawling for young men on The Loving Cup might arouse suspicion."

She laughed nervously. "One would hope so."

"Do you know any young Asian women who'd be willing to pay on my behalf? I'd reimburse them…"

She thought for a moment. "There's a couple of girls in chambers. I'm sure I could persuade one of them."

There was a pause while she took a few deep breaths as she realised what she had agreed to.

"Nathan, this conversation has been bizarre. I may have to phone you back to check that we've just had it."

I laughed. "Phone me back anyway, with some credit-card details."

***

She called the following morning to say that an intern in her chambers was willing to pay for my membership of The Loving Cup. Or, to put it another way, my daughter-in-law had conspired with me to entrap a young man and in order to do so she had pressured a subordinate into helping us. It might not have been a criminal act but it was certainly unethical of her, a Queen's Counsel, and me, an ex-Detective Chief Inspector. On the other hand, how would I have felt if Jodie had refused?

She also mentioned Alessandro Scutari, Suyin's lawyer. He was driving her mad, ringing twice a day to find out if there was any news about his client, which roughly translated meant had I found her yet? Could I by any chance phone and reassure him that I was doing everything possible, Jodie asked? I said maybe.

When Sandy Zhang logged onto The Loving Cup, she soon discovered that Charles Beaumont was still a member of the dating site and she immediately began to reel him in. His interests ranged from music to clubbing, when he was in town on business, via cinema, sport, reading and 'country pursuits', whatever they are. In his photo he was standing in front of his parents' sizeable mansion, leaning back against a vintage sports car, arms folded. He was six feet tall with sleepy dark eyes and a milky coffee skin. Predictably, he had been educated at Charterhouse and Cambridge.

Sandy played it cool to begin with, as if a romance was the last thing on her mind. And then, a week later, Charles suddenly stepped closer and asked if they could meet. Sandy was hesitant but agreed to it, choosing the Djanogly Café at Tate Britain as their first rendezvous. Upmarket, credibly artsy, lots of people around, safe.

Come the day of our first date, I arrived at the gallery an hour in advance, having zigzagged through human chaos from Victoria station. I'm not sure if the madness of the crowd was relieved or compounded by the William Blake exhibition that Laura suggested I take in.

I usually spend the first ten minutes in art galleries expecting a security guard to grip my shoulder and whisper that such places aren't for the likes of me, so would I kindly leave? And then a change occurs. I start to be drawn in to the artist's world and invariably leave a gallery hours later. Consequently, when I managed to force myself away from the exhibition and went down to the Djanogly, I spent twenty minutes trying to extricate myself from William Blake's terrifying imagination. As the Tyger roamed my head in disjointed phrases I returned to the main purpose of my visit.

The place was bustling and I'd taken my coffee and croissant, standard fare when undercover, to a far table. As I waited, my mind wandered back to the day I'd first met Maggie. It was a blind date, arranged by a colleague at Hendon Police College, and there in the Djanogly I could feel my stammering insecurity rising, hear myself laughing too loud as a small part of me hoped she wouldn't come. More powerful, though, was the thrill that she would, that I would at last meet the girl I'd only seen in an old school photo my friend had shown me. Dark, voluptuous and beautiful. The café we'd arranged to meet in wasn't anything like this place. It was North London budget, formica tables too close to each other for privacy and metal chairs that squeaked at every move you made. I was wearing my trademark black leather jacket, pockets on the chest with money in one of them. Twelve pounds fifty. Jeans. Tennis shoes. When she walked in, she looked round and spotted me. How could she fail to? I was the one waving like a clown. Somewhat disconcertingly, she glanced at her watch. She came over and I stood up. We shook hands and a year later we married.

When Charles Beaumont entered the Djangoly, he looked round only to discover there wasn't an Asian in sight, at least not a lone female one. He was a credit to his profile photo on The Loving Cup: pretty rather than handsome and expensively clad in a bomber-type jacket. From the way he nursed it between tables, it was almost certainly new. He settled three aisles across from me, took out his mobile and texted Sandy. My phone vibrated. The message said that he was there at Tate Britain, waiting, looking forward to meeting her. He propped the phone up against the sugar bowl and sat back.

I gave it a minute before I crossed the café and ambled down the aisle he was on. When I reached him I looked down and smiled, held it long enough to unsettle him.

"Hi, Charles. I'm Sandy Zhang."

He stared up at me, trying to deconstruct what I'd just said.

"I'm sorry I'm not as pretty as my photo," I went on. "Unless you tell me otherwise."

He tensed up and turned away, making ready to leave in a hurry. I snatched his phone off the table.

"Hey, what the fuck are you…?"

His voice was strangled and screechy as he tried to keep the conversation just between the two of us. I sat down opposite him and explained.

"Charlie, I've seen blokes make a run for it and leave behind wives, mothers, even their kids. But no one ever abandoned their phone." I started to flick through his apps. "Don't worry, I'll give it back when we're through."

He was looking round, maybe hoping to spot someone who could rescue him.

"If you make this awkward for me, I'll slap you, so let's be friends."

"What do you want?" he asked, reasonably.

"Two questions. One: did you kill Opinder Pandeshi? Two: where is Suyin Qu? She's missing."

His face screwed up in horror to a point where I thought he was going to cry, but he held off. He slumped back into his chair as if a string running through his limbs had suddenly snapped. Eventually he said, "I haven't seen either of them for a year."

I nodded. "That's when you broke up with her, right? I take it you've heard about Opinder Pandeshi's murder?"

I could see him wondering if that was a trick question. He struggled to sit up straight again. "I heard it on the news."

"You didn't think to come forward, see how your ex-girlfriend was taking it?"

"Listen, Mr… what did you say your…"

"I didn't. Hawk. I'm an ex-copper."

He nodded at my hands crawling all over his phone. "Can you stop doing that?"

"Lot of Chinese girls on your contacts list. You've got a thing for them, I hear."

"So what?"

"Quiet, submissive, beautiful… usually well-off."

He laughed, nervously. "Submissive? You don't know Suyin."

"She doesn't fit the stereotype?"

"No way, man. Missing, you say?"

"I think Opinder wanted her to go back to Shanghai, maybe for her own safety. You any idea why she'd be in danger?"

"Not a clue."

"What's your real name, Charlie, because it sure as hell isn't Charles Beaumont. Oh, here it is on your preferences. Francis Stevens. Oh, look, and you're not from the country. You're a West London boy. Mum, 4 Harrow Way, Pinner. Where's Dad?"

"Dunno. They're divorced." He took a few deep breaths before asking, "Why come to me?"

"I don't have much to go on, Frank, so tell me something about Suyin."

He took the request apart in his mind before saying, "You think she killed Opinder?"

I slipped his phone into my inside pocket and leaned forward. "What kind of stuff was she into? What sort of company did she keep?"

"How am I supposed to…?"

"People always know more than they think. Tell me one thing about her that I can get my teeth into. Something that made her unhappy, nervous, different, strange… maybe something that pissed you off."

He considered my request for a moment or two before responding to it, moodily. "She started to get up herself, kept hauling me round London to poncy art places. I reckon she fancied the bloke who owned this one joint…"

"Which joint?"

"In the King's Road. Mandrake's, or something. Smarmy git." He did a bad impersonation of a lounge lizard. "'Hallo, Suyin, how lovely to see you again.'" He changed to Suyin. "'Oh, hallo, Taylor, yes, likewise.' She never bought anything. Couldn't afford it. She just… looked."

I smiled. "Was it her or this… Taylor, did you say? This Taylor Mandrake who pissed you off?"

"She was a student, right? A nurse." He sniggered. "With ideas above her station…"

"You're a fine one to talk, Charles Beaumont!"

"Couple of weeks before we broke up she told me she'd invested in a British company. Fifty quid, she said. She was going to a board meeting the following day, at their head office in Norfolk."

"Norfolk? Bloody hell!"

"Where the turkeys come from. I drove her to Liverpool Street. She came back two days later, chuffed to buggery."

"What was the company called?"

He shrugged. "Don't remember. They make vegetarian pet food, somewhere near Cromer. Where the crabs come from."

I wondered what someone like Drusilla Ford would make of Charles Beaumont. Insecure and unhappy in the skin of Francis Stephens, certainly. A liar. A fantasist. A murderer? It was difficult to add that to his profile, but stranger things have been known.

"They make jackets there an' all…"

I reached out and grabbed his arm. "I know where things come from, Frank. How'd you get on with the Pandeshis?"

"They didn't like me, or at least the old man didn't." He suddenly heard the implication of what he'd said. "Doesn't mean I killed him though…"

"I never said you did."

I slid his mobile across the table. Before I took my hand off it I said, "4 Harrow Way, should I ever need you again."

He wasn't listening. Reunited with his phone, he was greeting it like a long lost friend. Had he been alone in his bedroom he would have kissed it.

Given that few people invest a mere fifty quid in a business and, even if they do, are unlikely to go all the way to Norfolk for a board meeting, I was intrigued. It's also a universal truth in my line of work that the biggest outcomes often derive from the silliest of details.

That evening I typed 'vegetarian pet food' into Google and honed my search down to Norfolk. It gave me a handful of retail outlets in this eco-conscious county, but only one manufacturer. The name was Richard Bennett. I confess I didn't read the web page beyond the first paragraph, probably out of indifference to such a lunatic project as dog food made from organic plants. Whatever next? Gluten-free? No, no... I was way behind the curve. Gluten-free dog food was already on their menu.

Whenever I travel eastwards beyond the Mile End Road my mind jumps immediately to the coast. My father had a strange emotional tie to the East Coast having been billeted there on his return from Dunkirk, still a boy and with bits missing from his left hand. In the coastal village of Walberswick he'd been taken under the wing of the local blacksmith, and Dad took me to meet him one summer, thirty years thereafter. I remember walking into the forge and watching my father greet this huge, aproned man who leaned down like a god out of the clouds to shake my hand. I can smell the sizzling bone as the shoes burned into the horses' hoofs. I can hear the ring of the hammer as the nails were driven home. I can feel Dad's hand reaching down to take mine when, for a brief moment, we became Father and Son.

As I coaxed the Land Rover up the A1065, just after the turnoff to Mildenhall in fact, I spotted a car in the rearview mirror and it set me on edge. It was a silver-grey Volvo estate, one of dozens you pass in an average day, but this one stood out because it *didn't* stand out. The driver maintained a distance between us, a mile, sometimes two, and I could hardly speed away to test if he was tailing me. My suspicion subsided when the Land Rover overheated and I had to pull off to let the engine cool down. The Volvo sailed past me.

Due to the Land Rover's bad behaviour, I was ill-disposed towards the White Horse Hotel, just outside Cromer, long before I reached it. It stood alone in lifeless surroundings, not a ripple in the landscape apart from a thin lip curling upwards at the coastline. Beyond that was a shingle beach with a view of the North Sea. Grey sky meeting grey water.

Next morning, I summoned the AA breakdown service and a technician, whose stomach was barely contained by his khaki shirt, shook his head at my engine and asked how far I was hoping to go. Seven miles, I said. To a place called Tricks Farm in Weybourne. He closed his eyes as if in prayer and told me not to expect miracles. He did what he could and I set off.

I took the coast road, a ribbon of sameness broken by sudden views of the North Sea, but when I turned off at the road for Tricks Farm the landscape became more interesting. It began to rise and dip, and the land around was in visible use, being planted, ploughed, some of it even grazed by sheep.

At the main entrance to Tricks Farm, I rattled over a cattle grid and up the newly gravelled driveway. Beyond the railed fence to my left, three horses were grazing. In one corner of the field stood a brand-new combine harvester affair, possibly for root vegetables. My knowledge of farm machinery is minimal, but over the years I've had to endure Martin Falconer complaining about the price of it. The last combine he bought cost three hundred thousand pounds.

I parked in front of the house and began to recalibrate my attitude to Tricks Farm. As I did so, I glimpsed an elderly man in the rearview mirror, creeping up on the Land Rover with exaggerated stealth, trying to stay in its blind spot. At a guess he was in his eighties, stooped at the shoulders and dressed in an old tweed jacket, grey flannels and cut-down wellingtons. A candy floss of white hair. So far, so scarecrow, but the baseball bat in his hands troubled me. He held it as if, given the chance, he would launch my head out of the stadium.

When he drew level with the driver's door he kicked it to let me know he was there. I wound down the window and within moments became aware of the sea somewhere beyond a slight rise in the terrain: the smell first, then the distant sound of waves stroking the shore.

"I was told to be civil to visitors," said the geriatric striker.

"I think that's good advice."

"Who are you?"

"My name's Hawk."

"I know a man called Peregrine. Any relation?"

I was quick to deny. "None. Do you mind if I get out, stretch the legs?"

"Frankly, yes, but it's a free country."

He skipped backwards and the wellingtons made a gulping sound. He watched as I stepped down from the Land Rover and took a few exaggerated breaths of sea air.

"Nice bat," I said. "What's it made of?"

"Wood."

"Yes, I meant what kind? Ash, maple, hickory? May I see?"

I held out my hand and he stared at me for a moment before slowly handing it over. Once it was in my grasp I threw it as far as I could. He watched it spin in the air and clatter to earth twenty yards away.

"Can we start again?" I asked.

We were interrupted by a brand-new Range Rover gliding up the drive towards us. It braked with a crunch and the driver stepped onto the gravel, unfolding to a spindly six feet four. He too was armed and dangerous, with a fancy shotgun broken over his arm. In his early forties, he had a sickly face, long and bony, fair hair whitening at the ends. He was wearing the inevitable check shirt of his profession, waxed jacket, brown cord trousers and lace-up leather boots.

"You must be Richard Bennett?" I said.

"Must I?"

"Er... vegetarian pet food?"

He thought he'd got a handle on me. "Sorry, we don't sell it here. You can buy it online or the village store does a token range of..."

"No, no, I've come to see you, actually."

"What about?" he asked, sharply.

How had I offended him, I wondered? Was it the battered vehicle I'd turned up in, the equally battered leather jacket, the battered face which I hadn't shaved that morning? While he waited for an answer his wife opened the rear door of the Range Rover and stepped down. She reached back to a child seat, more complicated than a dentist's chair, and extricated a small girl.

"My name's Nathan Hawk. I'm a retired police officer. What's with all the weaponry, Dick? Shotguns, baseball bats?"

"What's with the visit... Nate?" he asked.

So the guy had a sense of humour, aggressive though it was. "Point taken. I'd like to talk about Suyin Qu."

Mention of the name made him even less friendly.

"What about her?" his wife asked.

"Can we do this inside?" I asked. "Over a coffee maybe?"

Her husband and I waited for permission to be granted. His wife nodded and led the way over to the house, carrying the child. Having retrieved his baseball bat, the geriatric striker followed us.

The front door of the place opened into a vast, beamed room, full of 18th-century Heath Robinson repairs, the odd oak pillar rising from the flagstones to support the rooms above. The walls were a junk shop of prints, paintings, photos, masks, old farming implements, clocks. In a corner, far away, was a kitchen area, 18th-century open plan, where the small daughter was being fastened into a highchair by her mother. I ambled over to the table, trying to be friendly.

"Sorry, I didn't catch your name," I said to the child.

"Roberta," said her mother. "I'm Farrah. The dog's Clemmie."

She was referring to an old retriever lying on the hearthrug. Richard, Farrah, Roberta, Clemmie. A family with social aspirations, then.

Farrah was a country girl and no mistake, a couple of stone overweight, dressed in old riding breeches and boots, a sloppy sweater on her top half. She had a rather lovely face, spoiled only by the dagger looks she kept giving me. I gestured round.

"Lot of people don't go for three centuries of do-it-yourself. I love it. In fact I live in a house rather like…"

"Hawk," said Richard. "You anything to do with that actor, Jaikie Hawk, only you look a bit…"

"He's my son."

It's amazing what a dose of celebrity does for attitudes. Richard warmed a smidgeon as he removed two cartridges from the shotgun and placed it on a rack above a window. He turned back into the room.

"So, Suyin Qu?" he said.

"I heard from an old boyfriend of hers that she invested money in your business. Fifty quid, he reckoned. Which made me think you'd be a tinpot outfit, working from an allotment. How big's the farm?"

"Three thousand acres," said Richard.

I tried not to show my surprise. "That's quite an allotment. Suyin's a friend of my son, by the way. She's missing"

"What do you mean… missing?"

I laughed. "People always ask that question, and in those very words. Missing as in there's an empty space where she should be. I reckon she's gone to ground… and where better to do so than in a big old farm like this? Either that or she's dead."

He was on the verge of asking me what I meant by dead, but he stopped himself. I turned to Farrah, who was now spoon-feeding her daughter, trying to get an orangey gloop to stay in her mouth. I got the feeling that she wasn't as concerned by Suyin's possible demise as her husband was.

"Given that I'm looking for her, are you going to tell me something helpful? Let's start with how you come to know her."

Farrah nodded permission for Richard to fill me in. He went over to the kitchen range and moved an enormous kettle from one hotplate to another.

"Three years ago we had a rough time of it. So much rain in November and December you couldn't tell land from the sea."

"How biblical."

"That's what Farrah's dad said. He's a minister in Felbrigg. Floods here in the UK, fire in Oz, locusts in North Africa, plague on the horizon the Reverend was breathing fire. Anyway, rain washed out the October planting, drowned the livestock. Then after Christmas the land dried up and any crops that had survived were burned to dust. We'd started on the veggie pet food by then and that was struggling. Two years ago, an old schoolfriend of mine sent us an angel to rescue us. Suyin Qu."

"Who was the old schoolfriend?"

"His name's Taylor Mandrake. We thought she just wanted bed and breakfast, until next morning over her bacon and eggs she told us about her and Taylor. And that she was looking to invest in our business, reckoned there was a big future for it."

"How much did she want to put in?"

Richard looked at his wife.

"Twelve million pounds," said Farrah.

I gave it a moment before trying to rejoin the conversation.

"That clatter you just heard was my jaw hitting the floor," I said, eventually.

Nobody laughed, except Roberta. The striker had dozed off in a distant armchair. The dog hadn't bothered to wake up in the first place .

"You're surprised?" said Richard. "How do you think we felt?"

"I'd have thought she was trying to scam me for the B and B. What happened?"

He smiled. "Being British, we said we'd think about it. You see, what we've always needed is drainage, from the land into a lake about half a mile north of here. Private reservoir. So, dykes, ditches, diverting streams, it would all cost money we didn't have. Suyin had worked out a business plan, back-of-an-envelope stuff, but viable." He shrugged, as if recalling the leap of faith he took. "What had we got to lose? A week later we said yes. In the two years since we met her the business has taken off."

I held up a hand. "Where did her money come from?"

"A finance company in Shanghai called White Crane," said Richard. "You'll find it online, but it won't tell you much. Suyin drew up the legal stuff. Fifty-one percent of the shares went to White Crane, forty-nine to Farrah and me. We're still reeling from it."

"I expect the new Range Rover takes the edge off that."

He smiled. "That's what everyone singles out."

He led me across the room and I peered out at three, maybe four bolt-together farm buildings, the size of small hangars. A dozen cars were parked in a designated area.

"You're looking at five million quid in which seventeen people are working their guts out. Preparation, baking, drying, mixing, packaging, dispatching. Draining the land, three million. Machinery, pumps to draw water out again come the drought, two million. The Range Rover's a drop in the ocean, and by God I needed it. I'd been driving round in something even worse than yours."

He poured boiling water into a primed mug, set it down on the unit nearest to me then ducked into the fridge for a bottle of milk. As I stirred some into the coffee I said, "You still haven't answered my original question. Why all the firepower? Brace of shotguns over the window. His and hers?"

He glanced at Farrah, who busied herself cleaning up Roberta's face.

"We're farmers," he said, eventually.

I nodded at the old boy still dozing in the armchair. "And is your father Babe Ruth? There's a camera in the corner there recording every twitch, and the front door's got more heavy metal on it than Led Zeppelin. What are you scared of? Turnip rustlers?"

"We haven't seen Suyin since the last board meeting, a month ago," said Richard. "When I see her again I'll let her know you were looking for her."

He glanced at his watch like a man with a busy schedule which has been interrupted.

"Can I drink the coffee?"

"Please do."

"One last question. For you, Farrah. Girl talk. Were Suyin and Taylor… close."

"Yes, so if that's all…"

When somebody watches me drink something they've just made, it develops a funny taste. It's all in my mind, I'm sure, but I took just a few more sips of coffee and left the rest. The striker startled awake and stared at me.

"Who's he?" he asked. "I know him."

"No, you don't, Dad," Richard assured him.

The old man stood up and came over to me. "I'll see you to your…" He frowned and snapped his fingers, then lit up again as he recalled. "Land Rover."

We walked out onto the forecourt and he followed me across to where I'd parked. As I opened the driver's door, he grabbed me by the shoulder and turned me to face him.

"Bye, Mr Bennett," I said.

"Walter, please."

I climbed in and turned the key. The starter motor whined and flagged. I tried again.

"I can fix that," said Walter Bennett.

He galumphed round to the front of the motor, lifted the bonnet and propped it open. He fiddled with the mess of wires in front of him, then called out.

"Again! Again!"

As the battery began to die he yelled for me to give it one last attempt, at which point the engine spluttered into life. Walter stood back to admire his work, and as I leaned out of the window to thank him his face hardened, which for a moment made him seem younger. I'd seen the look before on the face of an elderly neighbour. A window of lucidity had opened in his mind and he spoke quickly, knowing it would close again soon.

"You asked them what they were scared of."

I smiled. "I thought you were asleep."

"Two men came here looking for the Chinese girl. Father and son."

"How d'you know that?"

"One called the other Dad."

I smiled. "Dead giveaway. When was this?"

"Last month."

"D'you see their faces?"

He shook his head. "Ski masks, navy blue. Boiler suits, gray. They searched the house, made a mess…"

"Were they armed?"

"One had a… meat cleaver thing. He brought it down on the table, next to the baby."

"You don't know where Suyin is, by any chance?"

"I was told not to say."

"Does that mean you do know or don't?"

"If I ever did, I've forgotten."

I wanted to press him further but his facial features were slackening. He pointed at me.

"I'm sure we've met before."

"We have." I shook his hand. "Nice seeing you again, Walter."

The end occurred just north of a town called Brandon. There was no violence involved, no scream of fear at the moment of death, just a subdued rattle. I freewheeled onto a wide verge and applied the handbrake. Naturally, I tried to restart the engine, but to no avail.

As I began to reflect on our time together, I saw it again in the rearview mirror. The silver Volvo estate. It pulled onto the verge in front of me and a man in his early forties got out and walked towards me. At first glance he had the easy manner and bearing of a 1950s academic. I pick the date because of his clothes – sports jacket and cavalry twills, brown brogues. His face was that of a perpetual schoolboy, a forelock of hair falling over his right temple, in constant need of being stroked away. I rolled down the window and he leaned in.

"Need a hand?" he asked, in a gentle voice.

"No."

"I guessed you might say that. My name's John Smith." I gave him a withering look. "No, really. I can't tell you how often I've thought of changing it. Nice to meet you, Mr Hawk. Mind if I...?"

He walked round the corpse, opened the passenger door and climbed in beside me.

"How do you plan on getting back to Winchendon?" he asked.

"I'm now thinking of beating you to a pulp and nicking your car."

"No, don't do that," he said, chuckling. "I'll give you a lift and see to getting this thing towed away." He smiled at me before applying his particular brand of pressure. "I can get you another just like it. Or something a little upmarket perhaps. Personally, I'd go for the new Discovery."

"If?"

"We won't haggle yet. Hour and a half to your place? I could murder a cup of tea. Bring your things."

Our conversation during the homeward journey was more monologue on his part than duologue between us, and as a result I learned more about him than perhaps he wanted me to know. He'd read Oriental Studies at Oxford and had fancied the academic life, but it wasn't to be. He owned and lived in a house overlooking Ravenscourt Park in London. He had a cat called Kublai Khan. He was an only child of parents who'd had him late in life. Sadly they had both died eight years ago, within six months of each other. One of pneumonia, the other of a broken heart. Shortly after that, he got married to a girl called Sophia whom he'd met at university…

When we reached Morton Lane he parked beneath the big beech, got out and looked up at the house.

"The place suits you so perfectly," he said.

"By the sound of it, this isn't the first time you've been here?"

He smiled, grabbed his laptop and we crunched across a carpet of beech husks towards the back door. Dogge flew out past us and had a pee before sizing Smith up.

"Has she been on her own all day?" Smith asked, critically.

"If I'm away for more than eight hours a friend in the village comes and lets her out."

He nodded. "Your cleaner? Mrs Tindall?"

"Give it a rest, John, will you."

He followed me into the kitchen and, from the way he glanced round it, pausing at whatever caught his eye, I figured that while he'd visited the area before, he hadn't been inside my house. He didn't know where the downstairs toilet was.

"Other side of the stairs, first door you come to," I said.

We took our tea into the living room where he paused by a framed photo of Maggie.

"We have something in common, Mr Hawk. The way in which our wives died."

Though I tried not to, I nodded sympathetically and asked, "How old was she?"

"Thirty-nine."

"That is… far too young."

"Oh, I had good support," he said. "Neighbours, they scraped me up off the floor, put me back together again. Mammoth task. Not really over yet. Don't suppose it ever will be." He jollied himself back to the business in hand. "Suyin Qu. It must have occurred to you that she's gone back to China?"

"It's on my list of possibilities," I said.

"So you'll be going there to check?"

"Much as I'd love to, it's a long way to travel on a whim."

"I beg to differ," he said, quickly. "Thirteen hours from Heathrow to Shanghai. It'd take you that long to drive to John O'Groats."

"I wouldn't go there either."

He flicked his hair as he tried to readjust the conversation. "You've guessed that I'm not just a good Samaritan, picking you up from the roadside…"

"I've no idea who you are."

"We know you're looking for this woman."

"Everyone in the world seems to know, except her. Why is she important to you?"

He affected mild horror that I'd needed to ask. "Mr Hawk, a public servant, an officer of Her Majesty's Government, has been murdered. We don't let these things just fade away."

I laughed. "You mean it's nothing to do with the money Suyin's put into Tricks Farm?"

"What money is that?"

"You must think I fell out of that tree, John Smith. Why not handle China yourselves? You must have people on the ground."

He winced. "Several things against that. First, most of our people there are well known to their Chinese counterparts. You're not known at all. And, let's face it, you've been getting blood out of stones for thirty years, so we were hoping that while you're in Shanghai looking for Suyin you could…"

"I'm not going to China, not without knowing the reason you want me to."

"The other problem is, well, White Crane. We've looked for the address it operates from. It doesn't exist." He lowered his head and his voice. "Or at least we haven't been able to find it."

I nodded and thought for a moment.

"Suppose I were to take you up on your offer? What's in it for me?"

"Oh, we'd see to your visa, book flights, best hotels, first-class travel. Tour guide."

I laughed. "One of your lot, breathing down my neck?"

"As a matter of fact, no. Ex-police officer. Old acquaintance of mine."

"Who is this 'we' you refer to, John?"

"MI6."

He'd whispered it, not out of reluctance to acknowledge his paymaster, more out of… disenchantment, I fancied.

"Right, my guess is you're the lowest of the low, an Intelligence Officer." He didn't respond. "You fit the stereotype. The slight bagginess of personality, matching your clothes. I'd say you were a bit of a loner. They like that at SIS, don't they? Want you to work alone so they can disown you if you make a cockup. Do feel free to correct me."

He smiled. "No need."

"And two hours ago you mentioned a new Land Rover. A new Discovery."

"Well, yes, we can discuss that at the appropriate time."

With a purposeful slap of both knees, he rose from the sofa and missed an overhead beam by a fraction of an inch. He handed me a plain business card with the name John Smith on it and a mobile number.

"Think it over, call me tomorrow with your decision."

He reached out to shake my hand, fixing me with a pissholes-in-the-snow look that belied the shambling image he'd been projecting. Which was the real man, I wondered? The overgrown schoolboy, or this… national security lackey?

"I should remind you that you're a signatory to the Official Secrets Act," he said. "Pure luck on my part, but do bear it in mind. No nattering to friends. Not even to Doctor Peterson."

He all but winked, and left.

I didn't allow John Smith's intrusion into my life to alter my plans and next morning Laura drove me into Thame, where I hired a cake tin on wheels from Johnson's. It was cheap and far too small for comfort, so I drove it to Haddenham Station and went in by train.

In my twenties I used to love the Kings Road. I remember buying so much tat at the market, in the belief that I was getting a trendy bargain, until the T-shirt or jeans fell apart in the first wash. The place was always touristy. You could meet the whole world there. Nowadays the tourists come with more money to spend than my generation dreamed of, so the stalls have poshed up. One hangover from the past, or maybe it's just a fact of life, is that you can still get your wallet nicked without feeling a thing. In a way, I suppose, it's reassuring.

There was no market to distract me when I visited Taylor Mandrake's gallery and the trip felt like a minor replay of my experience at Tate Britain. This was not my kind of shop and the price tags on the merchandise meant it never would be. In the window was a poster of the man himself with a sincere look on his face, brows knitted together. Vote Green Party, the legend said. Vote for Taylor Mandrake in the forthcoming council election. In smaller print were some bullet points that I didn't bother to read.

As I entered, an old-fashioned bell, a relic from the days when the place was a bakery, tinkled rather than rang.

The gallery had all the charm of a walk-in freezer, the kind you might find in an abattoir. It was laid out in a series of rooms, all painted off-white with wide arches leading from one to another. The walls were hung with the works of emerging artists, a far cry from those of William Blake, which still flitted through my dreams. On various plinths stood sculptures, most of them the work of sculptors with a weakness for scrap metal. A few plants completed the setup, tall and twisted bamboo and a large purple orchid I wanted to touch to check if it was real. I changed my view of the place from walk-in freezer to dentist's waiting room.

The only living thing in the room, apart from me and the plants, was a girl with a high finish on her who appeared from behind a screen and came towards me, lipstick first, a cloud of perfume trailing.

"May I help you?"

"I'd like to speak with the owner, please?"

"I'll see if Mr Mandrake's available. What name shall I say?"

"Hawk."

Her manner changed in a flash from formal to silly schoolgirl.

"You're Jaikie Hawk's dad," she blurted out. "You look just like him!"

I smiled. "I don't mean to be picky but I think *he* looks just like *me*."

She giggled, went across to a side door and knocked on it. A voice from the other side sang out for her to enter and from the doorway she informed the owner I was here. He emerged a few moments later and stretched out a hand.

"Mr Hawk, how lovely to meet you."

My first impression of him was probably tainted by the ponytail, held in place by an ornate gold clasp. The cotton suit was beige and unseasonal, the embroidered shirt would have set me back a month's wages. Some people would have called his manner suave and elegant. I wasn't one of them.

"May I offer you a drink?"

I shook my head. The office was done out in the same style as the gallery, cold and untouchable. If George Smiley didn't trust a man with a tidy desk, he would have avoided Mandrake like the plague. He perched on his desk, brought one knee up to his chest and clasped it, not so much a poser as needing to give his nervous hands something to hold onto. He nodded me to an armchair and watched me take in the paintings. I recognised them all but could only name two. Vermeer's *Girl With a Pearl Earring* and a Renoir portrait of Jeanne Samary.

Mandrake smiled down at me from his elevated perch. "They're copies."

"You don't say."

"Sorry."

I nodded vaguely in the direction of the front door. "Green Party."

He smiled. "Yes. If you'd like to hear my campaign speech, I'll willingly give it to you."

"I'll pass. You know Suyin Qu?"

"I've done business with her. These days rich people in Beijing can't wait to put European art in their vaults for a rainy day."

"How *well* do you know her?"

He looked away, smiling. "Are you asking if we're *more* than friends?"

"Why so coy, Taylor? I have it on good authority that you were… close close. Farrah Bennett."

He smiled. "The eternal matchmaker."

"If it's true, then my next question is why are you so laid back about her disappearance? When did you first meet her?"

He sighed and shook his head. "She came into the gallery about a year ago, looked round and, well… liked what she saw. We chatted and… you know how it goes."

A year ago would have been round about the time Suyin gave Francis Stevens the heave-ho. She walked into a Chelsea art gallery, all set to spend money, and there to greet her was this absurdly handsome man, ten years older than her but so what? Her money, his looks… yes, I did know how it went.

"Did she invest in your business?"

He was unfazed. "She offered to, but I've sufficient resources of my own."

"D'you know, if someone had asked me the questions I'm asking you, I'd have told them to wind their neck in."

"It crossed my mind, until I remembered you're the father of a valued customer."

"The Dransfields. How much were they, if you don't mind me asking?"

He smiled for the umpteenth time. "You may certainly ask…"

I went over to *Girl With a Pearl Earring*. It was oil on canvas, with a persuasive patina of time and grime and, for my money, only an expert could've told it from the original. The same went for the Gainsborough beside it, depicting the artist's two daughters chasing a butterfly.

"Two possibilities explain Suyin's disappearance," I said. "One, she's dead, the other, she's gone back to China. What do you reckon?"

He laughed. "About her being dead? I'd say you're an ex-policeman, you're bound to think the worst. As for her going back to China" – he shrugged – "it's her home."

"Did she ever mention Opinder Pandeshi?"

"Who is that?"

I wagged a finger at him. "You just stumbled, Taylor. You knew straightaway it was a person, not a place. I think he was killed by someone looking for Suyin."

"Again, the ex-policeman in you."

I so wanted to reach behind his head, grab the ponytail and bring the side of his face down on his redundant blotter. It wasn't exactly a Map situation, but the bunch of sweet peas I conjured up instead wasn't much help. Laura Peterson thinks of poetry when in danger of losing her temper. Di-dum-di-dum-di-dum.

"I wish I could help you, Mr Hawk, but I repeat: such dealings as I had with Suyin were strictly business, and there wasn't a vast amount of that."

"I don't believe you."

He laughed. "You know, you'd be far better off talking to a guy called Alessandro Scutari. He's an immigration lawyer I've known for years. Used to work at the Home Office. If you'd like his number…"

"I've met him. He made the same impression on me that you have. Dodgy."

He tried to find an amusing riposte but failed. He went over to the door and opened it.

"I think it's time for you to leave."

As he ushered me out of his office we were both distracted by a large man wearing an expensive suit and with visible extremities bespattered with jewellery.

"Mr Abdullah," said Mandrake. "How lovely to see you. Excuse me one moment." He called out to his glossy assistant. "Caroline, would you give Mr Hawk Alessandro's address and number?"

"I told you, I've met him…"

He smiled. "Just in case. Mr Abdullah, are you back to give the Carl Lederman a second look?"

The two men strolled off into the depths of the gallery. Caroline had returned to her pitch and jotted down Scutari's address on a compliment slip, which she now handed to me.

"Can I ask you something, Caroline?"

"No problem."

Another of my linguistic loathings. I let it pass.

"Has the gallery been broken into recently? I'm thinking two men in ski masks, grey overalls?"

She froze immediately and the skin on her face went white and stiff. Poor kid had probably been here, working, when it happened, and no doubt Taylor had asked her to keep quiet about it. Keeping secrets didn't come easily to her.

"Why do you ask?" she blurted.

"Well, the cameras here are state-of-the-art, the shutters out front are brand-new…"

She began to draw from a prepared script. "The insurance company… they insisted we update to the latest system."

"When was this?"

"A month ago. Now any break in the circuit goes straight through to the police station. They turn up in two minutes."

"Good job I left his hair alone, then." I turned to the tinkling door. "Nice meeting you."

"You too," she called out. "Give my regards to Jaikie."

***

Next door but one to the gallery there was a trendy coffee bar, where I ordered a latte and a sandwich and took them to a dark alcove. A young couple who had chosen the same recess for its privacy weren't bothered by my sitting within earshot and that irked me for some reason. I blamed it on Taylor Mandrake who had tried to fob me off royally.

Nevertheless, I'd managed to extract a few things from our conversation. Top of my list, I was now sure that Taylor and Suyin were an item. Of some kind. When I'd asked him how well he knew her he immediately denied they were lovers. I hadn't suggested they were. On top of that, he seemed unmoved by the idea that she'd gone back to China. He was even more casual about the notion of her being dead. Even a passer-by would have asked for more details. Taylor didn't need any. I reckoned he knew exactly where she was, dead or alive.

He had also tried to point me towards Alessandro Scutari. Did he believe that Sandro was the *deus ex machina* who drove the father-and-son combo round London trying to find Suyin, killing anyone who got in their way? Did Taylor want me to prove that, to get Scutari arrested and charged? Or did he simply want me off his back?

I took an Uber south of the river, to the address which Caroline had given me.

It had been built by the Victorians as a warehouse but there was no indication of what they might have stored in it. Being close to the river and with Waterloo Station a stone's throw away, it could have been anything from anywhere in the world. Now it was a honeycomb of offices and Alessandro Scutari rented one of them.

The outside of the place had been perfectly preserved, I suppose to some people's delight. Not mine. I've never been keen on the yellow brick which South London is built from. Cold and off-putting. Not that there was time to examine my finer feelings about architecture, because parked up on the kerb outside the place were three police cars, one with a blue light ticking over. My thoughts bounced from low crime to high, from a broken window to murder, but I've yet to work out how I knew the victim would be Alessandro Scutari. Maybe it was just that his name was the only one I recognised from the forty-odd on the board outside.

A cobbled slope ran down to what was once the basement, now the front entrance to Brougham House. Outside the fancy doors, the kind that open if you breath too hard, there was a dozen uniformed coppers and at least four others in plain clothes. An older, heftier man was in charge and I made a slow beeline down the incline towards him. At a certain point they broke off from their chat and turned to me, almost in unison.

"Help you, mate?" said the boss.

I'd put on my worried face by then. "I'm here to see someone."

"Name?"

"Mine or his?"

The boss took a few steps towards me. "Both, while we're at it."

"He's Alessandro Scutari, I'm Nathan Hawk. Ex-job, as it happens."

He looked me over without brotherly feelings. "You got an appointment?"

"Open invitation."

He nodded gently before making up his mind. "His office was broken into sometime last night."

"Poor bugger," I said, with credible concern.

"Nothing taken, just turned over, made a mess of. We're nearly done here, so knock yourself out. He's in the rest area having a drink. First landing you come to."

"Thanks."

I made to walk round him but he raised a hand. "Ex-job, you say. You seeing him for something personal or on behalf…?"

"On behalf of a friend of a friend."

He smiled. "I'm DI Mark Jackson. Hawk? Rings a bell, but I can't place it."

"Put the Nathan in front of it and you will, sooner or later."

"Can I have your mobile number?" he said.

I smiled. "We've only just met."

"Yeah, but you know… chemistry."

I gave him my number and went into the building.

***

I would have called him a commissionaire in the days when he might have worn a uniform, but this was just a guy bulging out of a tight-fitting suit. I told him I had an appointment with Alessandro Scutari and he directed me to the rest area which turned out to be a tarted-up balcony with a licensed bar running along the back wall and a general livery of railway green, the better to hide any dirt. Tuneless music was playing in the background. I could see people offering sympathy to Alessandro, who was slumped in a sofa. He spotted me out of the corner of his eye and sprang to his feet, his face taut and the muscles in his neck rippling with tension.

"You heard what happened?" he said as we shook hands. "God knows how the bastards got in. I mean He probably does. And so do I. Well, I think I do. I'm guessing…"

I tried unravelling sense from that but nothing came.

"Take a breath and try that again," I said.

He fiddled with the diamond stud in his ear and lowered his voice. "There are forty offices in this building. Don't ask me what they all do. But somebody from one of them's given the door codes to… whoever."

"Who's whoever?"

"My money's on the same bastards who broke into Jaikie's house looking for Suyin. Nothing taken from there, nothing taken from my office. They just emptied every bloody cupboard and slung the furniture round, hacked off because what they came for wasn't there."

"Information about where to find her? You told the police about her?"

"As little as I could."

"Mind if I have a squint at your office?"

He led the way up a wide staircase to the next floor, passing a young woman who was descending it. She paused and smiled. The recent lipstick she'd applied had smudged onto her front teeth.

"Sandro, bad luck," she said.

"Thanks, Dee. Drink maybe, after work?"

She screwed up her face in sympathetic agony and smiled through it, then carried on down the stairs. Alessandro held his gaze on her departing shape before turning back to the business in hand. At the third-floor landing he pointed to a row of small wood and glass offices, laid out like a milking parlour. Alessandro's stall was at the far end and he paid £900 a month for it, he said, even though he worked from home three days a week.

I stood in the doorway and glanced round. He was right about one thing, the place had been well and truly upended. Meticulously, you might say. The desk and his secretary's station had been toppled. Drawers in a filing cabinet had been taken off their runners and the contents emptied. Books, papers and a few ledgers had been swept off shelves and lay strewn across the green carpet. Even the dusty plant was lying on its side.

"Being a rubber plant you'd expect it to bounce back up again," I said.

"It's plastic. I get hay fever."

"Forensics been here?"

He nodded and looked round. "Maybe those two from the murder squad'll believe me now."

"Parfitt? Gadsden?"

He flopped back against the door jamb and folded his arms. "Yeah. Dropped in on me at home, never mind that I had my girls with me. Hour and a half. What did I know about Suyin? Not much more than you, I said. You're lying, said…"

"Their very words?"

"Verbatim. I could see how their minds worked. Pandeshi, immigration officer: me, immigration lawyer. Got to be a connection, eh?" He nodded round. "Now this!"

"Let's go back downstairs."

At the bar he bought me a scotch with prissy little shards of ice to the brim and ordered himself a soft beer, which he drank from the bottle.

"So, you told Parfitt and Gadsden nothing…"

"I'm as much in the dark as everyone else."

"Not even about Tricks Farm? And the twelve million quid she shelled out? And don't give me that crap about client confidentiality…"

He deflated with a sigh and began nodding as he worked up a response. "So you've found out about it… her… sorry."

"You asked me to, remember? Offered to pay my expenses?"

A young man in a gaudy waistcoat hailed him as he passed by.

"Sandro, bad luck, mate."

"Thanks, Chris."

The sympathiser moved on quickly, no doubt glad that it hadn't been his office.

"Could be any one of them," Alessandro muttered. "Him, the barman, Dee…"

"How long have you known Suyin was mega-rich?"

"Ever since I drew up the papers for Tricks Farm, a year ago. I swear to God that till then I thought she was a common or garden nurse. Then she made an offer for the lavender farm next door to the Bennetts'. Norfolk's known for its lavender, evidently, not just its reed or turkeys…"

I slapped the bar. "How much did she offer?"

"Twenty one million."

"What!"

"The twat turned her down to begin with, changed his mind two months ago."

"What's his name?"

"Peregrine Bailey."

That must have been the Peregrine Walter Bennett had referred to when we first met. Odd that Richard and Farrah had never mentioned it…

"How does your friend Taylor Mandrake fit into her life?"

He chuckled. "You've stumbled across him as well, have you?"

"I never stumble, Sandro. I fall like a Sumo wrestler. Splat."

He turned on the stool and signalled the barman for another beer, glancing to see if I wanted more scotch. I did, but said I didn't.

"Listen, this'll sound cheesy, but I think Suyin came to the UK to do business. To invest, Chinese-style. Then she met Taylor and… well, he's that good-looking I could fancy him myself!"

"Has she put money into anything else?"

"Two friends of Taylor, raving loonies. They run an outfit in the Cotswolds called Abiding Earth. She didn't put in millions, just a paltry nine hundred grand."

"Why didn't you tell me this before?"

"To be honest, I thought she'd turn up by now." He paused for a moment. "I've been thinking, since she disappeared. Abiding Earth would be an ideal place to hide out in, or keep someone under wraps… or even to dispose of a body."

"What's so special about it?"

"Go see for yourself."

I downed the dregs of the scotch and stood up to leave.

"I gather you worked at the Home Office in a former life," I said.

"Yeah. Couldn't wait to get out."

"Did you keep your contacts?"

"The useful ones. Didn't you?"

I shook his hand and left.

***

I envy anyone who can read a book on railway journeys. With all that rocking from side to side, I can't even think properly on a train. I latch onto a problem at the outset, try to work through it, and then somebody gets on at the next station and grabs my attention.

The tall, leggy woman who boarded the train at Harrow and sat on the seat opposite me was determined not to catch my eye. She was ugly-beautiful.

From a certain angle she was mesmerising, from another downright horsey-looking. She was early thirties and classily dressed, and her indifference to the rest of the world, especially to me, was probably due to her day at the office still swirling round in her head. She had a bony face that reminded me of someone I knew. I couldn't place who and kept on looking, more than I should have done for the poor woman's comfort. A broad, high forehead and beautiful eyes, the whites exceptionally clear. Prominent cheekbones and a proper nose. Christ, I felt like a pathologist measuring her skull... and then, thanks to the medical connection, it dawned on me. She was a younger version of Laura Peterson. So, strike 'horsey-looking' and replace it with 'a curiously striking face'.

The redolence had broken my train of thought about Alessandro Scutari. I went back into my mind and stood at his office doorway, glancing in at the chaos. Meticulous, I'd thought at the time. Careful chaos. Papers, books, ledgers on the floor. The desk on its side. The secretary's station overturned. The rubber plant lying on its side as if it had been taking a nap...

At Gerrards Cross the young woman alighted. By the time I reached Haddenham I was sure my suspicions were well founded.

***

At about nine that evening I got a call on my mobile. I didn't recognise the number. Expecting it to be a cold call from India, I grunted my standard response.

"Uh?"

"Mr Hawk? This is DI Mark Jackson. We met outside Brougham House this afternoon."

"Hi, Mark. Believe it or not, I know what you're going to say."

He paused before laughing. "Go on, then."

"Alessandro Scutari's office wasn't broken into. He faked it."

He laughed quietly. "Once a copper, eh?"

"Question is, why?"

"If I had the time I'd find out."

I decided to tell him what I knew about Suyin's disappearance and Opinder's murder, with special reference to the father-and-son machete-wielders. I ended by giving him DS Gadsden's number.

"I'll give him a call, courtesy," said Jackson. His voice seemed to lean back a little. "While I've got you, Nathan, was it a left or a right?"

"Was what?"

"The punch you threw at your guvnor?"

"Straight left."

"I shall dream about it. G'night."

"G'night."

Abiding Earth either had something to hide or harboured deep suspicions about the internet. Its website said it was an 'eco-research facility' and left it at that. It gave no details of what the company was engaged in. There were photos of the main building, taken years ago if the graininess of the images was anything to go by, and at first glance I thought it might be a present-day tax dodge, a way of making a large house affordable by using it commercially. Then again, if Suyin was the canny operator I was beginning to believe, she was unlikely to invest in a scam. Not even a paltry nine hundred thousand pounds. Did I just write 'not even a paltry nine hundred thousand'? It shows how easily you can start thinking in millions and discounting thousands as small change.

I drove to *Cider with Rosie* country, ever hopeful that the romance I associate with that story would prove to be real. It never does. Too much traffic, too many garden centres, not a horse and cart in sight. Just before Chipping Camden, I turned off towards the village of Arkway and pulled up outside the wrought-iron gates of Abiding Earth. I half expected them to creak open on rusty hinges or a disembodied voice from one of the stone pillars to ask what I was doing there. Instead, there was a notice on one of them saying the company was sorry but the motor operating the gates needed repairing so would visitors leave their cars on the verge, enter by the pedestrian gate and walk up to the house.

It wasn't so much a gravel drive I found myself walking on as an obstacle course where sinkholes had opened up over a half-mile stretch. The reason for that, I imagined, was the stream running under a humped bridge, which turned back on itself and disappeared underground. Quaint though it was, I began to walk with extra care.

Despite the time of year, the trees were still heavy with leaf and held in place by an overgrowth of hops. As anyone who has ever grown them will tell you, they never die, they just multiply year on year. The effect at certain points was of a minor rainforest: thick undergrowth and a darkening canopy of leaves overhead, drip, drip, dripping. Apart from the water, there was no sound at all.

An occasional clearing in the undergrowth gave a glimpse of the house itself. It was eighteenth-century, built of the area's mellow stone, and it comprised three front gables, all fighting off various creepers, with ferns and other plants growing in the mortar. From the tiled roof rose eight chimneys. Had I been approaching at night, I would have expected a storm to be raging with flashes of lightning giving a tantalising glimpse, but as things stood on that drab and dreary October afternoon, I could see that the building was fighting for its life. I reconsidered my tax-dodge theory. If the owners were getting perks from it being a business, they weren't guarding their investment.

The drive narrowed, and as I found myself in another tunnel of vegetation, I heard a crack beneath my feet. I'd stepped on something, a crude wooden lever as it turned out, which triggered the descent of a huge rope net, heavy enough to knock me off balance.

I clawed at one of the squares of rope and, as I pulled, so the netting tightened and twisted around me, scuppering any chance of escape. I froze, and as the net slackened I considered my position. This antique booby trap was made of rope, and in my back pocket was the penknife I always carried but seldom used. I opened it and began to cut my way free.

I paused when I heard boots crashing through the undergrowth nearby and a male voice telling someone to stay back, stay back. Seconds later, a man in his sixties appeared and stopped dead, three feet away.

"I might have to rethink this, Barbara," he said to the woman who had joined him. "See what's wrong, my love? He's cut his way out with a simple blade. Keep still, man! She won't hesitate!"

He meant his companion wouldn't hesitate to use the rusty billhook she was holding.

"Get this thing off me!" I yelled.

"Few questions first, if you don't mind."

The man had a baboon face with a gingerish beard running under his chin but making a wide detour round his mouth. The hairline was receding and the two of them appeared to have bought their clothes in a buy-one-get-one-free offer. They were identically dressed in anoraks, denims and working boots.

"What are you doing here?" the man demanded.

"Looking for Suyin Qu."

The woman passed the billhook from her left hand to the right. "What do you mean?"

They both had similar accents to go with their attire. Refined and precise.

"How many ways can I say it?" I raised a square of the net with my elbow. "What's the purpose of this… contraption?"

"Our first line of defence against bio-spies," said the woman. "Bio. Spies. We've had trouble with them."

"Whatever they are, I'm not one, so could you move this fucking thing?"

The man paused before stooping to find the edge of the net. Barbara joined him and together they gathered it up before lifting it over my head and stepping back.

"It's a new device," he said. "Prototype."

"New? Tell that to the Cherokee nation. Am I its first victim?"

"You're the first person who's been here in over a month, apart from staff. They walk round it."

"Very wise. How big is this place?"

"Fifty-four acres. It used to be a mental hospital."

It was a perfect conversation stopper, not that we'd really been chatting. When the hospital had been decommissioned had Barbara and the baboon been patients who'd refused to move on? Were they soldiers in the jungle who had yet to hear that the war was over?

"My name is Nathan Hawk. I'm a retired police officer. I'd like to talk to you about Suyin."

The man held out his hand. "I'm Professor Kenneth Blake. My wife is Doctor Barbara… well, Blake."

I smiled at her, and she moved the billhook from her right hand back to her left.

"Suyin…?" she asked. "Suyin?"

"I think we should talk somewhere more comfortable." They looked at each other, as if for a translation. "The house, maybe?"

Professor Kenneth nodded and set off back through an alley of bindweed and brambles until we arrived at the front of the house. To one side of the overgrown gravel were three wooden buildings, such as might have housed prisoners of war in the last century. Lights were on inside them and I could make out at least two people at work. I paused.

"The old dormitories," said Kenneth. "The patients here weren't so much dangerous as challenged. My father wanted them to have as much freedom as possible."

"Your father?"

"He was a clinical psychiatrist with many a fresh idea on how to unlock the psyche. Bought the place in 1953. Not many people shared his views, of course, but he espoused them right to the end."

"And you inherited?"

He tapped his nose as if keeping the world's biggest secret up his right nostril. "Oh yes, and we've put it to a very different purpose."

We arrived at the front door. It was made of heavy oak and sat lopsided in its frame. Over the years, a quarter-circle had been gouged out of the flagstones. Barbara put her shoulder to it and the door opened in stages.

Inside, I expected it to be oppressively dark but on the contrary there was an abundance of light coming from neon strips, relics from the house's clinical days. A small, dark-skinned woman of fifty emerged from what I assumed was a kitchen, since she wore an apron and a hairnet.

"*Señora, Señor*," she said, as if reminding her bosses of something, in this case their manners.

"Oh, yes, thank you, Maria," said the Professor. "Would you like something to drink?"

Maria gave me the options. "Tea, apple juice, home-brew."

I wondered which would be the safest. "If you are, Professor, so will I."

"Bring us beer, Maria." He smiled at me. "I love the way it rhymes. Beer. Maria. Probably why I drink so much of it…"

Maria headed back to the kitchen, but not before relieving Barbara of the rusty billhook.

"We've a sitting room down the corridor," said Barbara. "Not much, but it suffices. It suffices. It suffices."

Kenneth led us down a pokey corridor, on either wall of which hung prints and paintings, most of the latter so blackened that the subjects had been obscured.

The sitting room was about as sittable in as a 1950s police cell and the fetid smell was equally overpowering. Through the window I could make out broken guttering hanging at an angle, and beyond that lay more jungle, specimen plants in their day that had run wild. As far as getting comfortable went, there were two church pews and a leather sofa, the latter worn down to the horsehair and no doubt home to God knows what. I opted for one of the pews.

Professor Kenneth went to a light switch just inside the vast inglenook and a neon strip flickered and then burst into life, illuminating centuries of tar on the stonework. A cast-iron grate still contained ashes from the previous winter.

"These… bio-spies. What are they after?"

"Valuable secrets," he said. "Our research."

"Two men? Masks, overalls?" I turned to Barbara. "Meat cleaver?"

"Which one of them wielded to terrifying effect," said her husband. "He held us captive in the kitchen while the other man ran round the house, charging into every room. Then they did the laboratories. Poor Mansur, a timid soul at the best of times, thought his end had come…"

"Did they mention Suyin?" I tried.

"They asked if she was here. I said no, and informed the police once they'd gone. A whole squad came and went, and, well… no doubt they're extremely busy so I took matters into my own hands. The booby trap."

"When did you last see Suyin?"

"July the seventh," said Barbara, immediately.

There being no door to this room, Maria called out from the corridor and entered, carrying a tray with a pub pint glass and a porcelain jug on it.

"We only have one beer glass," Maria explained to her boss. "You drink from jug."

"Thank you, Maria, most kind."

She nodded and left the room. I took a sip and Professor Kenneth waited, as if to see how long the poison would take to kill me.

"That is pretty good," I said, meaning it. "Doctor, may I ask why you remember the date, July the seventh, so readily?"

"I have that kind of mind," she said, coolly.

"Why did she visit?"

"She came with a friend and, well, a supporter of ours," said Kenneth. "Taylor Mandrake. He wanted Suyin to learn of our work. She was sceptical to begin with, then gradually warmed to it."

"And gave you money."

He shifted in the sofa and scratched his thigh for a moment. "I discovered, rather late in life I'm afraid, that if we're to get anywhere we need finance. So I took courage and asked her for some."

"And she wrote a cheque for nine hundred thousand pounds." Professor Ken flinched, alarmed that a close secret had been revealed. "It's okay, I prized the figure out of Alessandro Scutari."

"Sandro," said Barbara, brightening for the first time. "Such a good-looking chap. I mean, don't get me wrong, Taylor is pretty, despite his namesake being highly toxic, but I do love a fine musculature."

I held up a hand. "Just dally there a second, Doctor. Namesake, highly toxic?"

"The root of the mandrake plant, *Mandragora officinarum,* would kill you were you foolish enough to eat it. Don't tell Taylor I said that. I think he's blissfully unaware."

I nodded. "What exactly do you do here, Professor?"

"We anticipate the future," he said, grandly.

He rose from the sofa and beckoned me over to the French windows and, in spite of the dense foliage beyond, he pointed to where one of the dormitories would be.

"Under the Abiding Earth franchise there are three projects afoot. In lab one Mansur and his wife – they're from Uzbekistan, he's a botanist, she's a chemist – are working on fish proteins. I won't trouble you with the science, a layman like yourself won't understand. Suffice to say, it will be the source of a new kind of wrapping, for food in shops, for bags, tubs, containers, all of it biodegradable." He gazed into the middle distance, picturing a scene. "Just imagine, you bring home your shopping from Tesco, throw the wrapping in the compost and six months later it's fertilising your vegetable patch!"

I nodded my admiration. He pointed outside again.

"Next to that, an eco-warrior team from Australia, both highly qualified in their fields, are working on eco-bricks. I don't suppose you know what an eco-brick is."

"Not in detail."

"One stuffs a plastic bottle with soft plastic waste and when it's full to bursting you have in your hand the foundation of a new building material. A brick. Won't they be flammable, I hear you cry? Won't they be all different sizes? Won't some of them be less fully packed than others? These are the challenges the boys are addressing, but I have to say the eco-brick bothy they've built is impressive."

He pointed again.

"In lab three, a bunch of fashion designers from New York – where else? – is working on biodegradable clothes, to challenge the fast-fashion industry. In my mind I see me taking off my trousers at night and in the morning them not being there!" He chuckled. "Now come and see the jewel in our crown. Bring your beer."

He led the way, through more dereliction and crookedly hung paintings, to the farthest wing of the house and paused at a door on which a wooden plaque declared it to be the dining hall. He turned to me and lowered his voice.

"This isn't just a room, Mr Hawk, it's a place of science. It doesn't require masks and gowns and sterility and all the rest of it, but serious and rigorous work goes on behind this door."

"I don't doubt it," I said.

Even if I'd made a wild guess as to what was in the room it would've fallen far short of the reality. He opened the door and more light flooded out at us. What I saw in the first few seconds of gawping was an ocean in a storm, the choppy water grey, black and beige with white tips as if waves were about to crash on the shore.

I was looking at an area the size of a cricket pitch, and the light came not from neon strips under which patients had once taken their meals, but hydroponic lights from units suspended over serried ranks of horticultural benches. And the trays they supported didn't contain water. They contained a collection of fungi.

"Barbara's the microbiologist," he said, clearly delighted by my initial amazement. "She'll explain."

"They're having lunch," she said with a straight face.

I thought she was referring to the two girls pouring pellets into a wooden plant box at the far end of the room. She wasn't. She was talking about the fungi.

"On the menu today, as every other day, is plastic."

I didn't hear what she said for the next few seconds but picked up her thread as she explained,

"…some are eating faster than others, depending on the species, the heat, the enzymes we're adding to their diet. This is teacher's pet."

She went over to a wooden container, lifted it and swung it round to show me.

"Meet *Aspergillus tubingensis*," she said. "I think it's rather handsome, in spite of being mistaken by the hoi polloi as a poisonous toadstool. One day, this little chap will help to rid the world of the most pernicious substance man has ever created. Plastic. The vast islands of it adrift in the oceans will be devoured. So too the acres of landfill piled high with the stuff. Even in your own back garden you'll be able to make it disappear. The earth will abide, you see, with a little help from Kenneth and me."

She replaced the box on its bench and turned back to me with her first smile since we'd met, and her demeanour wasn't so much unhinged as evangelistic.

"And guess what! If I have my way, we will be able to eat the fungi! Which makes this the ultimate recycling project."

When you're out of your depth it's often advisable to stop flailing and raise a hand in the hope that a lifeguard will see you. I turned to her husband for help.

"It's all true," he said. "Who would have thought it?"

"Indeed."

"Doctor Barbara Blake did!"

I took a swig of the beer I was still holding. There was nothing to say. I simply had to accept that, before my eyes, a collection of fungi was eating plastic.

"Let's leave these chaps to their lunch, shall we?" said Kenneth. He called out to the two workers. "Michaela, Affra, sorry to disturb you."

They waved to him and he led the way back to the sitting room. Once the three of us were settled he said, "I've quite forgotten why you came here."

"Suyin Qu," his wife reminded him. "She's missing. Has she been… kidnapped?"

"Anything's possible," I said. "I'd be interested in what you know about her."

"Not a great deal," said Professor Kenneth. "Chinese, wealthy, beautiful…"

His wife disagreed on the last point. "She's satisfactory in that department, but, well… each to his own."

"You agree with me on the first two points?" he persisted.

"I would say they are incontrovertible facts. However, beauty is in the eye of the beholder. What do you say, Mr Hawk?"

Unwilling to be part of a verbal scrap, I tried to divert it. "How well do you know Alessandro Scutari?"

Professor Kenneth hesitated before answering. "The man's done us several good turns, but, you know… lawyers."

"Good turns?"

"Apart from drawing up our legal agreement with White Crane he obtained longterm visas for Maria, who is Argentinian, and for the Uzbeks who come from… well, Uzbekistan. Visas aren't cheap these days, and depending on where you come from, ka-ching, as they say…"

It might have been whatever lived in the sofa that was crawling up my neck, but it was more likely to be the spiders. I was beginning to rely on them as warning signals.

"I thought visas cost the same, no matter where you come from."

He closed his eyes, like teachers do in the face of disagreement. "Not so. Maria's was cheap but Mansur and his wife were fifteen thousand pounds apiece." He tapped the side of his nose and raised his eyebrows. "Sandro has a contact in the Home Office, did what they call a speedy deal. Worth every penny, of course." He paused. "They are the family we never had."

They weren't the first couple I'd met whose brilliance in their field was overshadowed by their naivety about everyday matters. Thirty grand for two visas? How far would Alessandro Scutari go, I wondered, in order to protect such a lucrative sideline? Would he murder someone who got in his way?

"You wouldn't happen to know the name of his Home Office contact?"

He turned to his wife. "Dirk somebody-or-other. Can you remember?"

"We were never party to his surname," she said. "Just Dirk. As in Bogarde." She smiled. "Now there was handsome for you."

If thirty grand would buy you two visas, I wondered what you could get with the ninety I'd found in the stuffed crane.

On the drive back from the Cotswolds I indulged in a long think, and not just about the who-dun-wot-and-why of Opinder's murder, nor how it tied in with Suyin Qu's disappearance.

I wondered why I'd jumped into the fray of it without taking a breath. I'd tried to fool myself that it was on account of her being a friend of Jodie. That wasn't strictly true and soon lost its appeal. I moved on to having felt 'morally bound' to poke around in the affair. That might have been true once, but not any more.

The real reason for getting involved was darker and forced me to consider that I, an ex-police officer who had been dedicated to his job and then forced to retire from it, needed people like Suyin Qu to go missing in order to give me a reason for getting up in the morning. And did I really need people like Opinder Pandeshi to be murdered, to give me the same buzz?

I tried to shake off the thought, only for Drusilla Ford to take its place. She would have a therapeutic means of guiding me towards writing my memoirs, maybe standing for election to a parish council or to a minor political role like Taylor Mandrake. Drusilla wafted out again.

It was dark when I reached home. Ahead of me was an evening of eating alone, watching telly alone, going to bed alone. The blip of self-pity faded as I scooped up the post from the front doormat. Among it was a folded note written in an impressively neat hand.

"Guvnor, I'm up in your local," it said. "Can you join me? Tom Gadsden."

Maybe the rest of the evening wouldn't be so bleak after all. The thought of cocky DCI Jim Parfitt being all at sea and sending his sidekick to ask for help certainly gave me a boost. I showered, fed the dog and wandered up to the Crown.

Gadsden was over at the bar, sharing a joke with Annie's husband, and in my current frame of mind I wondered if I'd been the butt of it. I had a sudden urge to turn and walk out, but Andy McKinnon spotted me and waved. Gadsden turned to shake my hand.

"Guvnor, great to see you! Give this man his usual, Andy, and I'll have another Remy."

"How is she?" I asked Andy.

"Big. Another week and that's it. No more kids."

"You said that last time. You eaten, Tom?" He shook his head. "Try the shepherd's pie. Two specials, Andy. Put 'em on the slate."

I led the way to a free table and we sat down either side of it. Gadsden smiled.

"I've learned a lot about you in the last couple of hours, guvnor. I wasn't digging, it just came spilling out: you, the kids, the doctor, your successes…"

"Oh yeah?"

"And an acquaintance of yours rang me in the car. DCI Mark Jackson. He thinks Alessandro Scutari's got something to answer for."

"Like why break into his own office? He reckons being the victim of a crime means you can't be a suspect as well…"

"We ran him through the PNC and his name came up. Nothing to bowl you over but worth a mention. Taking and driving away, four counts, when he was eighteen."

"So twenty years later he kills Opinder?"

He smiled. "We tried going there but he went all lawyer on us. Clammed up."

"So, I guess you never got round to Suyin Qu…"

"Tried to."

"…and the fact that she's as rich as Croesus."

"Really?"

"I doubt he mentioned Tricks Farm, either. Or Abiding Earth."

He swallowed, wiped his lips and asked, "Er, what are they?"

"Christ, what have you been doing? They're two places she invested in. One's in Norfolk, the other's in the Cotswolds."

"When you say *invested*?"

"What does anyone mean? She put money in. Millions."

As briefly as I could I filled him in about both places and included the visits by the meat-cleaver men, father and son. He wanted to quiz me but I'd caught sight of Annie McKinnon emerging from the kitchen, leaning backwards at a dangerous angle. She was carrying a tray with two plates of shepherd's pie. She reached our table and set it down, then nursed her aching back.

"Er, sorry to be so male about it, Annie, but shouldn't you be… resting?"

"Probably." She smiled down at Gadsden. "Have I had the pleasure?"

"This is Tom Gadsden; Tom, Annie McKinnon."

He half rose to shake her hand, but she gestured for him to stay put. She took napkins and cutlery from her apron and laid them down on the table. She smiled. Looking back, it wasn't so much a smile as a wince of pain.

"Normally, I'd ask if there was anything else I could get you," she said. "Like a refill. At this moment, though, I couldn't give a tuppenny fuck."

"It looks fabulous…" Gadsden tried.

Annie turned and began the long haul back to the kitchen. Halfway across the bar she paused, the tray clattered to the floor and she reached out to a customer's shoulder. The Gorbals accent came bursting through.

"Oh, Christ… not right now…"

The bar went quiet as she tensed up in agony and leaned over her stomach, as far as she could, to examine her feet. Fluid was trickling down her legs and onto the floor. Nobody spoke, nobody moved. They gawped instead. Then the man whose shoulder she had clasped vacated his seat and eased Annie down into it.

"Andy, phone for an ambulance!" he called out in a screechy voice. "Her waters have broken!"

Andy hurried from behind the bar and went over to his wife. She looked up at him and said, "It's okay, hen. Just do something, will you!"

I'm sure he'd have gone into action straightaway if his feet hadn't been nailed to the floor.

"Is there a midwife in the house?" I muttered to Gadsden.

With a parting glance at the shepherd's pie I rose and went over to Annie. Gadsden was right behind me.

"Breathe," I said. "Big, deep, long breaths. Andy, car round the front. We're off."

Annie snatched at my hand and held on to it. "Nathan, I don't think I'm going to make it…"

"Oh, well… never mind." I signalled to a neighbour. "Ring Laura Peterson."

"You sure?" said another neighbour.

"Someone just do it!"

A lone voice recited Laura's number from memory and the neighbour jabbed it into his phone.

"Andy! You got a first-aid kit?" I asked.

"Erm, yeah. No. I've got an emergency birthing kit."

"Even better." He stared at me. "Get it!"

He jemmied his feet away from the floor, hurried behind the bar and ran upstairs.

"Nathan, please…" said Annie, gasping for air.

"You, keep breathing." I looked round. "You two, off the sofa!"

The young couple I'd referred to leaped to their feet and moved away. Gadsden and I steered Annie towards it and lowered her down. She looked up at me.

"Have you… done this before?"

I sniggered. "Annie, I used to be a policeman. Lie there, try and relax, keep breathing…"

"What do you think I'm going to do? Suddenly stop?"

"Tom, crowd control. Get the onlookers behind the barriers!"

Gadsden started fanning the punters back to a reasonable distance. I slung my leather jacket over a chair and hurried behind the bar, where I rolled up my sleeves and washed my hands. The barmaid threw me a clean tea towel.

"Where's Laura?" Annie whined.

"She's on her way," said the neighbour who'd phoned her. "She's in Thame."

She looked at me. "You sure you've done this before?"

"You want a list?" I said, tetchily.

Her husband had returned with a small suitcase. He stood looking down at Annie, a rabbit in the headlights.

"Open it, you berk!" I snapped.

The case appeared to contain everything I might need. I put on a pair of plastic gloves and Annie groaned out loud as a contraction swept through her. Given the fact that Andy was stricken with terror, I lifted his wife's apron, then her skirt and pulled down her pants. What on earth would the neighbours say about that, I wondered. First he leaves Laura Peterson in the lurch, then he takes liberties with Annie McKinnon…

"How far away is Thame?" Gadsden asked, casually.

"Five miles. I've often wished it were nearer."

"What happens now?" Andy managed to ask, taking his wife's hand.

"We wait. Babies give birth to themselves, usually. Annie, tell me when you feel like pushing… and, well, go for it."

Just five minutes later Carla McKinnon came whistling down her mother's birth canal, landed in my hands and started yelling the place down. I laid her on Annie's stomach and reached into the suitcase for two clips, applied them to Carla's cord and invited Andy to cut it with the scissors. He froze again so I did it myself. That's when the applause began. Maybe they didn't hate me after all…

I cleaned up Carla as best I could, wrapped her in a tea towel and moved her up to her mother's breasts. She pursed her lips and clamped on. A moment later Laura Peterson came hurtling through the door, bag at the ready. She looked round and our eyes met. I shrugged, as if to say that her help wasn't needed. She went over to Annie who was miles away by then, in that mysterious land where a mother greets her child for the first time and those who witness it go weak at the knees.

And as the applause died down I said to Gadsden, "I guess the drinks are on me."

***

When all the fuss was over, and Annie, Andy and Carla had been dispatched to the local hospital, Laura joined me and Gadsden back at Beech Tree. We'd agreed that he would stay the night in Jaikie's old room, so we made for the living room where I poured three brandies from an expensive bottle of the stuff Jaikie had given me the previous Christmas. It hadn't been opened and but for Laura's hand on the cap it might not have been closed again. She raised her glass.

"So, here's to Carla Natalie McKinnon."

We echoed the sentiment and drank.

"Natalie?" I said. "Not very Scottish."

"It's the nearest they could get to Nathan."

I let it sink in, then muttered, "Ridiculous."

***

Carla Natalie McKinnon had thrown Gadsden off course and I was still keen to know the reason for his visit.

I came downstairs next morning to find that he'd made himself at home. There was coffee brewing and he'd worked out how to use the toaster properly, which is more than I'd done in three years.

"Hope you don't mind," he said.

I shook my head.

"Your friend Laura lives nearby then?" he went on. "Didn't work out between you?"

"You're as bad as my neighbours, Tom."

"Nice-looking woman. But then intelligence always looks beautiful."

I poured some coffee and joined him at the table as he began spreading marmalade onto his toast with geometric precision. He saw me watching him.

"My father was a painter and decorator," he explained. "Had a thing about neat edges and corners. Don't you eat breakfast?"

"No."

He was about to lecture me on the subject but I held up a hand to prevent him.

"Listen, you might be onto something with Scutari," I said. "Everyone I've met who had anything to do with Suyin has been visited by the meat-cleaver men. Everyone except Alessandro Scutari, who'd like us to believe they've done him over as well."

"Why?"

"He's got a nice sideline in pay-as-you-go visas. He'd like to keep it, I'm sure."

"Would he kill for it?"

I shrugged. "He works with a contact at the Home Office, an old colleague. Dirk somebody."

"Do people really call their kids Dirk?"

"Derek, presumably. Which means I already know one thing about him. He fancies himself rotten."

Gadsden smiled. "Parfitt still reckons Suyin Qu for this murder. 'Our missing prime suspect', he calls her. I'm not convinced, but we can't just write her off."

"Fair enough, but why has she disappeared?"

Gadsden started spreading the toast in accordance with his father's principles, glancing up at me occasionally.

"You haven't found her, we haven't found her. We wondered if she's gone back to China. I mean, *we* can't do it but if you were going there to look for her…"

"What good would it do? I can't bring her back with me."

"No, but there are diplomatic channels."

"With China? Good luck with that."

"Well, are you or aren't you? Going?"

So, first MI6, now the Met police. Both wanted me to be their man in China, as it were. I gave him the only answer I had. "No plans at the moment."

He nodded and started on the toast, taking small bites and chewing properly, unlike most coppers who shovel their grub in and swallow.

Jaikie, Jodie and Grogan were due to attend an evening drinks guzzle at Pinewood Studios, the purpose of which was to celebrate a new series of *Warrington* being commissioned. All it needed now, Jaikie said without a hint of irony, was to be written and made. He phoned in the morning to say they would make a detour and visit me afterwards. Maybe they could even grab something to eat while they were here?

I phoned Laura, with malice aforethought, and invited her to join us. I would be serving grilled salmon with chips and greens, I said. I could sense her wincing, but rather than ask if I knew how to cook anything else she offered to make a casserole. And to defrost a cheesecake she had in her freezer. Mission accomplished.

The car pulled up beside the big beech and Dogge went into her 'get off my land' routine until she heard Jaikie's voice, at which point she squealed with delight. He was talking to Grogan,

"Of course, I was consulted about casting," he was saying. "People told me I should beware of choosing someone too good to play my adversary, in case they put me in the shade." He laughed at the very idea of it. "I said bollocks, I need a good actor to spark off, not some tired old…"

He entered through the back door in typical form, a bottle of wine in each hand. He paused and breathed in the aroma of the casserole, then smiled.

"Dad, you shouldn't have asked Laura to go to all that trouble."

She went over to him and they double air-kissed, then she turned to Jodie, then to Bill Grogan. For all that living with Jaikie and Jodie had… socialised him a little he was still wary of Laura. They shook hands and she noticed right away that he was somehow… different. He was dressed in a dark grey suit that had been literally taken out of mothballs for the drinks party. It fitted him rather well. I pecked Jodie on the cheek, conscious that I needed a shave and was underdressed in jeans and T-shirt. Jaikie bore down on me with a bear hug.

"Good to see you, mate. What's new?"

"I delivered a baby the other night."

"What the hell for?"

I pulled a pain face. "What a stupid bloody question! It was due and no one else stepped forward. Annie McKinnon's. Carla, her name is. Middle name Natalie. After me."

The kids laughed. Laura clapped her hands to get our attention.

"Everyone, we're eating in the dining room. Supper will be five minutes so grab a glass of wine and take it through." She handed me the corkscrew. "Natalie, will you do the honours?"

***

It was an odd picture. The five of us seated round the oak table, placemats, silver cutlery, crystal wine glasses, Irish linen napkins. Grogan had tucked one into his shirt collar to protect the suit. He declined the glass of wine Jaikie offered. I didn't and at my first sip I could taste the small fortune it had cost. It struck me, in one of those interloping moments, that I was becoming like my father, a man who priced everything. It used to be just coffee. Bean to cup 19 pence, cup to lip in Starbucks £3.50 minimum. I promised myself I would stop.

Laura doled out the casserole and told us to help ourselves to the veg. As we began the meal I eased them into the subject of Suyin.

"I take it no one's heard from her? Jaikie, Jodie?" They shook their heads despondently. "Two government agencies believe that she's gone back to China."

"They've told you that?"

I smiled. "Sounds good, doesn't it? 'Nathan, just phoning you to say we think she's gone home. Thought you should be in the loop, old chap.'"

"Difficult," said Jodie. "Her passport's with the Home Office."

"I'm sure she'll have more than one. Your friend Alessandro would've seen to that. Him and his mate at the Home Office."

Jodie squared up behind her knife and fork. "Nathan, whenever you get doubts about Alessandro, he suddenly becomes 'my friend'."

"No offence, but he does have a sideline. Visas. I met this tree-hugging couple the other day. They run a research centre. Mad as hatters. Only not, if you know what I mean. Are you aware that a certain species of fungi devours plastic? Or plarstic as these two insist on calling it. *Aspergillus tubingensis* eats plastic and loves every mouthful. To make it even more interesting, we humans might be able to eat the fungi. How about that?"

"You were talking about visas," said Jaikie.

"Suyin's put money into their research projects, which is… peculiar. Alessandro got at least two of their workforce visas." I looked at Jodie. "Fifteen grand a pop."

She stared at me. "That is outrageous! I knew he was a bit casual but…"

"Is that lawyer speak for bent? Ask yourself this: would he kill if he had to? To keep a lucrative sideline going?"

She turned away and Jaikie said, "He's a family man, two daughters…"

"He's divorced with a criminal record. TDA – taking and driving away."

"That is so old copper of you, Dad!"

"Why are you defending him?"

He sighed. "I don't know."

"Anything else we should know?" said Jodie, frostily.

"As a matter of fact there is. Suyin bought the lavender farm next to Richard Bennett. Which means it's not only turkeys, crabs, reeds and jackets that come from Norfolk. It's lavender."

Grogan stopped eating and looked at me. "When you say the farm next to…?"

I sighed, inwardly. "Adjacent, Bill. Like side by side."

"How much did she pay?" he asked.

"Twenty-one million. I'd love to know where it's all coming from…"

Grogan half rose from his chair and paused as if about to ask permission to leave the table. "Have you got a laptop I can borrow?"

"Kitchen dresser."

With his napkin still under his chin, he left the room. I looked at the others, who were as baffled as I was. A few moments later Grogan returned with the laptop and asked me to bring up a map of Tricks Farm.

"You'll probably say I've lost it, Nathan, but there's no harm in thinking big, seeing as how thinking small isn't getting you very far."

"Thanks, Bill, but it's a process as you very well…"

"Tricks Farm." He leaned round the screen and indicated Richard Bennett's land. "Notice anything?"

"It's big. It's next to a lavender farm. Which is also big."

Jaikie chipped in. "Dad, maybe suspend the old disbelief for a moment?"

Duly admonished, I gestured Grogan to continue.

"They both reach all the way to the coast," he said. "And her investment in that part of the world now stands at thirty odd million pounds."

He tapped a few keys to bring up a map of Sri Lanka and expanded the southern tip.

"The Chinese built an airport, billions of dollars, right there. Mattala Rajapaksa it's called. One problem: nobody uses it. Likewise, on the coast they built Hambantota Port. No one uses that much either. I don't suppose many people travelled the Silk Road to begin with."

I laughed. "You think Suyin Qu is land grabbing? To build a port on the Norfolk coast?"

He leaned back and began to fold his napkin fussily.

"In the West we see our future running to what? Fifteen, twenty years from now? That stems from our ability to change things, almost at will: governments, social structures, alliances. In China they think dynastically. They see life going on forever and I'll bet you that 50 years from now Mattala Rajapaksa will be buzzing with aircraft, military and commercial, and the port at Hambantota will be awash with traffic. Most of it Chinese. Just think what they're capable of, even now. They say they can build a dam between Denmark and Scotland to hold back the North Sea! Do we, who gave the world the Industrial Revolution, ever think that big? No, we leave the future to the Chinese."

He set down the folded napkin and looked round at us. I was still reeling from the amount he'd said, never mind the substance of it. I'd never heard him speak in paragraphs, and rarely in sentences, only phrases.

"So who has she bought it for?" I asked. "Herself or China? The invisible White Crane or the CCP?"

"That's China for you," said Grogan. "You can't tell one from the other, people from state."

"You've been reading up, Bill."

He shrugged. "Fills the time."

I was starting to join up a few dots. If what Grogan had proposed was true, maybe that was the reason John Smith was so keen for me to visit China? To get chapter and verse on White Crane? He certainly didn't care about Opinder's murder. The next bunch of dots, when brought into a straight line, suggested that he'd leaned on Parfitt, persuaded him that if Suyin had gone back to China then I was the best man to find her. Why me? I certainly had the necessary skills and a motive to the job. Better still, from the MI6 and police points of view, if nothing came of it, or worse still I was arrested on some charge, they could both disown me. I could be dismissed as a barmy Englishman with a mission to solve a crime. Nothing to do with either of them.

But what if it was true, that the Chinese were empire-building on the east coast and their woman on the front line had killed a British citizen in the process? Shouldn't I at least go and see? Didn't I owe Shirina Pandeshi that much after the promises I'd made her?

Or was I still looking for an excuse to visit China, all expenses paid.

I rose from the table and began to wander about, avoiding the central beam in the ceiling, and the room went quiet as the four of them watched me. True to his profession, Jaikie couldn't stand the silence and broke it, albeit in disbelief.

"But she's a girl," he said, quietly. "She lived in the flat upstairs. She sat on the bottom stair crying when immigration tried to take her away. Now she's a Chinese oligarch who kills people?"

"You know anything about her family, Jodie?" I asked.

"We've been through this before. No. Will you go there?"

"Hell of a big place to search… but if she's connected in any way to Opinder Pandeshi's murder, I owe it to his wife to find out."

"Then what?"

"God knows." I smiled. "First things first, though. A visit to that Land Rover dealer in Queen's Park. Test-drive a Discovery."

I called the number John Smith had given me. He answered in the way that I do, as if it isn't really me on the other end of the line.

"Hallo," he whispered.

"John, this is Nathan Hawk."

His manner changed immediately and I sensed that he was congratulating himself for knowing I'd soon be in touch.

"My dear fellow, how good to hear from you."

"I'd like us to meet."

"Certainly. I can come to yours or you can visit the wedding cake in Vauxhall. What's your pleasure?"

Offices and pubs are anonymous. People's houses can tell you most of what you need to know about them.

"Your place. Give me the address."

***

27 Ravenscourt Lane was the last house in a no through road that overlooked Ravenscourt Park. It was Georgian and had once been a single dwelling that would've looked more at home as a vicarage in the wilds of Yorkshire rather than being surrounded on all side by thirty miles of London concrete. The most striking thing about it, at first glance, was the garden. It was immaculate, almost obsessively neat, and in high summer it must have been ablaze with colour. As I approached on foot, a woman who'd been arguing volubly with a clump of dead dahlias straightened up and turned to me. She smiled and ran her hand across her forehead.

"You must be Mr Hawk?" she half stated, half asked.

"Yes, er…"

"Johnny asked me to keep an eye. Won't shake hands. Mucky. I'm Grace Fournier, by the way."

She was in her mid sixties, according to her hands, though the skin on her face belonged to a younger woman. My father, with his apolitical correctness, would have called her a 'titchy little bitch'. I'll rephrase and say that she was… petite but stern, the kind of headmistress who made pupils flatten themselves against a wall as she passed by.

She trod the small fork she'd been using into the ground.

"He's doing a Costco run. We take it in turns."

I gestured lamely to the house. "This is his place, though…"

"We're the neighbours. And the gardeners. And mates, really. And, well… we love him."

"We?"

"My husband and I." She glanced at her watch. "He said he'd be back midday. Oh, have you come by car? Only you'll need a parking permit. The wardens are a nightmare. Good in some ways, bad in others."

"I came on the train."

She smiled. "How terribly old-fashioned of you. Or how modern. Which is it these days? Came in from where, may I ask?"

"Near Thame."

"Don't know it. Would love to. Care for coffee while you wait?"

"Thanks, no." I nodded over to the park. "I'll go for a stroll."

She paused, as if I'd given her the wrong answer, but then she smiled. "If you change your mind, just come back and holler."

She returned to the dahlias. I wandered into Ravenscourt Park.

***

It was a full hour before John Smith returned from his shopping trip, by which time I was browsing the park's garden shop. What had drawn me into the place was a display of bonsai trees. They were hardly the work of bonsai masters in Hokkaido, more the product of a nursery in Holland, but they served to remind me of the tree taken from Jaikie's draining board. Or more precisely the fact that I'd yet to place it in my inquiries. On the phone a day or so previously, and in an actorish frame of mind, Jaikie had suggested that it was a McGuffin, a mere device to trigger the Suyin story. I was sharp with him. We weren't making a bloody film, I said, we were investigating a murder. Fact as opposed to fiction.

"Mr Hawk, Mr Hawk," said a voice behind behind me. "I am so, so sorry. I really meant to be home before twelve and..."

It was John Smith, hurrying towards me, hand outstretched, his face puckered with remorse.

"Not at all," I said. I gestured to the trees. "It's been rather pleasant."

He gestured in the direction of the café, from where the sound of plates and cutlery and other people was coming.

"Shall we chat here, perhaps?" he said.

"I'd prefer your house."

***

The fork was still there in the front garden but Grace Fournier wasn't. She had doubtless gone indoors to deal with her share of the Costco shop. I glimpsed John Smith's half of it piled on his kitchen table as he ushered me into the living room, which was in semi-darkness.

A large tabby cat looked up from the sofa and ran his eyes over me. Smith introduced him as Kublai Khan and, as I reached down to fuss him, he began to purr. Then he must've caught a whiff of Dogge, as he jumped up, straightened his back and walked out in a huff.

Smith went immediately to the French windows and drew back the curtains to reveal a large garden with flowerbeds as finicky as those in the front and a lawn close-cut and weedless enough to play croquet on.

"Your next-door neighbour's work?"

"Yes, God bless her. It's more Grace than Nick. But yes…"

His voice tailed off with an affectionate smile.

It was a large room: part library, part office, part lounge, part music room, part… museum with a host of Chinese and Japanese artefacts dotted around. There were also numerous feminine touches to the place: pink velour cushions on the leather sofa, floral-patterned curtains, a collection of delicate mobiles hanging from the ceiling. Photos of Smith's wife cluttered the walls.

In her mid-thirties, Sophia Smith had masses of studiously disarrayed hair which fell around an intelligent face. The only image of her smiling, though, was a photo propped on an eye-level bookshelf: smiling in gracious acceptance of her fate, I thought. The face was chemo-ravaged, bony and drawn. The hair was no more. Despite my suspicions of John Smith, the photo reminded me of our commonality.

A Georgian desk stood in the bay window. It was a landing strip for office-type debris rather than a workstation. Aside from the unmarked blotter there was a desk calendar, wildly out of date. The Victorian inkwell had dried up long ago. In a turned wooden pot a selection of pheasant quills stood ready for action but had never been used. Pens, pencils, old bills, cutouts from magazines, invitations, a few business cards, and three empty beer bottles had all been placed there over time, and not by design. Beside the door, as if at a staging post en route to the washing machine, was a balled-up tracksuit and a selection of sports shirts. A layer of dust had settled on them. The place needed a Jenny Tindall to… straighten it up. When he went out to the kitchen to fix a whisky for me and a beer for himself, I took some photos, more out of habit than necessity.

"You didn't fancy meeting in my office, then?" he said on his return.

"All that security, all those cameras recording every twitch and sniff for posterity?"

He laughed. "You're in danger of believing that we're more than we really are. Or maybe you think *you're* more than *you* really are? Anyway, cheers! What can I do for you?"

"I know why you want me to go to China." He looked at me down the barrel of the bottle he was sipping from. "The two farms in Norfolk. You think White Crane is building an outpost of the Chinese empire in East Anglia."

He paused to get the tone of his response right. "Concerned rather than scared," he said. "Concerned enough to close down Suyin's operation if she is."

"I hate to tell you, but I think the deal is done and dusted and she's gone back to China."

He took a swig of his beer and wiped his mouth on his sleeve.

"In some ways that's irrelevant, of course. I mean she can buy up Britain with an iPad from a cabin on Mars. But we do need to know who's behind the money." He set his bottle down on the table between us and leaned back in his chair. "So, that's why *we* would like you to go. Why do *you* want to?"

"Who says I do?"

"I doubt if you'd be here if that wasn't the case."

"I promised Opinder Pandeshi's widow I would find her husband's killer. The police believe Suyin Qu is behind it. But then you know that. You've been leaning on them, hoping they would lean on me."

He smiled. "Do *you* think she killed him?"

"I'll ask her when I find her."

"Er, we'd prefer that you didn't communicate with her, otherwise" – he snapped his fingers – "poof, into thin air she goes again. We'd like you to locate her, drop in at the consulate and brief them, then come back to Blighty."

"Blighty? The old country? My dear chap? You're as out of date as the clothes you wear, John."

He smirked. "You think a leather jacket and a pair of jeans makes you trendy?" He moved the fallen forelock back into place and gave me the pisshole stare I'd seen before. "I need your assurance, Mr Hawk. Tell me you won't speak to her. Leave her to us."

"And if I decided she's a murderer, what about getting her back to the UK?"

"I'll do my best, but the chances are he'll be written off as a casualty of the new… lukewarm war. Your word, Mr Hawk."

I set my glass down, went over to him and leaned down to grab his tie – Oxford Rowing Club. I pulled him towards my face. He let it happen without flinching.

"You jumped-up fucking uni-boy, that's three times you've asked me not to speak to her and three times I've refused. Whoever killed Pandeshi is also terrorising new friends of mine, to say nothing of my son and his wife. I don't care if it's down to one single girl or the entire Chinese Communist Party. I aim to find out and blow the fucking whistle." I let go of his tie and straightened up again. "I'm changing the terms of my engagement. I want the new Discovery you promised me and I want it before I get on that plane. Delivered to my house. Registered in my name. Keep me posted."

I turned and left. It was the third time in a month that I'd walked away from an unfinished drink.

Keen though I was to visit China, the prospect of decamping to a different culture always puts me on edge. My fear is of being mistaken for a gawping tourist whose charabanc is parked just round the corner. It's a secondary definition of old age. Clearly, I would never be able to disappear into a Chinese crowd but surely with a little research I could add to what I already knew of the place… and maybe blend in a fraction.

In the fortnight leading up to my departure not only did I discover how little I knew about the Chinese way of life, but my own *modus vivendi* was thrown into relief as well. It had changed dramatically in the previous ten years. For a start, I'd been widowed, something which altered my relationship with the rest of the world profoundly. It began when a grief counsellor half my age had suggested that I didn't "hold back my feelings". I took the advice and wound up breaking a senior officer's jaw. I was invited to retire, a police-service euphemism for being sacked. Death of a spouse and retirement, two of the most stressful life events anyone will ever experience. I capped it with a third and moved house.

Thankfully, it wasn't long before people began asking me to solve their problems, to find missing children, to avenge wrongs done to them, to solve the odd murder or two that the police had abandoned. Then my children left home. Then Laura Peterson came and went and…

I'm digressing. It's always been a weakness.

There are two Chinas in my mind. The first is the China of news reporting, television investigations and social media. They portray a culture where truth, far from being a moral imperative, is a commodity rather than a necessity. Anything I read about China is laden with conscience-pricking phrases: abuse of human rights, genocide, Tiananmen Square, the plight of the Uighurs, Hong Kong. Why, then, as an upright citizen of a democracy, have I never criticised such a repressive society, other than to tut about it with Martin Falconer on the odd Friday night? One possible answer is that much of it isn't true. Another is that half of what I own is Made in China. As is the Land Rover Discovery…

The other China is less controversial and it settled in my head during childhood. It has a soundtrack of erhus, pipas and dizis playing soulful music over footage of winding rivers, tall haystack mountains and terraced farms like isobars on a windy day. If human beings ever appear in the picture they are benign, wise and content.

So, at Laura Peterson's suggestion, I began my two-week wait with a film that fitted neither of the Chinas I knew. It was called *The Last Train Home* and chronicled the greatest movement of people on Earth in a single forty-eight-hour period. No fewer than 130 million Chinese return home for New Year. If they all walked in step to their local train station they would surely shake the world as Napoleon had predicted.

The following evening, when we searched the Netflix catalogue for something harder-hitting, all I could find was tourist China in the shape of a wildlife documentary about Yunnan Province and a journey along the Great Wall, east to west, by a drone camera. No people, no voiceover, just bubbles of information floating within the frames. I came away thinking that real China was a secret, less and less well kept, but still a mystery.

"Good job you didn't go at the beginning of October," said Laura at one point. "Golden Week. The whole country closes down for a holiday and 1.4 billion people become tourists in their own land."

"I can't picture 1.4 billion of… anything, never mind people."

She leaned in towards me and leaned away again when she realised the implication of doing so. "This John Smith, he's arranged all the necessary? Visa, hotels? Who is he, by the way?"

"I told you. Special Branch."

I'd thought it best not to mention MI6. It would have worried her as well as being a breach of Official Secrets. Not that I cared too much about the latter.

"So when's the new car coming?"

"Soon. If it comes at all." She turned to me, assuming that I would elaborate. "My last encounter with him was less than civil."

"So there's a chance you may not go?"

"Slim."

She looked away. "You will be careful, won't you? I mean, no rattling on about the evils of communism and Tibet or Taiwan or…"

"Actually, I was planning to drop in on President Xi and give him a piece of my mind."

***

It arrived the next day, driven by a man in his forties who was in a hurry. I saw him from the bathroom window as the Discovery turned in at the five-bar gate and I managed to reach the front door before he rang the bell. Dogge went berserk anyway. I walked across the gravel to inspect my new toy and the man followed me.

It was silver and spotless, but it wasn't new. It was seven years old and had a doctored logbook saying it had done 30,000 miles. To be fair, I've never owned a car that has done so few.

"I asked for a new one," I said to the driver.

He shrugged. "I've sprayed it with new smell. You taking it or not?"

I reached out for the clipboard he was carrying and signed beside the X. He handed me the keys, suggesting that I get in touch with the company named on the fob if there were any problems. He reached across to the passenger seat for an A4 envelope.

"Everything you need's in there," he said. "A thousand pounds in yuan, visa, hotel bookings, plane ticket."

"When for?"

"Friday."

He zipped up his fleece, adjusted his tea-cosy of a hat and walked off down Morton Lane. At the far end he got into a waiting car and it sped off, leaving a trail of vapour to rise above the cottages in the cold morning air.

Two days later, at four-thirty in the morning, Laura drove me to Heathrow. We spoke very little on the journey, but I remember our parting words at the drop-off point.

"Be kind to my dog, won't you?" I said.

"Of course. You be kind to yourself." She smiled. "And here's a challenge. Try and enjoy it."

Somewhere over northern Russia the Chinese music in my head began to fade, giving way to the more likely hum and thump of a factory floor. The transition wasn't helped by the other passengers in business class, not one of whom was wearing a sampan, or sporting a long braided beard. Did the tourists among them feel excitement, as I did? Or were they like my children, who could travel to the four corners of the earth with the same indifference as a trip to… John O'Groats? The lights in the cabin dimmed and I nodded off, trying to keep my private romance alive.

Hours later, as the plane descended to Shanghai, I might have been forgiven for thinking the pilot had made a U-turn and doubled back to Heathrow. In that moment, my first glimpse of China through the cabin windows, all I could see were familiar brand names reaching up into the sky, calling for my attention. Had it not been for that terrifying bump of landing gear touching the tarmac, I might have fallen into a depression. As it was, I was glad to be still alive.

In Pudong airport, itself a never-ending chamber of horrors, three people at various stations checked my visa, passport and luggage, but only one asked my purpose in visiting the country. Tourism, I said. The woman looked first at my attire, then at my face, nodded once that she was satisfied by my response, only to follow me with her eyes all the way to the baggage carousels. She was my first example of Chinese caution.

At the final barrier, at the end of a moving walkway, I paused and looked round for my tour guide. He was holding a placard bearing my name. He raised a hand in greeting and beamed at me, later telling me that since most Europeans look alike he'd been informed that I was a tall man, probably wearing jeans and a leather jacket, and with very little hair.

"Mr Hawk? Good to meet you. My name is Chao Lin." He shook my hand, long and hard. "Good flight, huh?"

His accent was part Chinese, part American: he was a powerfully built man who might have been anywhere between thirty and fifty, slightly taller than most of his fellow countrymen. He was dressed in a black, collarless jacket, black trousers, black shoes. The only touch of colour to his attire was the grey shirt.

"Follow me, if you would be so kind."

He took my luggage and trundled it out of the building, out of the controlled climate of Pudong and onto a bustling pickup area where, on this late October day, the air was not so much breathable as edible. Most cars arriving and departing were indistinguishable from one another, but not in Chao Lin's case. He raised an arm and a white Mercedes cut between the moving traffic and pulled up at the kerb. He opened the rear door for me to get in, closed it and signalled me to put on a seatbelt. It was a foretaste of his admirable attention to detail. He put my luggage in the boot, slipped in beside the driver, then turned to me and beamed again.

"Your hotel. The Regency. One of the top in Shanghai. You want to shower, rest, order some food, a drink maybe? I will arrange all that…"

By the time he'd finished the sentence the ex-copper in me had decided he was more than just the tour guide John Smith had promised.

***

The most Chinese thing about the Regency hotel was the wallpaper. In my room it depicted a stylised landscape with many a black swan flying towards distant mountains. It was broken up by occasional fishermen with long poles and women in flowing gowns staring into the middle distance, no doubt afraid of unravelling their elaborate hairdos.

In spite of my protestations that I could work a lift and swipe a card to open a door, Chao Lin had seen me to my room. The lift had launched us skywards at breakneck speed to the thirty-fourth level from where, I imagined, I would have a perfect view of Shanghai. When left in peace I went to the window, drew back the gauze and looked out in the general direction of the East China Sea. There were no jostling zaws and junks in full sail. Instead I was reminded of the chorus to a Victorian music-hall song.

"Wiv a ladder and some glasses

You could see to 'Ackney Marshes

If it wasn't for the 'ouses in between."

What I did marvel at in that cluttered view of skyscrapers was the eternal miracle of bamboo, which not only feeds pandas and holds up Laura Peterson's runner beans but, if allowed to grow, serves as scaffolding. Pound for pound stronger than steel, every work in progress I could see was clad in it.

Thinking of Laura prompted me to email her to say that I had arrived safely. Would she kindly let the kids and Bill Grogan know. After that I must have dozed off for a while, to be woken by a gentle knock on the door. I shrugged myself into presentability and went to see who it was. There was no one there. I stepped out into the corridor. It was deserted. Persuaded that I had dreamed the tap, tap, I stepped back into the room and noticed that a business card had been pushed under the door. I picked it up and read the English part of it. "Company tonight?" it asked. "Tel: 742190-5". The reverse side bore a photo of a beautiful Chinese woman smiling out at me invitingly. Some would say it was an example of Chinese hospitality. Others, like me, would feel uncomfortable.

I blame jet lag for the Englishman abroad in me breaking through next morning at breakfast. The actual trigger for it was an absence of cold milk. The restaurant in the Regency, whose design owed more to nineteenth-century Vienna than anywhere else, served a very Chinese breakfast. The staple of it was congee, an overcooked rice pudding with flecks of meat and vegetables in it. There were dumplings and sweetened scrambled eggs on the side with squares of cold bacon. I settled for All-Bran, a Western cereal more akin to wood shavings than anything nourishing. I looked round for the milk. A smiling waitress directed me to an urn.

"Have you *cold* milk?" I asked.

She carried on smiling and beckoned the restaurant manager, a besuited young man in his thirties.

"Cold milk?" I repeated.

He in turn beckoned a colleague who would act as translator.

"Have you any cold milk?" I asked again.

"No."

"You must have. Before this milk was hot it was cold. Where do you keep the cold milk?"

The three of them exchanged a collision of words after which the translator said, "We have cook milk only."

It must have been their combined indifference to my request that set me off. I tapped the departing manager on the shoulder.

"I want cold milk!"

The restaurant fell quiet. The manager sighed and sent the waitress off somewhere. She left her boss and me in a state of suspended animation and returned thirty seconds later shaking her head. The manager stared at me.

"None."

I remember thinking that of the four effs available to me I had chosen fight. The waitress and the translator fell away from the danger zone and I set down my bowl of All-Bran. God knows what might have happened if, as I clenched my free fist, I hadn't heard a voice on the edge, sharp enough to cut through the red mist.

"Mr Hawk, Mr Hawk, there is no problem here."

On the edge of my vision I could see Chao Lin striding towards us from the doors to the lobby. When he reached me he placed a copper's hand on my arm.

"What is wrong? Tell me. I will put it right."

"There's no cold milk," I hissed.

He waited, expecting there to be more substance to my complaint. He and the manager exchanged some agitated diphthongs, after which Chao Lin said, "They have no milk left, Mr Hawk. Come. You and I will have breakfast in Starbucks."

Had I really travelled 9000 miles only to end up in a Starbucks? He released me from his grip and awaited my reaction. I nodded.

***

Half an hour later we sat facing each other in a Starbucks in one of numerous honeycomb shopping malls which Shanghai boasts. I had polished off a bowl of muesli and a waiter was bringing me two croissants. Lin had opted for coffee. No milk, warm or cold.

"Thank you," I said to the waiter.

Lin nodded the boy away. "You eat your rolls, Mr Hawk, and we will discuss the day."

"I should apologise."

He shook his head. "I understand. You…" He searched for a word but couldn't find it. Instead he mimed an explosion, complete with sound effects. "Me too. I was also a policeman."

I nodded. "I used to have this way of holding down my temper. A Map. Pretend. I would take it out whenever…"

He was smiling at me, trying to understand.

"A Map?"

"In my head. Imaginary. A Map of the world. I would choose a place to go."

"Did it work?"

"Most of the time." I leaned back in my chair. "So, if you're no longer a policeman, what are you?"

He smiled. "Tour guide. Where shall I take you?"

I took a page of a notepad from my inside pocket and handed it to him.

"Number 17 Dafeng Alley in Shikumen," he said. "I know this area. Is near Tian Zi Fang, only not so smart." He looked at me. "Who is here, you think?"

"The office of a company called White Crane."

He pulled a face. "These places are old China but Tian Zi Fang is now for the tourist. Shikumen is still poor. Very poor. No business there. Come, I will show you."

***

We crawled through the Shanghai traffic towards the old city with Chao Lin pointing out various buildings he thought would interest me. They did, but not as much as the traffic itself, or rather the accepting nature of the drivers. There can be no equivalent phrase in Mandarin for 'cutting in' or 'tailgating' because in Shanghai these moves are the easygoing conventions of driving to work. And those who are forced to fall back in the traffic queue as a result don't shake a fist or raise a British middle finger. They simply accept.

"You like motorbikes?" Lin asked, as we walked away from the car park we had ended up in.

"No."

"Mopeds?"

"Even less."

"Shame. Much quicker. "

He looked at me and waited for a favourable nod.

"I'll give it a go.," I said.

We strolled into a district called Changning and my impression of China shifted a degree or two. As if by some cinematic device, we had cut from a skyline of eternal skyscrapers to a location of narrow, crowded streets and low-slung buildings with scalloped roofs dipping all the way down to my Western head. It was a mirage. History was being preserved here for the visitors, most of whom were from China itself.

We crossed a tributary of the main river, a stretch of water no wider than an average canal, yet flanked by small shops whose owners called out for our attention. Everything was for sale, from gaudy tourist landfill to takeaway food. A gang of workers was sweeping footpaths that were already clean and Chao Lin noticed my surprise. This was Tian Zi Fang, the artists' quarter, he said, by which he meant the shops were full of photos, prints and paintings, models of terracotta soldiers and pandas galore. The whole area had been neatly wrapped and presented so that any visitor might still believe that Chinese history had not been rewritten, the culture not forgotten. The young Chinese couple walking ahead of us had certainly been persuaded and were anxious to record the fact for posterity. They stopped at a stone parapet and he stepped ahead, gesturing that she should pose for a photo. She giggled self-consciously but obliged him.

A while later Chao Lin led me into Shikumen and the view changed again as we found ourselves in what could only be described as a backstreet slum. The ex-copper in me tensed up in this pokey street of crumbling dwellings, boarded windows and roofs of corrugated iron. At our feet rubbish was piled alongside old bikes and broken white goods, while above our heads tattered laundry hung on a network of gantries. The residents turned to stare at us and Chao Lin avoided their eyes and quickened his step. This was old

China sure enough, a street full of skinny children and parents with shrivelled faces, suspicious of every newcomer who turned a corner. Doors stood open and the smell of human living seeped out onto the cobbled street. The raised voices were made all the harsher by me not understanding the words. Music was whining in the background. We turned again, into an even narrower street.

This was Dafeng Alley, Lin told me. He approached an old man who was seated on the cobbled ground, leaning back against the wall of a house. Lin asked him a question. The man rose with difficulty and hobbled away.

"I ask if he knows the office of White Crane. Number 17. No answer." He gazed into the distance for a moment. "A year from now, this will all be gone. You hear that noise beyond?"

I listened. Heavy machinery was at work close by.

"Bulldozers. This is the Shanghai which embarrasses, so new development is being built." He turned away and offered his own view, not the party's. "These people don't want it. They should be left alone. Come. We might get lucky."

As we walked on I asked, "You know this place from your working days?"

He shook his head. "Police do not come here."

As we approached the far end of the alley he asked one other person, a youngish woman, if she knew of a White Crane in the area. She thought for a moment, then raised an arm and pointed across the alley. At the entrance to a narrow ginnel, an outline drawing of something I recognised was painted on the wall. He wasn't white – he was grubby and peeling – but he was definitely a crane. Chao Lin looked at me.

"You want go in?"

I nodded.

He led the way down the passage, which was no wider than a man's shoulders, the ceiling so low that I had to stoop. We could barely see our way for darkness and at one stage I reached for Chao Lin's shoulder for guidance.

The end of the passageway gave onto a room no bigger than a garden shed, with grey light filtering in through a mossy ceiling window. The place was cluttered with everyday belongings hanging over makeshift furniture and the air was thick with cigarette smoke. Four men, two of them shirtless in the heat, were seated at a rickety table playing Mahjong. Behind them an elderly woman was stitching a child's dress. They looked up as we entered, alarmed but by no means afraid. One of them got to his feet and Chao Lin raised his hands in deference and spoke. The man stared at him, hawked up phlegm from his throat and spat into a brass container at his feet. In any language the gesture demanded that we leave. Chao Lin turned and ushered me back the way we had come.

***

We had lunch at a restaurant that overlooked the mouth of the Huangpu river. It was a terrace on the second floor of a building and commanded a view across this part of Shanghai that made the contrast between here and Dafeng Alley all too obvious. For the first time that day, there was a slight breeze, but the air seemed to cling to us rather than pass us by.

Chao Lin ordered fish, fish and more fish, assuring me that it had been caught far away from the oil-thick river below. I still had trouble eating it: something to do with the man in Dafeng Alley having spat so fulsomely into an already full spittoon. The sound of it would live in my mind forever.

"So, what next do you do?" he asked.

"I don't know."

"Is not an office, you agree?"

"You don't need Trump Tower to make a fortune," I said. "All you need is a place out of the rain. And a computer."

He smiled. "In Dafeng Alley? Maybe the address is a mistake? Or maybe old information. Out of date?"

"What happens if I send a letter there, Lin? Is it delivered?"

He shrugged. "Have you time to test?"

"No. I just wondered."

When we had put away the fish and most of the side dishes, Lin asked if I wanted coffee. I nodded and the waiter brought a pale imitation. No milk.

I decided to ask for my tour guide's help, even though he was an unknown quantity and the only example of his… independent thinking was his heretical view that Shikumen and its people should be left alone. I chose my words carefully and made no mention of the thirty million pounds Suyin had invested in Norfolk.

"I wonder if mail goes there, and then it's collected and forwarded?"

"What is… forwarded? Sent on?" he said. I nodded. "Who to?"

"It would be nice to know."

He thought for a moment, then walked across the balcony and threw his coffee into the Huangpu.

"I could arrange that," he said, returning to the table.

"You mean ask the postal service?"

"No, no. Then it becomes public record. Someone at number 17 takes the mail to the post office, you think? You and I cannot sit there and wait for that to happen, but I can get a friend to do so."

I smiled. "That would be good."

***

The next day, as part of my tourist cover, Chao Lin said, he took me to Xian. This was the home of the Terracotta Army, which Laura had insisted that I visit. Without referring to a map I imagined it would be a car or motorbike ride, but it turned out to be 750 miles away and a plane journey.

The 1800-year-old collection of clay soldiers is a lifeless parody of China, ancient and modern. The emperor, Qin Shi Huang, buried 8,000 effigies alongside him in three graves, each plot the size of a football pitch. Facially, they are all different but they are taller, broader and more inscrutable than the man in the street, and stand ready to obey any order given them. They were unearthed by two farmers, who sank a water well in 1974 and came across broken pottery faces. They kept quiet about their find for fear of state reprisal, filled in the well and began digging elsewhere. Again they unearthed broken faces and this time felt compelled to report their discovery. When the area was finally uncovered, the Army was in a pitiful state and a horde of archaeologists began the task of gluing the broken soldiers together again. They did so without a single join being visible and the results were displayed in serried ranks, no individual out of step with another.

The giant hangar of a building was packed with sightseers and it was difficult not to be in awe of the restoration. Even as we gazed down on the army of archers, foot soldiers and cavalry, more broken remains were being pieced together. Indeed, a chariot was being manoeuvred into position and then unveiled. Cameras and iPhones, including my own, clicked and flashed as their owners leaned over the guard rails. Among the faces, twenty yards from where I was standing, was one I recognised. It belonged to the young man who had snapped his partner on the parapet in Tian Zi Fang just twenty-four hours previously. At one point I was in his shot and I turned away instinctively. Lin glanced at me.

"The couple on the bridge yesterday," I said.

He glanced over to where I had jerked my thumb.

"How can you tell?" He chuckled. "We all look the same, no?"

"Who is he?"

More out of courtesy than anything he looked again. "I don't see."

I turned. The young man had disappeared. I looked down at the photos I had taken of the chariot and expanded them. He wasn't in any of them either.

***

I went down to breakfast the following morning and found Chao Lin in the restaurant, seated at a table with a box of muesli and a carton of long-life milk in front of him. I stared across at my adversaries of the cold-milk incident but they remained professionally aloof.

As I poured some muesli into a bowl, Lin's phone rang. He answered it in clipped and questioning phrases. When he finished the call, he reached across the table to me.

"We have to go. My man, Yong, he follows a woman from Dafeng Alley. She carries mail."

I gestured to the muesli and the milk and Lin paused, beckoned the manager and gave him instructions. The unfathomable man nodded, picked up the packet and the carton of milk and walked off with them.

It had been a long time since I'd ridden pillion on a motorcycle, let alone one as flimsy as Chao Lin's moped, and I clung on to the saddle for dear life. At the first junction a red light brought traffic to a halt in the dedicated bike lane and a hundred other bikes swarmed around, revving and twitching to be first off the mark when red turned to green. Even in this high buzz of tinny engines, Lin took a call from his friend and the screeched conversation gave him an update on the woman courier's progress. When the way ahead was clear, he swung left and headed to Tian Zi Fang.

He slithered to a halt on a gravel strip on the edge of Changning, propped up the bike and beckoned me to follow him at a run. No one paused to wonder about our haste. I remember thinking that in London the whole street would have stopped and turned to look at us, free to be as nosy as they liked.

As we turned a corner, Lin pointed twenty yards down the sidewalk to a sign above a building, the green-and-gold banner of the Chinese postal service. A man standing outside the shop visibly relaxed at Lin's approach, though he spared a moment to glance suspiciously at me. The two men spoke with breaks in their fluency, due, I later learned, to Yong speaking Shanghainese, a dialect peculiar to certain parts of the city. Lin translated.

"A woman, number 17 Dafeng Alley, came out with letters, all tied together. Yong follows her here. You were right, Mr Hawk. She sends them forward."

"Is she still inside?"

Lin nodded. "We wait, the other side of the street."

We crossed over and, with it being difficult to conceal a six-foot-tall European man anywhere in Shanghai, Lin suggested that I browse one of the open-fronted shops. Within moments of entering it a store assistant descended on me, offering bargains galore. I held him at arm's length on the pretext of wanting to see everything before I spent money and he transferred his attention to his next victim.

It was ten minutes before Yong reacted to the woman emerging from the post office. Over the garments I was flicking through I saw Chao Lin step forward with his phone and take a photo of her, another and then another. It was the elderly woman we had seen in the back room at number 17, stitching a child's dress. When she was out of sight, Lin beckoned me and I followed him into the post office.

It was much like a post office anywhere in the world, with queues of people for various services. Lin hurried to the front of the mailing queue, to the mild surprise of those waiting patiently, and spoke loudly to the clerk on the other side of the counter. He showed her the photo he'd taken of the woman and asked if she'd been here minutes ago. Yes, she had. Good, the letters were Lin's, he said, and he wondered if he'd given the old lady the correct forwarding address. The clerk turned to the the shelf behind her and lifted down a bundle of letters. Lin's display of relief was impressive. He took a photo of the address on the top package, then turned to smile at the queue he had disrupted.

Out in the street, the three of us settled on a stone parapet over a square of turgid water and Lin brought up the picture he had taken.

"Flat 5/40, Jinyu Residential Block, Shizhong District, Leshan, Sichuan Province, Postcode 7300169."

"It sounds good but I'm none the wiser…"

"No name of who will receive it. Leshan is a city near here."

By which he meant two thousand kilometres away.

***

We checked out of the Regency and headed for Leshan later that same day. Once again, my papers were examined at every stage of the journey. Passport, tourist visa, flight ticket. Even on the Shanghai underground, en route to Pudong Airport, my bags were scanned, my body too, and it left me with the uncomfortable feeling that on a cloud in the Chinese sky every thought I had ever had was recorded.

On the plane Lin tried to reassure me that Leshan was a more agreeable place than Shanghai, being set 'in the mountains' and for a moment I imagined the China of nature documentaries, of haystack mountains, gentle rivers in which old men fished. As it turned out, in spite of the air being cooler and fresher than Shanghai's, Leshan wasn't a village, not even a small town but a city of three million people. The streets were wider than those of Shanghai, the river less polluted, but the tower blocks were just as tall and stretched as far as the eye could see.

Lin hired a car at the airport and drove the fifty miles to the suburb of Shizhong, where we booked into a hotel. It was nine o'clock when we finally sat down at the bar and, like most of his fellow countrymen, Lin was ready to eat. I declined.

"Tomorrow we work," he said, summoning a passing waitress.

I nodded my agreement and turned in.

Seven o'clock the next morning saw us walking towards the centre of Leshan along the banks of the Min River. It was twice the width of the Thames in London and much faster flowing, yet for all its heaving currents three men were swimming downstream close to the bank. Lin paused to watch them pass.

"Buddhist monks," he said.

He took a pair of binoculars from his rucksack, handed them to me and pointed a mile or more downstream. At a place where the river forked I could make out the features of a giant Buddha carved into the red stone cliff, seventy, eighty metres high.

"You see a boat, a ship?" he asked.

"Indeed."

"He takes tourists to see it. If you pay the monks who live there you can climb up wood stairs to Buddha's head. Very high." He smiled. "You fancy we go there?"

"Not today," I said.

He laughed and we turned away from the river into the bustle of Leshan on the move. Cars were hooting their way down wide freeways, not in Western bad temper but simply to announce their presence. People were strolling along pavements towards their places of work. Nobody seemed to begrudge the early hour, the stress of the day ahead, the presence of so many others around them.

The seven towers of the Jinyu complex were set at angles to one another in a parkland of tall trees and exotic plants, forming a village in the sky. Had I toppled them sideways they would have fallen as a row of terraced houses and taken up forty times the space. The defining factor to this conurbation was money, and unlike some of its counterparts in Beijing or Shanghai, this place was well heeled enough to be gated. Lin hadn't reckoned with that and signalled me to wait as he approached the barrier.

It's odd how you don't need to know a language or even hear the intonation in order to understand what's being said. Lin asked the gatekeeper if we could speak to whoever lived in Flat 40 of Tower 5. The man reached back into his booth for his glasses in order to read the address and then shook his head. Lin asked again, his hands together, prayer-like, then suggested the man phone the occupant. The head still shook. In a final bid to change the stubborn mind, Lin reached into his inside pocket. The gatekeeper was offended at the prospect of a bribe and backed away in disgust.

At that point, a young man I hadn't noticed before wheeled his pushbike towards Chao Lin, all smiles and Chinese bonhomie. The three men conversed for a few minutes, after which the gatekeeper reached for his mobile and made a call. He handed the phone to the young man, who spoke to whoever had answered. A minute later the barrier rose. Lin beckoned me to follow him and his new friend into the village. The young man was delighted to make my acquaintance.

"Hi!" he said, reaching out a hand. "I know Qu Kueng."

The name stopped me in my tracks. "Who?"

"Qu Kueng. The man you wish to meet. I teach him English. He is delighted to meet you…"

Qu. Given the Chinese style of putting family names before the forenames, were we about to meet a relative of Suyin? Given that a million other Chinese share the name, it was by no means certain.

The teacher pointed up in the sky, to the top of the furthest tower, and we set off towards it. It was like walking into a well-frequented London park – asphalt paths, short grass and specimen trees, benches to sit on beside a small lake. A large notice bore a dozen icons telling you what you couldn't do. I could not dig a hole, light a fire, pick flowers, ride a motorcycle, drop litter, scale a wall, roller-skate, play music, smoke or spit. Even though I'd no intention of doing any one of them, it was as well to be forewarned.

People were coming and going, mainly parents with small children carrying books and satchels heading towards a school where, as far as I could tell, each child was received individually and steered towards a row of basins where they washed their hands and faces.

"I am Junxian Li," said the teacher. "Where are you from in England?"

"Winchendon."

"Ah, I have not been there."

I feigned surprise. "Really?"

"London, yes, Win…"

"Winchendon. It's a bit like this place, only set at a different angle."

Junxian Li lowered his voice. "Heh, you know Jeremy Clarkson?"

I stopped, surprised to hear the name of a well-worn British television presenter so far from home.

"Not personally."

"He is a really funny guy, don't you think?"

"Each to his own. I mean it's a free country…" I wished I hadn't said that. "How do you know him?"

He lowered his voice even further. "A friend of mine has a VPN. I have seen the television show *Top Gear*. It's good. And funny."

Chao Lin smiled. "Your *friend* has VPN, or *you* have?" he asked.

"Friend, friend…"

We reached the curve of steps to Tower 5 and Junxian parked his bike. He tapped a code into the panel next to the front door. It slithered open and we stepped into a plush lobby where Junxian summoned a lift. It arrived in seconds and launched us up to the fortieth floor, dragging my stomach in its wake. At the landing there were double doors leading, I presumed, into the penthouse, but Junxian pointed to a small flight of stairs. We followed him up them.

We emerged into the China I had dreamed of throughout my life, perched 150 metres above ground in an area no bigger that my own garden at Beech Tree. A flowing stream twisted between clumps of trees, creating the illusion of it going on forever. Even at this late stage in the year flowers were in bloom. A beaten path led to a cat-stretch bridge that straddled the water in front of an open pavilion, inside which a man of about fifty rose from a wicker chair. He was dressed for gardening in old clothes, with an open-necked shirt and a straw hat. He removed a pair of gloves from his hands and laid them aside.

"You are from England, yes?" he called out.

"I am."

Junxian tried to manage the introductions but the man waved him aside.

"My name is Qu Kueng. I am pleased to meet you. Who are you?"

It was textbook English, precise and clear.

"My name's Hawk."

He reached out to shake my hand and held it while he scrutinised my face. "Welcome, welcome."

He looked at Chao Lin and gestured for his name. Lin told him and tried to say more but Kueng held up a hand to silence him.

"This is… just beautiful," I said, looking round.

Qu Kueng laughed. "It is the fashion now in China. We move the countryside to the city. No room on the ground so we place it on top of buildings."

He pointed across to the nearest tower, which also boasted a roof garden where fruit and vegetables were being harvested by a middle-aged couple.

"One day we will join all the gardens together. Pathways in the sky. What do you think, Hawk?"

What I thought was too critical to voice. Mao's successor, Deng Xioping, had urbanised China, only for its people to wish they were back in their villages.

I laughed. "I think whoever built these apartments was courageous, to say the least."

"That was me. I built them. My company built them."

"Your company being White Crane?"

His pride blipped and the almost permanent smile began to fade. He turned to the young teacher. "Thank you for your help, Junxian Li."

"I can wait. Maybe translate…"

"No, no. Class dismissed."

"Tuesday?"

"Goodbye."

Junxian bowed to his employer and left, somewhat reluctantly, I fancied.

"He is a good teacher," said Kueng when he was out of earshot. "Or maybe that is for you to say."

"From what I can tell so far he's done an excellent job."

"He likes it here." He smiled. "He likes it too much."

He gestured for me to follow him back across the stream to the pavilion. Chao Lin tagged along. On the bridge, Kueng leaned over the rails and pointed down to the water where a shoal of koi carp raced towards him as if he had called to them. He reached into his pocket for pellets of fish food, threw them in and the water below seemed to boil.

Once in the pavilion he removed his hat and seated us, Lin at a distance, me close by. He took out a phone and spoke in Mandarin to whoever picked up.

"I ask for tea. Rice tea, Hawk? Is that to your liking?" I nodded. "So, Hawk… this is a bird, hawk, yes? You have other names?"

"Hawk is my family name. Given name, Nathan…"

"How do you know of White Crane, Hawk Nathan?"

I decided to leave the name dyslexia till later. I took a deep breath and leaped in.

"I used to be a policeman. I'm now looking for a young woman called Suyin Qu."

His eyes drifted back to the stream. The fish had calmed down and were moving away.

"She is my daughter."

"I guessed. Do you know where she is?"

He shook his head, wearily. "You have children?"

"Four."

"You know where they are?"

"Nepal, New York, London and… Haiti, perhaps."

"Where in Nepal? Where in New York?"

"I get the point."

He smiled. "Why do you want her?"

"She hasn't been seen for a while. Her friends, my son included, are worried."

He smiled and shook his head. If her disappearance bothered him he didn't show it.

"You thought she would be here?"

"When did you last see her?"

"A year ago."

"You don't keep in touch? Facebook, Zoom…?"

"Not so much."

"But she's your child."

"My only child. My only relative. But it is her life. I let her live it. What do you know of her?"

"I know she's spent a great deal of money in England. Investments in the name of White Crane."

He gave a sceptical nod and his English began to fray at the edges. On purpose, I thought. "This does not surprise. I make her White Crane Head of International Business. She spread the wings… like a hawk."

"Two big farms on the English coast."

He pulled a face and shrugged. "She is fond of the country. Like me. We have house in Yunnan, her mother's family. You know Yunnan?"

"I've heard. So there are no plans for… Norfolk?"

His eyes brightened. "Norfolk? Where the turkeys are grown?"

Christ, I thought, not you as well. I repeated the question. "Plans?"

"She has not told me."

"You don't seem bothered by her… absence."

He paused for a moment. "You policemen always think you see what people feel from their faces. You cannot. Not from mine."

"Why don't you answer my question…?"

"You are in danger of offending me, Hawk Nathan. I would not like that. I would prefer friendship."

I nodded. "Just one more thing. Can she drive?"

He looked at me in bewilderment. I thought he hadn't come across the word 'drive', so I mimed turning a steering wheel.

"I know what is drive," he said. "No, she does not drive."

He looked across to the steps that led down to the apartment, from where a young Chinese woman was approaching with a tray of tea and mooncakes. She was dressed in smart office black and white, the style of a personal assistant as opposed to a wife or mistress. Kueng spoke to her in Mandarin. She poured the rice tea into small cups and handed them round. She bowed slightly and returned the way she had come.

"You like?" Kueng asked of the mooncake I had bitten into.

I nodded through the crumbs. Chao Lin raised a hand, like a child to a teacher in a classroom, and asked in English, "Why is the address of White Crane in Dafeng Alley? Why not here?"

"To honour the past. My grandfather, he came from a village near to Russia. Very poor. He settle in Shanghai and started business. I like to remember that my family was not always rich."

"What business was he in?" I asked.

"Land. He bought land and he built."

His phone pinged and he glanced down at the message he'd just received. His face suddenly screwed up with excitement, a mass of lines radiating from his eyes and he hurried through the greenery behind us, beckoning me to follow. I joined him at the very edge of the roof and summoned the courage to look down at the ground forty stories below.

Kueng pointed to the barrier, which the gatekeeper had just lifted. A security van of some kind, lights flashing in a sequence, began to make its way towards Tower 5. Kueng tapped me on the upper arm and I grabbed at the safety rail.

"It is the courier," he said. "Special, special delivery. Come see."

He hurried back down the path, crossed over the bridge and almost ran to the steps down to his apartment. We followed.

At the landing the double doors to Kueng's penthouse were open and the smart tea lady was beaming at him. I stepped in and gazed around. My first impression was of a museum of Chinese antique furniture and ceramics. Wherever my eyes landed there was a priceless artefact dating back God knows how many centuries. The main room was dominated by a round mahogany table with eight barrel-shaped stools around it, each one exquisitely carved with rural motifs. Around the walls were cabinets, coffers and dressers, some carved, some painted, all of them bearing untouchable ceramics. The word Ming seemed to echo round the room, price tags fluttering behind it.

Whoever had bought the pieces in this place – and I assumed it was Kueng – had been trying to reach the past, but with so many tributes to it the place had the feel not of a treasure house but a cluttered junk shop.

"You like?" Kueng asked, noticing my amazement.

"Very much."

The lift beyond the double doors pinged and slid open. Two security guards emerged. They were dressed in garish uniforms and were seemingly armed to the teeth. The younger man carried a crate with extreme care. It was the size of a small cabin trunk, protected by wooden battens and spattered with warning notices in every language possible. His companion took a small crowbar from his belt and asked Kueng if he wanted the seal broken and the first layer of protection prized apart. Kueng nodded, holding up his hands as a warning to be careful. Like a Russian doll, there was another layer of packaging under the first but Kueng insisted he could handle that. His assistant signed for the delivery and the two security guards left.

Together we lifted the package onto the table. When it was settled Kueng held his arms wide, fingers drumming in midair as he savoured the delay in opening it. Then he gently began to peel away the outer wrapping, taking note of every label, every instruction as he went.

"You guess what this is, Hawk? I give you clue. Made in France."

With a long, slow tear of the final layer of packaging Kueng revealed the contents of the delivery. Made in France, certainly, though not as recently as the phrase implies. It was a painting, maybe fifty centimetres by forty, oil on canvas and clearly in its original frame. He called his assistant to hold it upright on the table and he gazed at it for a full minute. It depicted two men in a Parisian café, playing chess. One of them was leaning back in his chair, waiting for the other to make his move.

"This man here, he is a poet called…" He pointed to the one leaning back and struggled to recall the pronunciation. "Charles Baudelaire."

"Who painted it?"

"Edouard Manet."

I paused before asking, "This is… original?"

He nodded, still mesmerised by the work. "It is one of four, the same subject, the same players. Chess, the international leveller, you agree?"

"Original?" I asked again.

Again he nodded and beckoned me to step even closer. From what I could tell, which at the best of times is very little where painting is concerned, it seemed authentic.

"I have the other three. Come."

I followed him across the room to a door where he placed his thumb against a small pad. The door swung open slowly. He gestured for me to enter ahead of him and as I did so a light came on, soft daylight that seemed to glow from the ceiling of this windowless room. The door closed behind us to preserve the temperature, which I presumed was set to accommodate the collection on the walls. He led me over to the three other Manets and shrugged his delight, hoping that I would share it. I pretended to do so and began to sidestep my way around the room.

The paintings were all named in their original language and I needed a Laura Peterson to take me through this rich man's paradise. The artists I recall were Henri Matisse, Jean Frédéric Bazille, Paul Cézanne and Henri de Toulouse-Lautrec. Kueng didn't want me to tot up the imagined price tags, he simply wanted me to enjoy the works themselves, and I became aware that he was watching me keenly as I moved round. When I'd finished I turned to him.

"Why keep them here?" I asked. "Why not some gallery in Beijing or Shanghai?"

He nodded slowly. "When I go…" He corrected himself quickly. "When I die they will be given to the people. Until then…"

He gestured his meaning, which in any language said that until his demise the paintings would remain on these walls. They would be his and his alone.

We returned to the main room, where Kueng instructed his assistant to hang the new arrival in its appointed place. As she picked it up and carried it into the gallery an odd feeling came over me, a kind of anxiety whose roots were in my frugality. This young woman, so polite, so efficient, so good at making tea and serving cake, had been entrusted to hang a work of art that must have cost millions. I half expected to hear a hammer banging a nail into a wall followed by a crash as the painting fell to the floor…

"Where did the painting come from?"

"It is found for me in Sweden by a London art dealer. A close friend of my daughter."

"Taylor Mandrake?"

"You know him?"

"Not as well as I thought."

Kueng nodded. "He bought this at auction, in May."

He stared at me as if willing me me to read between the lines. He counted the months on one hand.

"May, June, July, August, September, October."

We spent the next hour in a conversation that Kueng directed with such subtle efficiency that I couldn't once break his hold on it. Each time I came close to the subject of his errant daughter or my suspicions about White Crane, he swerved us away to much safer topics. And as we small-talked our way along he revealed a love and a loyalty to the country of his birth and gentle praise for its leaders. Had I breathed a word of criticism, I'm sure he would have taken offence and no doubt smiled me towards the lifts.

At one point, Chao Lin asked to use the toilet and Kueng directed him to a bathroom at the other end of the apartment. When he was safely out of earshot Kueng asked casually, "Do you know who he is?"

For a moment I thought he was going to tell me, but it was a genuine enquiry.

"Er, no. A tour guide. An ex-policeman like myself."

Kueng smiled. "As you know, Hawk Nathan, there is no such animal as ex-policeman."

"You don't trust him?"

He stared at me. "I would trust him with my life. Men of his profession, they are chosen for their integrity, their loyalty, their courage."

It sounded like a sentence from a recruitment web page and I looked away, slightly embarrassed for him.

"Meet me tomorrow, Hawk, at the quay and I show you the giant Buddha…"

"I've seen him from a distance."

Kueng was insistent. "We will go close. The riverboat. Let us say first trip of the day. Seven-thirty. Come alone. You will learn so much…"

"Fair enough."

We heard the toilet flush and Kueng cut the air with one hand. There would be no more questions. They could wait till the following morning.

***

Chao Lin and I left the Jinyu complex shortly afterwards and, in keeping with what little I knew about him, Lin was hungry. At the entrance barrier he asked the gatekeeper to recommend a café, whereupon the man pointed across a vast intersection of highways to a small establishment.

As we approached it, in broken stages on account of the perplexing traffic control, I saw Junxian Li emerge from the place and hurry towards his bike. I thought nothing of it to begin with. We were a good twenty metres away and, yes, he might well not have spotted us. His haste suggested otherwise. He unlocked his bike and pedalled away.

I glanced back at the towers. Seated in that café he would have had a clear view straight to the barrier and seen us emerge. I put my suspicions down to the paranoia of being in a country where every move you make seems to be watched and logged. Uncharitable as my fears were, they were vindicated when we entered the café.

It was a cheerful, crowded place with a feel of the European coast to it. A large fishing net hung from the bannister right down to the floor and caught in it were plastic crabs and lobsters. A wooden skiff was hanging from the ceiling, photos of French and Italian street life adorned the walls, old pots and skillets hung from hooks. Sitting at a table by the window was the young couple who had crossed my path in Tian Zi Fang, then again when I'd visited the Terracotta Army in Xian. I stared at them and they turned away.

I never actually see red, although that's often how it's described by others who witness insurmountable rage. What I see is the object of my anger in tunnel vision and to the exclusion of all else. There's no sound, apart from my heartbeat banging in my ears and at that point I've no idea what my body does. Without intervention by a third party I emerge minutes later, bearing down on a head I've slammed on the nearest hard surface or looking up at someone who has thrown to me to the floor and held me there.

On this occasion there was intervention. As I strode towards the young couple, intent on God knows what, Chao Lin must've recognised the signs and stepped between my targets and me. He reached up and pointed in my face and yelled, "Map, Map, Map…."

I paused and looked down at him, conscious now of the background sound of people gasping, sliding back their seats as they waited to see what would happen next. I took a breath and reached into my inside pocket and took out The Map. I laid it on the table and carefully unfolded it, then donned the imaginary spectacles I always carry. I held up my finger and brought it down on that 'far more agreeable place', as Roy Pullman called it. Today it just happened to be Winchendon. Specifically Chestnut Cottage, where Laura Peterson handed me a drink and smiled. In my mind I told her what had suddenly dawned on me.

"These two kids, maybe the teacher as well, maybe even Chao Lin, they aren't interested in me! What an ego I have to ever think they were. They're spying on Qu Kueng. He worries them…"

With the drumbeat in my ear now subsiding and normal vision being resumed, I looked down at The Map and began to fold it again. I slipped it back into my inside pocket and removed the imaginary spectacles. As the noise level in the café rose, I turned to the young couple and asked, "What the fuck are you two up to? Ask them, Lin. What do they hope to learn? Are they working for the Secret Service or… who?"

As I lifted my phone to take a photo of them, the young man shielded his face, the girl likewise. They rose from the table and left the café, faces buried in their sleeves.

A moment or so later Chao Lin asked, "Hawk, you want food?"

"You think anyone here would grill me a salmon steak?"

Lin smiled. "I will ask."

I sat down in the seat vacated by the young man and my mouth began to water.

The next morning I rose at six o'clock and decided to skip breakfast, the better to avoid any disappointments regarding the menu. I slipped out of the hotel with nothing more than a long smile from the young woman at reception, whose eyes followed me to the main door and beyond.

I headed for the Min River, and at an iron bridge I turned to follow the sign depicting a riverboat. The water below was sluggish, perhaps in deference to the early hour. Riversides always disappoint me. In my mind I expect to see grassy slopes descending to shallow banks where trees stand half in the water, half on land, dipping their branches in the flow. What I get is stone walkways and concrete walls with the river, edged by detritus, twenty feet below me.

It was a five-minute stroll to the quayside and even at this early hour the place was busy. A market was being set up along the adjacent road and already customers were haggling with traders. I paused beneath an ancient Chinese elm, which was doing its best to rise from its surroundings. Slabs of stone had been cockled by its roots and a large warning notice was pinned to the bark. The graphic told passers-by not to climb the tree. I glanced round to see if I'd been followed. It would not be Chao Lin. I had passed his room in the hotel and heard the slight rumble of snoring. Junxian Li and the young couple were a different matter. It was their job to keep an eye on Kueng Qu and his visitors, but this morning they seemed to have fallen short.

I suppose I had expected to find the plushest of river cruisers, with all mod cons and its engine purring as it prepared for the day ahead. In its place were two of the most decrepit tubs imaginable, peeling and patched with rust abounding. The deck seating was downright hazardous, freestanding and rickety. The engine was suddenly fired and as it clanked into life it emitted a cloud of black smoke from the stack. Nevertheless, at the head of a gangplank tourists, mainly Chinese, were already queuing to take their place on board. I stood watching from a distance and turned when a voice called out, "Hawk Nathan, good morning!"

I turned to see Kueng Qu hurrying towards me, the universal Starbucks coffee in his hand. He pointed to it.

"You want?"

"No thanks. Morning."

"Come, we go on board."

He headed for the gangplank, where a crew member unhooked the chain and bowed him aboard like royalty. The queuing tourists simply watched as we trampolined our way onto the boat. Another crew member ushered us into the main saloon. It was hot and stuffy, with the smell of engine oil seeping from its every pore. I fancied I smelled a faint overlay of vomit but that could have been my imagination. We had it to ourselves. The crewman paused to ask Kueng if there was anything he wanted. Kueng shook his head and waved the man away. We settled at a plastic table, from where Kueng kept a watchful eye on the quayside.

"We talk when the boat leaves," he said. "You understand?"

I smiled. "Safer than talking in your apartment? No camera to see us, no microphone to hear?"

He nodded. "You are a true policeman, Hawk."

It now dawned on me that the crew had been waiting for us to arrive before allowing other passengers to board. One of them now unhooked the chain, and as the embarking tourists bounced their way onto the boat he studied them closely. At one point he stopped a lone male in his forties and passed him to a colleague, who immediately began to question him. He probably asked the same things I would have done. Show me ID? Where do you live? What is your job? Why are you alone? The man became irate and his inquisitor turned towards the saloon window. Kueng shook his head minimally and the passenger was ushered towards the other riverboat, protesting all the way.

I had just witnessed the power of wealth in action, even in this country where all are equal but the rich are more equal than others.

When the riverboat was finally untied and its engine below our feet cranked up, Kueng suggested that we go up on deck and join the other two dozen or so passengers. The boat crossed the river and went as close to the opposite bank as possible, enough that I could make out the faces of people hurrying to work, many on bikes, most on foot. Instinctively I kept a lookout for Junxian Li. China does that to you. It makes you believe that every face might belong to someone who will inform on you. A crewman directed us towards seats at the bow of the ship. They had been reserved for us. He waited for Kueng to dismiss him, then bowed and withdrew.

As we progressed downstream Kueng drew my attention to various waypoints of interest: a temple here, a house there, a bridge, even a sacred tree. I found none of it as interesting as the possible reason he had asked me to join him that morning. When he ran out of monuments to share he turned and smiled.

"Hawk, you are a man who does what he says he will do. Is this so?"

Flattery – it's usually the opening gambit of anyone who is about to put you down. "I like to think so."

"You will find my daughter… because that is your promise… to yourself, your family."

He was picking his words carefully, and not just because English wasn't his first language. He was sounding me out.

"In searching for her you are in danger of… uncovering things… about us."

"Spit it out, Kueng. That's slang for get to the point."

He turned away for a moment, nodding.

"You know about the farms in Norfolk. Their investment possibilities?"

"A friend of mine believes you could build a port there, like the one in Sri Lanka."

He laughed. "This is good. Good! Your government believes this?"

"A small cog in the big wheel of it does."

"It's good," he whispered. "Is excellent that your cog believes White Crane will build a hub for commerce and all things related." He reached for my arm and laid his hand on it. "But it is not true, Hawk. And now I confide in you."

"You're sure you want to?"

"I have no option. You will find out my true purpose and then there is danger that you reveal it. I hope to persuade you… no." I turned and gave him my trustworthy look. "In the spring I will seek asylum in your country."

I laughed. "I had several explanations for what you were up to, but that wasn't one of them."

"Even more excellent."

"Dangerous, though."

He nodded. "Men like me have been hunted down and murdered, years after they leave China. Their families tortured. I have no family except Suyin."

"Kueng, somebody is *already* after her. Are they Chinese, do you know?"

He chuckled, nervously. "Nothing so big. They are small people with ambition. Opinder Pandeshi, he learned that someone knew who Suyin was… that she was rich."

"Hardly surprising, given the money she spent. Who is the 'someone'?"

He shrugged. "I have no idea, but he thought she was in danger of being taken."

"Kidnapped? Held for ransom? Is that why he wanted her back in China?"

He nodded and reached for my arm again. "I ask you this, Hawk. Find her, look after her. Then find whoever tries to catch her. You can say your price."

I moved his hand away. "Everyone wants to give me money to find your daughter. There's one small hitch. What if your daughter killed Opinder? By accident or design. What then?"

"She says it was not her. You will prove this for me?"

"When did you last hear from her?"

"Three weeks."

"And where was she?"

"England. England for sure. I don't know where."

I leaned back in the rickety chair and it slid a few inches away from him. He shuffled his own chair closer to me.

"You will do this?"

I wondered what would've happened had I refused. There were at least three crewmen on board who were in Kueng's pay. Would they descend on me at a sign from him, take me to the stern of the ship and heave me overboard? Whenever I'd envisaged my death, down the years, it hadn't been by drowning in the Min River.

The riverboat was approaching the Buddha, a vast effigy carved into the rock. Once completely red, the stone was now partially blackened with pollutants, and even at this early hour tourists were climbing up to the Buddha's face via the narrow stairway clamped to his body. Why anyone should want to increase the distance between themselves and the ground has always puzzled me.

"I might have got there on my own," I said. "You, coming to England, I mean. The Edouard Manet. Bought at auction in May, arrives now in November." He smiled and urged me to expand on that. "Where was it in the intervening six months? Being cleaned, authenticated, the frame refurbished?

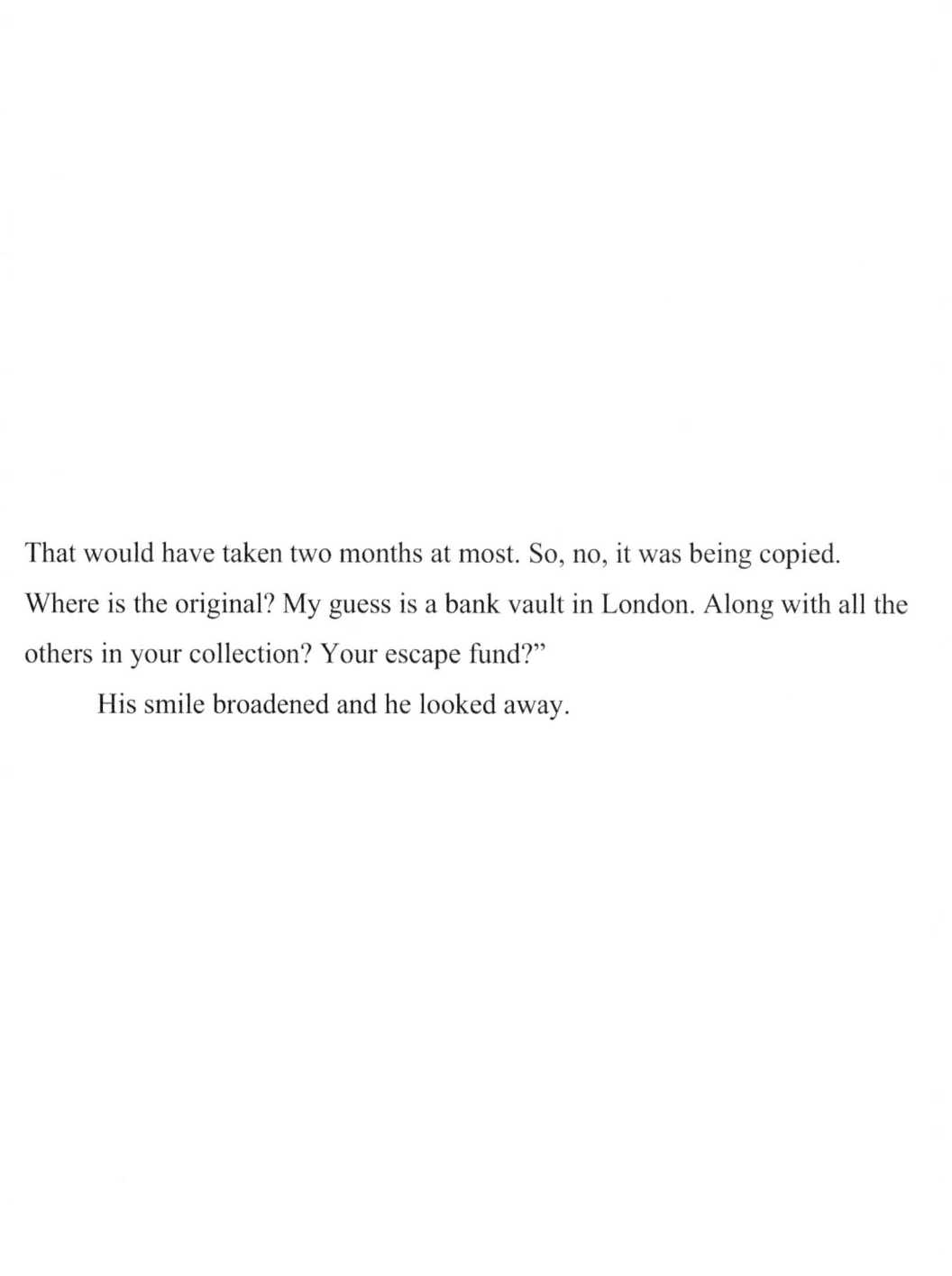

That would have taken two months at most. So, no, it was being copied. Where is the original? My guess is a bank vault in London. Along with all the others in your collection? Your escape fund?"

His smile broadened and he looked away.

Chao Lin had a dozen questions he wanted to ask. I could see in his face they were lining up to be voiced but he didn't put one of them, not even when I told him I was leaving China as soon as possible. He certainly didn't ask where I had been for three hours that morning before breakfast. Perhaps he already knew.

We flew back to Shanghai the following day and stepped out into the treacly air.

Later that afternoon he drove me to the UK consulate, a building that cowered among a collection of tall Western hotels and shopping malls. It reminded me of an old Whitehall office of state, fashioned from large blocks of stone, all sharp corners and sudden recesses. Inside was busy enough, despite it being late in the working day, and the security was efficient, though markedly less severe than anything I'd experienced in the previous ten days. At the reception counter a woman in her forties with a Yorkshire accent, of all things, adjusted her glasses and smiled.

"Good afternoon. How can I help you?"

"To be honest, I'm not sure who I need to speak to."

"Well, give me the bare bones and we'll…"

"Is there a duty officer?"

"I can certainly ask if he'd come and… some idea of what it's about would help…?"

I lowered my voice. "I was asked by an MI6 intelligence officer to come and be debriefed here… when I'd finished doing what he… had asked."

I corkscrewed my forefinger in midair and she ran what I'd just said back through her mind.

"Yes, there is someone who'll come and have a word with you," she cooed. "Do you think I could have your passport and visa? Have you got them with you?" I handed them over. "Thank you. If you'd like to go and wait over there, Mr… Hawk?"

"I'm a retired police officer."

That seemed to endorse her view that I'd slipped a cog. She smiled and pointed to a huddle of wicker chairs set beneath a huge carved mirror. She followed me with her eyes as I strolled over to it and stuck my tongue out at my reflection, before slumping into a chair and gazing round at portraits of past Consul Generals. I waved at one. God knows why I was behaving so childishly, but I've since realised that with this small piece of China being so British I had to reestablish my freedom to behave as I chose. I was also exhausted. I closed my eyes, and the next thing I remember was a hand gently shaking my shoulder and a male voice saying, "Sir, wake up, sir. Mr Hawk, wake up."

I opened my eyes and stared up at a man who, like me, hadn't shaved that morning, mainly on account of him being so young that he didn't need to.

"My name is Troy Palmer. I'm third secretary to the Consul General."

"That doesn't sound very high up the food chain."

"High enough, sir, for your purposes."

He beckoned me to follow him through a large heavy door, the other side of which was an open-plan office, laid out with heavy desks, leather chairs and tall feathery palms. At the windows, long plush curtains were tied back with gold sashes, all of it overlooked from the walls by yet more dead diplomats.

Troy led me across the room to his pitch and rolled a chair from a neighbouring desk towards me.

"So, an intelligence officer in MI6?" he said, once we'd settled. "What is his name?"

"John Smith."

He raised one eyebrow. "You know his section? You have an extension?"

"I have his mobile number."

I handed him the card John Smith had given me. He glanced at it, turned it over and handed it back.

"With all due respect, sir, that could be anyone. Especially with a name like Smith."

"Why don't you check? An email, a phone call to the right person in London."

He smiled. "Mr Hawk, it's now half past midnight on the South Bank. Come back early tomorrow. We'll sort it out then."

***

At nine o'clock the following morning I was first in the queue at the consulate, and after the security square dance the Yorkshire woman rang through to Troy Palmer and directed me to the wicker chair to wait. Palmer appeared before I had chance to reach it, which told me that he'd… reassessed my assertions of yesterday. For my part I had shaved.

Troy led me through to the open-plan office. He'd arrived early that morning, he explained, and just in case there had been anything to my story he had contacted MI6 via a series of intermediaries. He had discovered one or two interesting things…

"I commend you for your diligence, Mr Third Secretary, but the way you put it, 'just in case there'd been anything to my story', implies that you doubted it?"

He smiled. "Pinch of salt, shall we say. Yes, do sit down." He steepled his fingers together, something which has always annoyed me. It bespeaks an attempt at precision that more often than not the steeplejack isn't capable of. He looked over them. "Say again why he asked you to visit us."

The scepticism in his voice had alerted the spiders, though I wasn't quite sure why. It felt as though Troy knew something I wouldn't like.

"He just wanted us to shoot the breeze, me to tell you how…"

"There's a couple of John Smiths in MI6, Mr Hawk, as you might imagine. None of them has ever heard of you."

"You've spoken to them?"

"No, that isn't how it works…"

"You've called the mobile number I gave you?"

"Yes. Number unobtainable."

The spiders were on the move. At best, John Smith had taken me for a long ride. At worst…

I confess that momentarily I considered smacking Troy's face, but this was neither the time nor the place. I smiled instead, with great difficulty.

"I think it's time I headed home, don't you?"

"Good idea. Passport, tickets all in order?"

"Yes… yes. Shall we?"

He escorted me out to the foyer, and as we passed the Yorkshire woman at reception he raised an eyebrow. His mission was accomplished, the gesture said. Their behaviourally challenged fellow Brit was about to exit the building and, with luck, would never return. I do believe he was puzzled, though, to see Chao Lin pull up in a Merc outside the building, jump out and open the passenger door for me. I waved to Troy, fingertips only, as we drove away.

***

I had one final Chinese experience at Pudong airport. As my luggage went through security my name and flight number came up on an overhead panel and I was called aside to be grilled by two men in a bombproof bunker, somewhere in the basement. They were uniformed and efficient, but not personable. The taller of the two, who spoke a shortened form of English, showed me the X-ray of what bothered him about my suitcase.

"What is, please?" he asked.

"It's a reading light." He looked at me. "A light to read by… with…"

"Open, please."

I opened the suitcase and the silent one fished around in my clothes for the folding light. He placed it on the table between us. He and his colleague examined it from all angles without touching it.

"Made in Taiwan," I said.

"How does work?"

I extended it to its full height.

"Switch on, please."

Again I obliged, and it didn't explode. He opened and closed the battery case, then looked at me.

"Is for reading?"

"It's something you do with books."

"You have books?"

"Kindle."

"Where?" I pointed to the man-bag hanging from my shoulder. "Take out, please."

I opened the Kindle and switched it on and off. He held out his hand for it and navigated his way to my homepage, and from there to my search history. He scrutinised every item and then glanced at his watch.

"The plane leaves in forty minutes," I said

"Sit down, please."

"The plane…"

"There is another flight, four hours time."

He nodded to where I should take a seat and I slumped into a steel chair that groaned in a universal language. The silent one left the room and returned two minutes later with a uniformed woman who had left her personality at home that morning. She too examined my passport, then took me through the whole business with my reading light and Kindle. Once assured that I wouldn't be able to board the plane I was booked on, let alone blow it up, she gave me the all-clear with a nod.

"Is there a seat on this… next plane?"

"Not business class. Economy. Also, go via Amsterdam."

I smiled. "Great. I've never been there."

"Enjoy."

It was Chinese diplomacy at work, circuitous but unmistakable in its meaning. Go home, it said, and don't come back again.

Ten hours later, somewhere over Siberia, I emailed Jaikie to put his and Jodie's minds at rest. I said I believed that our mutual friend was alive and well and living in China. I asked him to pass on my flight numbers to Bill Grogan and ask him to meet me at Heathrow. And to bring a bag of Suyin Qu's dirty laundry from the basket in his attic room. Jaikie responded by asking if I'd meant that. I sent him a fistful of emojis: green ticks, thumbs up and then the word 'yes'.

Grogan was there at Terminal 4 that evening. He'd turned up in Jaikie's brand new toy, a patriotic Jaguar. Made in China. He looked at me in bewilderment as I paused to breath in a lungful of West London air. Normally I might have pretended to choke on it, but not after Shanghai.

"You well?" I asked.

"Fine. You?"

"Fine. You bring the dirty clothes?" He jerked his thumb at a Tesco carrier bag on the rear seat. "Thanks. Harrow on the Hill, please, mate. I'll take the train from there."

"I was all set to drive you home…"

"Just need a few words, that's all."

***

Grogan parked outside a pub called The Heathcote, the kind of watering hole my father always gravitated towards, especially at this time of day. The designer grime, the relic chairs and tables would have appealed to him, so too the leaded windows with their original black lettering. The only thing he would have balked at was the TV monitor the size of a door clamped to the far wall. A couple of elderly regulars were seated beneath it watching the loop of silent adverts. Trendier people were leaning at the bar being… trendy.

I ordered a double, ice all the way to the brim, from a bald thirty-year-old with a handlebar moustache. Grogan settled for a coffee and went over to a table, where he sat with his back to the wall.

"What does The Job tell you about murder, Bill?" I said, as he poured fake sugar into his cup. "Three reasons for it. Revenge, sex and money. Why are you looking at me like that?"

He blinked and looked away. "You're simplifying."

"Stop being sensible, Bill. Of course there are other reasons people get killed, but mainly…"

"Go on."

"In Opinder's case it isn't sex, it isn't revenge, so it must be money. But nothing to do with Chinese investment on the Norfolk coast."

I knocked back my drink and signalled across the bar, pointing to my glass for a duplicate. Grogan gave me another kind of look.

"Bill, you're not my mother, you're not my wife, you're not…" I paused. "Fuck it, I'm sorry, mate. I guess I'm just annoyed with myself…"

"Jetlag."

"That's kind of you, but no. I've fallen foul of the popular narrative that everything about China is suspect, when mostly it's people trying to live day by day. But it's a dangerous place to escape from, especially if you're an oligarch. And that's what Suyin's father is trying to do… to get asylum here, with his daughter. It was all going to plan until someone twigged that she was rich and tried to kidnap her."

"And along the way Opinder Pandeshi was murdered?"

"It was British greed, not Chinese skulduggery that got him killed. She went into hiding, hoping, believing that either Parfitt or yours truly would catch the killer, who by any stretch is also the kidnapper."

"So, you found the father, by the sound of it, but not *her*?"

"I didn't find her because she isn't there. She's in England. Don't ask me where, but I'm back where I started. Looking for her."

Grogan took a mouthful of the coffee. He didn't like it. "And you reckon there's no chance she killed Opinder… fit of pique, by accident?"

"Like I said to John Smith, when I find her I'll ask her."

The moustache bore down on us with another double scotch and ice. I wanted to say he should put the animal stuck to his top lip out of its misery, but I held off.

"Another coffee, sir?" he asked Grogan.

Grogan placed a hand over his cup and shook his head. The moustache swung away back to the bar to serve an incoming group of thirty-somethings, greeting them like old friends. Someone else switched on a few more lights and lifted the gloom a little.

Grogan unwrapped the Amaretti biscuit and downed it in one. "Where will you start?"

"Dunno. Apply your mind, Bill. Where will she be?"

"Well, I doubt you'll find her in the penthouse suite of some hotel. That's the first place anyone'd look."

I nodded. "I wondered about Taylor Mandrake's. I mean, she's closer to him than I thought."

"As in *close* close?"

I explained about Kueng's collection of masterpiece copies and the part Taylor had played in buying the originals. He turned his nose up.

"She may be in love, Nathan, but she isn't stupid. That's the *second* place they'd look."

He leaned back and went into a mini trance. When he returned from it, he said, "If I were Suyin Qu, I'd go somewhere I knew, somewhere I had control, influence…"

"A farm on the Norfolk coast? Maybe among the lavender?"

He shook his head. "How about Abiding Earth? From what you've told me it's big enough and barmy enough to get lost in. Rambling house? Raving eccentrics? Fifty-four acres of jungle? You might get lucky."

It was a decent suggestion, and even if nothing came of it I could cross it off my list. He must have heard me thinking about another scotch.

"Drink up, guv, I'll drive you to the station."

**

It was pitch dark when the taxi from Haddenham Parkway dropped me off at Beech Tree. I trundled my luggage, with the Tesco carrier bag attached, over the gravel and round to the back door. It occurred to me, momentarily, how little I used the front door. A habit from childhood. The front was for formal use, the back door was for family. The taxi pulled away and left me in nighttime silence. No Dogge to greet me either. Just a security light on the side wall, glaring down at me.

After a trip away, it always takes me a couple of days to warm back into the place and I tried to help it along by making a cup of tea. As the kettle boiled I opened the fridge, expecting to find leftovers to graze on. There were none. Jenny Tindall had… tidied them away. I defrosted a loaf, opened a tin of tuna and took the resultant sandwich through to the living room. I switched on the telly, but the late news felt alien enough to have come from Mars. I abandoned it and settled for checking my phone messages.

The only one that stood out was from Alessandro Scutari, who wanted to know how my inquiries were progressing and to tell me I shouldn't hesitate to invoice him for work to date. I read it as a roundabout way of asking how much I knew about his visa scam.

I phoned Laura, who was still up.

"You're back," she said. "How was it?"

"Fine," I said.

"You found her, then?"

"No, but she's here. England. How's Dogge?"

"She's fine. God, we're both beginning to sound like Bill Grogan. Dogge is in the rudest of health and can't wait to see you. How's that?"

"I'll pop round for her tomorrow. I missed you, by the way."

She waited, perhaps for me to add something a little more romantic.

"Well, I missed you too," she said, eventually.

In the unnerving way of these things, the moment I put the phone down my mobile rang. It was John Smith. I didn't answer it and it went to message. He didn't leave one.

***

Next morning I was up and drinking breakfast by six-thirty. As I prepared to leave the house the phone rang. It was John Smith again and I let it go to message.

"You're back, I hear," he said. "Wonder if you could give me a call, earliest convenience. Need to chat."

He sounded keen, maybe even anxious, to keep me on side. I looked at the phone as if it were him. "We sure do."

I went round to Chestnut to pick up Dogge, who went berserk for two minutes and then flopped down in the back of the Discovery, exhausted.

"I wonder if you've still got it in you?" I asked her.

"Got what?" Laura asked.

"You know she was a sniffer dog, drugs – failed the exam. With any luck it's a skill you never forget… if you're a dog."

"I won't pretend to know what you're on about, but I do like the car. Insofar as I like any car. I know it's your night with Martin Falconer, but supper this evening?"

"I'll put him off."

I went close and pecked her on the cheek. She reached out a hand to me and dropped it quickly.

"Have a good day," she said. "Sorry. Hate the phrase but like the sentiment."

In spite of the 30,000 miles on its clock, the Discovery was an easy car to drive in that it didn't need coaxing up inclines or easing round corners. However, slave to sentimentality that I am, I missed the clunking and grumbling of the Land Rover, to say nothing of the dubious smell, which had been replaced by new-car aroma fresh from a can.

As the novelty of the Discovery wore off I became aware of the traffic around me, mostly juggernauts from Europe and sleek saloons, overtaking me at high speed. That's probably why he stood out: the motorcyclist who was half a mile back and doing sixty, the same as me. Normally, bikers zip past but this guy was keeping his distance. I was sure it was paranoia on my part, or possibly the China effect where every move you make is observed. Whichever it was, I lost the biker just before Stroud, but he stayed with me in spirit, so much so that when I drew up outside Abiding Earth the sudden silence was overtaken by my heartbeat drumming in my ears. I turned to Dogge, who had just woken up.

"You ready for this, girl?"

The wrought-iron gates at Abiding Earth had not been repaired and the side entrance had been chained and padlocked in several places. A hand-painted notice hung from the top finials.

"Danger!" it said. "Gas leak. For your own safety please extinguish all naked flames."

It was a nice touch. Slightly better than a rope-netting booby trap.

I took the cutters and walked a few yards farther on to where the outer growth seemed conquerable. I cut a man-sized hole in the chainlink, then collected a few tools from the car, together with the bag of Suyin's laundry. Once the other side of the fence, I sat Dogge down and invited her to get a noseful of her quarry. She stuck her head in the bag and seemed to recall what was expected of her. After ten seconds or so she looked up at me.

"Okay," I said, excitedly. "Got it? Find it, girl, find it! Seek! Seek!"

She set off ahead of me, nose down but not really inspired, and I suddenly began to feel silly. I wondered why that was, then realised. Searching for Suyin in the Gloucestershire outback had seemed like a good idea from a distance, even late at night, but like all plans, daylight gave it perspective and made it seem daft and desperate. As I slashed my way through any overgrowth which impeded us I wondered what on earth I'd expected to find. Suyin camped out here? Living in a treehouse? A hollowed-out cave? Or in one of the POW huts? Maybe the attic of the main house itself? The eco-brick bothy? I didn't believe any of it. But true to my character, if not my current instinct, I soldiered on, though I did ask myself one question. If I'd discussed this jaunt with Laura before setting out, would she have made a better suggestion?

Dogge seemed to have recaptured her youth. Once or twice she sprang up above the height of the vegetation to check that I was still following. The distance between us soon increased and I called for her to wait. The sound of my voice startled a muntjac deer to our right, and with a crackle of broken twigs it leaped up and took off. Dogge followed immediately, deaf to my protests that she should keep her mind on the job in hand.

I hacked my way on until I reached the point where the greenery merged into the gravel at the front of the house. I stopped and called to Dogge, but to no avail. I would have given way to slight panic had not the door to the nearby dormitory been opened by a young woman. As she leaned out, I saw that she was dressed in a white lab coat over jeans and a sweater, and was clearly surprised to see an unknown face. She called to a companion inside the hut who came to the door and took in the scene: a man with a hand scythe in one hand and a Tesco carrier bag in the other.

"Wait there," the man said, pointing at me.

He descended the wooden steps and strolled towards me.

"What is your business here?"

The English was slightly stilted, the accent probably Uzbek. These two people were no doubt the fish protein couple working on the biodegradable packaging, who Professor Ken had paid fifteen grand each to acquire the services of.

"Have you seen my dog?" I asked. "She's a mixture. Bit of Staffy, bit of collie. She took off ten minutes ago…"

It might have been the hand scythe giving me a Grim Reaper appearance that made him suspicious.

"Who are you?"

"Nathan Hawk. Friend of Ken and Barbara."

"They expect to see you?"

"Er, no…"

"Wait there."

He exchanged a few words with his partner, who ran over to the house and banged on the front door. Between them, the girl on the outside and someone else within managed to haul it open. Maria, the housekeeper, stepped out and caught sight of me.

"Hi, Maria!" I said, taking a few steps towards her.

"Wait there!" said the fish protein man for the third time.

I froze.

"No, no," Maria called out. "He is good."

"Are they at home?" I asked.

"*Si*. I will get them." She turned and called out in voice like a bullfighter's. "*Señora, Señor!*"

Fish Protein Man gestured that I could move and I reached the door just as Professor Ken appeared beyond it.

"What's all the kerfuffle…? Ah, Mr Hawk. How nice to see you."

I tucked the scythe under one arm and shook his hand.

"Back at yer, Professor."

"Pardon?"

"I'm actually hoping to find Suyin Qu here. Right at this moment, though, I've lost my dog." His face told me I was in danger of losing him. "I brought my dog with me and she broke away, chased after a muntjac. I haven't seen her for…"

"I'm sure she'll be fine. She can't get out. What's her name?"

"Dogge."

"Yes, but what's her name?"

I spelled it out for him and he looked at me as if I was the eccentric-at-large, not him. At a sign from Maria he beckoned me into the house.

"Yes, yes, come along in." He waved to the fish protein couple. "Thank you, Zarif, Yulia. Mr Hawk, shall Maria get us some of the home-brew you so approved of? No, leave the door. It saves opening and closing it. Come through…"

To Maria's irritation he led me to the kitchen, which turned out to be the cleanest room in the house. Two hundred years out of date, but spotless. I set down the scythe and bag of clothes and sat at a wooden chair by the table from where I took stock. The only thing I could think of to say was, "How is your wife, Professor?"

"Splendid!"

I smiled. "And the fungi?"

"They are even better… Here, ask her yourself."

I rose from the chair and reached out to shake Doctor Barbara's hand as she entered the room. She smiled. I'd no way of knowing it right then, but she was about to deliver the luck Bill Grogan had tantalised me with.

"Remember Mr Hawk?" her husband went on. "He wants to know how the fungi are."

"Delicious," she said. "They need a lot of garlic, but I consider that to be a business opportunity for those who grow the stuff."

"He's lost his dog out in the gardens, dear."

I went through the explanation again, feeling sillier by the syllable, but I was clearly among friends who saw nothing odd about a man carrying a bag of dirty laundry. Maria asked for more information on the clothes as she set down the beer glass in front of me. She didn't verbalise; she just pointed at the bag.

"Yes, it's some of Suyin Qu's clothes. The dog – the one I've lost – she used to be a police sniffer dog. Terrific sense of smell…"

"Thanks to her vomeronasal organ." said Barbara.

"And I wondered if… well, if Suyin was here Dogge would be able to track her down."

"Why do you think she'd be here, Mr Hawk?" asked Professor Ken.

"I think her life is in danger, and if I were her I'd go to ground in a place like this. Enormous, rambling house, extensive grounds, closed off from the outside world. I planned on sending the dog on a woman-hunt but it wasn't the great idea I imagined it to be." I suddenly felt disloyal. "She has helped me before. The dog, that is. Younger days."

Barbara was looking at me oddly. "Bit of a fool's errand. I mean, I'm pretty sure she isn't here."

"With all due respect…"

"It was my birthday last week."

Professor Ken tapped his nose. "The one number she *can't* remember."

"I had a card from Suyin."

There they were. The spiders were back, crawling up my neck.

"Posted to you?" I asked, feebly.

"Yes, of course." She reached across the table to a small pile of greetings cards and sorted through them. She took one from near the top and handed it to me.

"May I?" She nodded and I opened it. "Many happy returns," it said. "To Barbara from Suyin."

I hardly dared to ask. "You don't still have the envelope, do you?"

With a bad grace Maria went through to a cupboard and returned with a cardboard box full of wastepaper. She dumped it on the kitchen table in front of me.

"We make paper logs for the fire, come winter…" Ken tried to explain, but Barbara and I were already sifting through it for envelopes. She found one, pulled it out and handed it to me. It had been franked, but that was illegible. What was plain as could be was the logo, hand-stamped on one corner of it.

"Happy birthday," I said to Barbara.

And as I downed the home-brew I caught sight of Dogge over the rim of the glass. She had wandered in and now stood at the kitchen doorway as if asking where the hell I'd been for the last half-hour.

On my way back from Abiding Earth I was feeling pretty good about myself. True, I hadn't actually caught up with Suyin but, thanks to the birthday card, I had a pretty good idea where she was. I had an urge to phone Bill Grogan and tell him that his words had been prophetic. I had got lucky.

And then at a single glance in the rearview mirror all that sense of achievement was dashed by the sight of the motorcyclist I'd noticed on the outward journey. It wasn't paranoia this time. I recognised the red flashes on the bike's bodywork and the streak on the rider's helmet. He was trying to stay in my blindspot and might have been successful had I been driving the Land Rover. The Discovery was a different matter.

My first reaction was to slew the car into the path of the vehicles between us, get out and confront him with a tyre iron. My second was to pull over and see what he did. Either of those moves would have alerted whoever he was working for, and since I had a pretty good idea of who that was, I drove on.

He kept his distance and followed me for the next thirty miles, almost to Oxford, where we hit traffic and he was forced to close the gap between us. At a set of lights, when the cars in front of me surged forward on green, I changed lanes and took the one for Kidlington. The biker followed suit. Twenty yards farther on I swerved towards the Summertown turning. Middle fingers were raised and windows lowered the better to swear at me, but the biker had been trapped between a white van and a school bus.

He hadn't lost me, of course. He knew exactly where I was, but not where I was going…

***

I headed to Petrie's, a small bodyshop in a rundown business park off Cowley Road. I forget how I came to know Ted Petrie, but as he approached me across the cinder patch I could've sworn he was wearing the same overalls as thirty years ago. His trademark rollup was dangling from his lips and it bobbed up and down when he spoke. I had worked out that he was mid-fifties, but the heavy load he appeared to carry made him seem ten years older. We shook hands. His were still hard and rough, in spite of the patina of grease.

"New motor, Nathan? Things must be bad."

"Pre-owned, as they say in your trade. 30,000 on the clock."

He smiled. "Would you like it to have done less?"

"No, thanks. Perfectly happy. How you doing, Ted?"

"Fair to lousy. What's your pleasure?"

"I'd like you to sweep it for tracking devices."

"Now you got me interested. Who's tailing you, eh? Someone's husband?"

"If I told you it was MI6, what would you say?"

"I'd say I wish I hadn't asked."

He went into the workshop and crashed around a bit before returning with a crawler board and a box the size of a beer crate. He lay down on the board, pulled himself under the car and ran a small handset over every inch of its guts until it crackled. He wheeled himself out from under and showed me a device the size of a matchbox. It had been attached to a flange by a small clamp, the kind you can buy in B & Q, ten quid a pack.

"It's out of the ark," he said. "And whoever fitted it's an amateur. You want it or will I crush it in the vice?"

"How much life in it?" I asked.

The unlit rollup quivered. He drew on it and blew out non-existent smoke. "Three weeks maybe."

I looked round at the other businesses that shared the yard with him. "Anyone here you don't like?"

He nodded towards a Portakabin in the far corner. "Over there. Rents out portable cludgies. They hang around unemptied for days."

"In a quiet moment, clamp this under his van."

I gave him a fifty-pound note and he examined it as if it might be fake. He drew on the rollup again.

"Ted, you do know the fag isn't…"

"I'm quitting. In stages. Stage one is pretend."

I wished him good luck with it and left.

***

Over supper I told Laura about the trip to China and, to begin with, she was politely interested. She became properly interested when it came to the art collection and paused me in my story to look up online those paintings she didn't know. She also had a host of questions about the roof garden, most of which I couldn't answer. How on earth did the building support the weight, how deep were the soil beds, did the water in the koi pond circulate?

As I moved on to the British Consulate she suddenly smiled and said, "What are you hiding, Nathan?"

"Nothing."

"Don't be silly. I've been diagnosing people for twenty-five years. Reluctant people. And you're holding something back."

I laughed. "I promise you I'm not."

She gave me an old-fashioned look and we returned to the British Consulate. When we'd worn the subject out, I asked if she was free tomorrow.

"Well, I had planned on clearing the garden but…"

"But you're not at the surgery. Only I wondered if you fancied a trip to London?"

She didn't jump at the idea so I made it irresistible.

"We could spend the evening with Jaikie. And Jodie, of course. And Bill."

"That sounds lovely. Any particular reason for the trip?"

"Yes, we're going to meet someone. She doesn't know we're coming and I'm not sure she'll be pleased to see me." She looked at me. "Suyin Qu."

She slapped the table. "I knew you were hiding something!"

I pulled up outside 26 Ventnor Road at around four-thirty. The light was fading. Another week and the clocks would go back and pitch us into winter. A bolt of sadness hit me, not the misery-guts kind but the Seasonal Affective Disorder kind. According to Laura, the symptoms range from persistent low mood to feelings of despair, guilt and worthlessness via irritability and a craving for carbohydrates. When I told her that I felt that way all year round, she said there was no hope for me.

I opened the Discovery tailgate and Dogge got to her feet. I helped her onto the pavement and reached onto the back seat for the bag of laundry. Having heard the car pull up, Mrs Pandeshi opened the front door and smiled, behind which I believe she began to worry. I heard Maya call out from the kitchen, "Mata, who is it?"

"It's Mr Hawk and, er… a lady."

Laura stepped forward and shook Mrs Pandeshi's hand. "I'm Laura Peterson," she said. "I was so sorry to learn about your husband. Please accept my condolences."

"That's kind of you. You are the doctor, yes?"

"Yes, and I gather your daughter is…"

She broke off when Maya emerged from the kitchen, sleeves rolled up and wearing an apron.

"Maya, this is my friend, Doctor Laura Peterson."

Maya nodded and looked down at Dogge. "And what is this?"

"I don't believe you've just asked me that, Maya."

"What is she doing here?"

"The longer you both keep us on the doorstep, the more I'm convinced it was a good idea to bring her."

"I'll wait in the car, perhaps…" said Laura, sensing trouble ahead

"No, no, not at all," said Mrs Pandeshi. "Come through to the kitchen and bring your… dog."

Between them they corralled us into the kitchen and guided us to a pair of wicker chairs in the corner. Maya began to strain a pan of rice into a china bowl, then moved a cast-iron pot to the simmering plate. Her mother filled the kettle. It was a show of busy-ness, the aim of which was to distract me.

"You would like tea, Mr Hawk, Doctor?" asked Mrs Pandeshi.

Laura said yes, I said no.

"Your… dog would like something?"

"She's more of a coffee person but it gives her wind…"

"You should not give a dog coffee," said Maya, sharply. "It is dangerous."

"I know. I was just trying to lighten the mood." I paused, still looking at her. "You know where Suyin is."

"I've told you before, Mr Hawk…"

"That wasn't a question, it was a statement of fact. Tell me where." I glanced back and forth at their tightening faces and I felt Laura squirm. "Let's start with here, 26 Ventnor Road…"

Maya raised an arm and pointed back at the front door. "This is so out of order. I must ask you to leave…"

"We won't play games, Maya," I said. "You slipped up. You made a mistake you'll kick yourself for. Ten days ago Suyin asked you to post a birthday card to a new friend of hers, Doctor Barbara Blake." I showed her the envelope I'd found in the Blakes' wastepaper box. "You put it in Barts Hospital's outgoing mail. They franked it and stamped it with their logo." I waited. "Well, don't both shout at once, just tell me where I can find her."

Maya gestured to the rooms above us. "Not here, if that's what you think."

I turned to her mother. "Would you mind if I checked?"

"No, please, if it will put your mind at rest."

I beckoned Dogge. "Ex-police sniffer dog. Drugs. Not that I expect to find drugs here." I pointed down to the Tesco carrier bag. "This is Suyin's laundry, left at my son's house."

"I promise you won't find…" Maya began.

I opened the carrier wide and Dogge shoved her head inside it. I led her to the foot of the newly carpeted stairs and pointed up them. "Go on, girl. Go have a look. Go find."

She took the stairs two at a time and for the next few minutes we heard her running around and getting nowhere. I went up after her and opened whichever doors were closed. She entered the rooms, did her stuff, nose right down, tail going nineteen to the dozen. Eventually, she emerged from the bedroom that had been Suyin's and stood looking at me with a blank look on her face.

"Downstairs, girl. Go on, down you go."

She lumbered down them and began to quarter the sitting room, then moved on to the gurdwara. Her vomeronasal organ, or whatever Doctor Barbara had called it, was doing overtime, but to no effect. It was either kaput or Suyin wasn't there. I went back to the kitchen, annoyed that my chance to show off to Laura had been scuppered. I avoided her eyes.

"Satisfied?" said Maya, her arms folded.

"Yes, yes, she isn't here. But I still believe you know where she is."

"I think it's time you went, Mr Hawk. If you don't I will call the police."

"I wouldn't. Your friend DCI James Parfitt wants to find Suyin as much as I do."

Her mother had decided to appeal to me through my stomach. "Mr Hawk, sit at the table. I am about to serve up the chilli. Doctor, can I offer you?"

I answered on behalf of both of us. "You sure can."

We took places at the table and Dogge tried to settle on the coconut doormat.

"I've been unmannerly," I said. I held up a hand to prevent Maya agreeing. "How have things been?"

"Difficult, but life must go on."

She smiled at Laura and gestured to the pot to confirm that she would like some of its contents. Laura smiled back.

"Help yourself to the rice, Doctor. I've made far too much, as usual."

"It will freeze, Mata," said her daughter, quickly.

"Where is your sister, Maya? Where is Jasnam?"

"School. Homework club."

They fell silent for a moment or two. I was hoping that as we worked our way through the meal one of them would drop their guard. My money was on Mrs Pandeshi. Laura made an attempt to normalise the conversation and turned to Maya.

"So, Maya, where are you at? What are your plans?"

I'm not sure how keen Maya was to share her ambitions, even with a fellow medic, but it was better than me harping on about Suyin.

"Next year's my last... After that I'd like to go abroad. To South Africa."

"How exciting. Why there?"

"A friend of mine, he went and... ended up almost running a small hospital with five others. He said he learned more there in one year than he had in the previous five..."

Laura nodded. "Here you're channelled all the time, there you do what's needed. Which is everything..."

They carried on talking medicine, though Maya kept one ear on me and her mother, small talk though it was.

"How is your sister, Mrs Pandeshi," I asked, "the one who has helped you so much?"

"Rosa. She is good… yes."

"Tell me again, where does she live?"

"Er… Potters Bar…"

As much as Maya was tuning into our scintillating conversation Shirina was trying to keep tabs on the one between Laura and her daughter.

"You know Potters Bar?"

"By name only. She has children?"

"Two boys, who work for their father. Something to do with IT."

I smiled. "Are they coming here for dinner?"

She froze. First Maya, then Laura turned to us.

"Why do you ask?" said Mrs Pandeshi.

"One reason is you've made so much food. The other is that you've laid four places at the table."

She struggled minimally. "Of course. We expect Jasnam soon, with a friend."

I smiled and shook my head. "My dog thinks otherwise."

I nodded to where Dogge was up on her feet and staring at the back door, as if mesmerised by it. She dropped her nose to the floor, then reached out and tried to bat the door open. I got up from the table and went over to her.

"What is it, girl? You got something? Good, good! Find it, find it!"

I opened the back door and she trotted out into the garden to follow whatever scent she had picked up. She led the way across the lawn. Across to the air-raid shelter. When she reached the door she sat in front of it and barked twice. The door opened and a girl of fourteen or thereabouts stooped down to Dogge before she noticed me. She smiled.

"Hallo, you must be Jasnam," I said. "I'm Nathan Hawk. Is Suyin with you?"

From her crouching position Jasnam turned and glanced back into the room. A moment later a soothing voice said, "It's alright, Jasnam. Come in, Mr Hawk."

I stepped into the air-raid shelter and looked across to where Suyin Qu was seated at a small table. She rose from it and Dogge rushed over to greet her like a long-lost friend.

"This is… Dogge, yes?" I nodded. "Jaikie told me all about her. She is a drug dog. You rescue her."

I turned to Jasnam. "Dinner's ready. Tell Mata we'll be in soon."

Maya had come to the doorway and now held out a hand to her sister.

"You'll bring her too?" said Jasnam, pointing down at Dogge.

I nodded and closed the door behind them before looking round at Suyin's hideaway. It was a far cry from my grandfather's shelter with its dark corners and scurrying mice, garden tools hanging on rusty hooks. There was no wheelbarrow here, no lawnmower, no workbench to remind me of him. The walls were pristine, painted off-white, the rug on the floor was an Indian weave, so too the silk counterpane on the bed. The only nod towards China was a fluffy crane propped up against the pillows. It made me smile.

"He isn't white," I said.

"They are not white when young. They are… biscuit?"

"You even have blackout curtains. Quite in keeping."

She frowned. "With what?"

"The room's original use. An air-raid shelter." I gestured to the table. "May I?"

I sat down at it, skew-whiff, and eventually she joined me on the opposite side. I picked up an exercise book and flicked through it. Equations, algebra, geometry… all of it a mystery to the young Nathan Hawk. To say nothing of the middle-aged one.

"I help Jasnam with her maths homework. I am good at maths."

"I'll bet you are."

It was a truly beautiful, tapered and expressive face, belying the inscrutability attributed to her fellow countrymen. It wasn't the frightened face I had seen in the dawn raid tape, any more than it was the reluctant one photographed for *The Guardian*. On the contrary, it was the face of someone who wasn't afraid of much at all. Like anyone else, her eyes were the voice of her inner feelings. Right now they said that she didn't trust me.

"Why hide away, Suyin? The police believe it's because you killed Opinder."

She glared at me in indignation. "Why, why would I do such thing? He was my friend…"

"He wanted you sent back to China."

Her eyes were still staring, mouth slightly open. Then her features softened into a frown. "If I kill him, why would I hide here? That is sick, sick!"

I nodded. "You came here because it's the last place your pursuers will look."

She thought for a moment. "If you think I murder him, it means you do not know who really did?"

"I'd say I'm pretty close." I gestured round the shelter. "Why hide out here? Why not in the house itself?"

She shrugged. "Jasnam has many friends. They are a big family. Uncles, aunties, cousins."

I smiled. "So, forgive me, but… where do you pee?"

She smiled and nodded in the direction of the house. "In the bathroom, like most people."

I twisted round, square onto the table and leaned forward.

"Why didn't you get in touch with me? I'm Jaikie's father, for God's sake, and you must have known I was looking for you! Taylor Mandrake will have told you as much."

She nodded. "I am sorry, but you might have told the police. You might do that now. You might do 'the right thing'?"

I laughed. "I haven't done 'the right thing' for forty years. Taylor Mandrake, you trust him enough to handle your money? Millions of pounds. The paintings."

She shifted in her chair, disturbed that I knew about his involvement with her father's escape fund, but she soon settled again. And waited.

"Suyin, you've led me on a merry dance. Up to Norfolk, Tricks Farm, back to the King's Road, over to the Cotswolds, then to Shanghai and Leshan." I paused. "Don't you want to know how your father is, by the way?"

"Of course."

"He's looking forward to coming here, I imagine. To live. To be with you. That's the plan, isn't it?" She nodded. "Tell me this: why do *you* want to live here? Is it Taylor Mandrake?"

She chuckled. "You mean do I love him? I will tell you for sure one year from now, by which time I will have decided to marry him or… send him packaging."

"Packing. Meantime he's on probation? I like that. I take it he's asked you?"

She smiled at the question then stood up, turning away as if to make a confession to the space in front of her.

"When I was at school I was taught many things which are only half true. One example in Western minds – Tiananmen Square?"

"I even remember the date. June 4th. 1989."

"My history teacher told us that a few terrorists try to bring down the economy of China. The People's Army killed three of them, by accident. I come to the West and learn that thousands died, thousands wounded, and those who organise executed. There were no terrorists, just students who want democracy. Among them was my aunt. My father believed what was told to their parents. She died. It was a accident."

"What makes you think we don't lie in the UK?" I asked.

"Maybe." She turned back to me. "But if I don't like your queen or prime minister, nobody brings a tank and kills me."

She sat down at the table again and took a few breaths.

"I want to live in a place like that. I want my father to."

"I think you came here to buy up bits of Britain."

"That was the reason I gave to my government when I apply for an exit visa. Foreign investment."

"But why two farms in Norfolk? Why an eco-research facility?"

"You know a lot about me, Mr Hawk. I know something of you. You hit a man and broke his jaw. Your boss. In China you would be in prison."

"How the hell did you…?"

"And Laura. I know of Laura." She laughed at my amazement. "Are you back together?"

"You're digressing, Suyin…"

"What is digressing?"

"Straying from the point. Two farms near the coast. I get that anyone watching from afar will think it's something strategic, of benefit to China. You say that's not so… but but I'm not so sure."

She slapped the table. "What if I say I believe in Green, Mr Hawk? Will you laugh? You will not laugh ten years from now. Today pet food from plants. Tomorrow people food. If we are still friends, I will… cut you in."

"I'll hold you to that. Meantime, I think whoever's trying to find you wants you in one piece. They want to ransom you, and get money from your father to let you go free. I know he would pay. Who wouldn't?"

She lowered her voice. "Why do they kill Opinder?"

"Because he got in their way. I think he heard on some grapevine that people were after you. He wanted you back in China for your own safety. Did he ever say who he thought was after you?"

"He just says they are dangerous. You hint you are close to catching them…"

"I have a shortlist of possibles. Tell me, did you like Farrah Bennett?"

Mention of the name surprised her. "Yes. Why?"

"When I spoke to them I thought she might be jealous of you." She put her hand to her mouth to stifle a laugh. "Why's that funny?"

"You put Richard Bennett in a room with Taylor Mandrake, who do women notice?"

"A wealthy, beautiful woman walks into their lives, turns their business around. Maybe Farrah thinks he's fallen under your spell."

"Next you will say that Doctor Barbara is afraid I run off with Professor Ken? Where to? A treehouse in the jungle?"

I laughed. "I'll tell you who I really don't like. Alessandro Scutari."

As if there were an easy explanation for that she said, "He is a lawyer. Does anyone like lawyers?"

"This one has a scam, fixing visas for people. Yours, the people who work at Abiding Earth and one for your father? Does that explain the ninety thousand pounds I found in the White Crane?" I paused. "He's an old friend of Taylor, yes?"

"So now you think Taylor is part of some plan to kidnap me? Why has he not done so yet?"

"Because he's still raking in your father's money. I take it he knows where you are?" She answered me by not answering. "You may be a wizard at business, but when it comes to love we're all mugs. Don't let his charm and good looks blind you to possibilities."

"I have said he is… probation."

"Have you ever met Alessandro's contact at the Home Office? A man called Dirk?"

She shook her head. "No."

"And one other. His name is John Smith, the third most common name in England."

She laughed. "Maybe I know him, then. I don't think so."

I leaned back in the chair and chewed over my options for a moment. "You're right about one thing. This was a safe place to hide. I'd like you to stay here while I find who's after you. For sure they're the same ones who killed Opinder." She nodded. "There will be a slight change… in the domestic arrangements."

"How so?"

"Nothing major… leave it with me." I paused. "Suyin, while I have it in mind… Remember what you bought Jaikie and Jodie? How much did it cost? By which I mean how much is it worth?"

"I pay £3000. Is very old. Please do not tell them."

"I don't think I could get the words out," I said, wincing. "Three thousand? Anyway, I left a plate of chilli in the kitchen, half eaten. There's plenty left and there's someone I want you to meet. Laura Peterson."

She smiled her smile again. "Ah, so you *are* back together."

Dogge had stood up when I moved and now executed a downward dog stretch. Suyin stooped down to stroke her.

"This dog, she finds me. How?"

I tapped my nose. "You left some clothes in the laundry basket at Elwyn Road."

She withdrew her hand from Dogge's head instantly. "You mean… dirty… clothes?"

"Her favourite."

I called Jaikie soon after we left Ventnor Road. He was in an Italian restaurant, Paganini's, just off Ealing Broadway, celebrating something else to do with *Warrington*. Hadn't they exhausted all excuses for a party? I asked. Wasn't it time to get on with the job of making the series? It turned out to be a cast member's birthday, an actress who was playing the wife of the man Jaikie's character relieves of his fortune. Needless to say, they end up having a passionate affair that ends in disaster.

Right at this moment, however, the lady seemed smitten with Bill Grogan, with whom she was having a proper conversation. I'd never thought of him as a chick magnet, or even an old broiler magnet, come to that, but there'd been a transformation in him during his time with Jaikie and Jodie. The suit helped, and I had it on good authority that Jodie had taken him to a top-dollar barber in South Ken for a cut.

The six new faces at the table were introduced to us in a Mexican wave of standing up and sitting down again. We were then offered food, which Laura declined on our behalf on account of Shirina Pandeshi's chilli still making itself felt.

"Well, isn't this wonderful?" said Laura to one and all as she was squeezed in between Jaikie and Bill Grogan.

"Laura, you've come at exactly the right moment," gushed the birthday girl, in a ladies' college accent. "These chaps have been trying to get me to reveal my age for the past hour. Short of them sawing me in half and counting the rings they will never know."

"That you're only thirty?" said Laura.

The actress dissolved into giggles. The wine waiter brought us a couple of glasses and poured and we toasted her thirtieth birthday. When the noise died down I toyed with the idea of telling Jaikie and Jodie that I'd found Suyin, but I held off. However, I wanted Bill Grogan to know as soon as possible, given the favour I needed to ask of him. I spent half an hour trying to prize him away from the birthday girl, without success, but eventually he needed a pee. I didn't, but pretended that I did and followed him through the restaurant to the toilets.

"Bill, you okay for a moment?" I asked, as the door swung shut behind us.

He paused by the hand basins and turned to me.

"What's up?" he asked.

"I've found her!"

If the news impressed him, he didn't show it. "Where was she? Abiding Earth?"

"Sort of, but right now she's at 26 Ventnor Road. In the air-raid shelter."

He slapped the hand drier, which burst into life. "She is something else, that girl! Scene of the crime. Who would look there?"

"Yes, but we can't look after her there… I mean *you* can't. I'm about to ask you to go the extra mile…"

"I can tell. Get on with it, I'm busting."

"If I bring her back to Elwyn Road, can you cope with all three of 'em?"

He nodded, headed towards a urinal and stood over it, waiting. I smiled.

"You want me to whistle, Bill?"

"I *want* you to give me some privacy, okay?"

I left him to it and returned to the table.

***

We got to Elwyn Road at about ten-thirty and I parked behind Jaikie's Jag. Grogan got out first, looked up and down the street for anomalies, then signalled us to follow him.

"Bring the dog in, Dad," Jaikie called.

"I won't, mate, not staying long."

Jaikie smiled at the Discovery. "How many miles on the clock?"

"Thirty thousand."

"Barely run in."

He chuckled and took Laura by the arm, steering her towards the front gate.

"Anyone for coffee?" said Jodie.

She always glanced in my direction when she offered coffee these days, presumably to reassure me that she meant instant. It would be the fourth cup I'd had in three hours and yet doubtless I would still wonder whyI had trouble sleeping...

Grogan was first up the garden path and the security light above the front porch failed to trigger. He paused. I couldn't see his face in the darkness, but knew he was questioning the sixth sense that told him something was amiss. He held up a hand to us and turned to the keypad beside the door. The backlight on that was also dead.

The next two minutes whipped past and yet every detail of what occurred seemed to last an age. I saw Grogan reach across his stomach for the Glock and, as he drew it out, a man in a ski mask and grey overalls yanked open the door and rushed out, knocking Grogan off balance. He staggered backwards but didn't fall. A second man, dressed like the first, charged out of the house. Grogan screamed to us.

"Down!"

As if performing some macabre tango Jaikie and I threw an arm round our respective partners and flung them to the ground. Jodie landed on what was laughingly referred to as the front lawn and began protesting, Laura ended up against the roots of the privet hedge. By then Grogan was out in the middle of the road, pursuing the two intruders. They were fifteen yards away and the gap was widening. He stopped, raised the Glock and aimed at the nearest.

"Hold it!" he yelled.

The man turned and faced him. Grogan walked towards him, the pistol raised, and a moment later a squeal of tyres heralded a car rounding the corner farther up the road, its headlights on full beam to dazzle us. The man who had frozen reached back his arm and hurled something in Grogan's direction. It fell short of him by yards, clinked and sparked along the newly metalled surface and caught him on the shin. Grogan fired. The man screamed and clutched at his right buttock as the bullet tore into it. His companion bundled him into the car, which took off, the door closing with the force of speed. Grogan fired again at the rear wheels and missed. The car turned into Chiswick High Road bringing down the wrath of at least two drivers who leaned long and hard on their horns.

"Fuck!" said Grogan under his breath. It was the first time I'd ever heard him swear.

"Inside," I said to Jaikie and Jodie.

Across the road a neighbour had come to his front door to see what the two loud bangs were all about. Another followed suit and walked to his front gate. A lecturer at Bramshill, the police staff college, told the class that fifty percent of people will always walk towards gunfire, not away from it.

I joined Grogan as he stooped down to the missile which had been thrown at him. It was a meat cleaver. He pulled out the tail of his shirt and picked it up.

"You're bleeding, man."

He looked down at his ankle and, in the glare of a street light, saw blood glistening in the torn fabric of his trousers.

"Ruined the suit!" he said.

I helped him into the house, where immediately he began to stress about making a mess on the floor.

Jaikie reached up to the fusebox above the hall table and flicked up the main switch. Several domestic appliances grumbled into life and from the kitchen Alexa said, "Good evening, how can I help?"

Laura removed her coat, slung it over the kitchen table and gestured Grogan to sit in one of the chairs. He slumped into the one Jodie turned towards him.

"Back seat Discovery someone. My bag."

When I returned with it, Laura was crouched on the floor and, scissors in hand, was cutting off the bottom eighteen inches of Grogan's right trouser leg. She pulled off his blood-soaked sock and though in considerable pain he continued to insist that it was just a scratch.

As she bound up his leg to staunch the bleeding I went upstairs, turning lights on as I went. The attic was the only room the intruders had bothered with, perhaps because we'd surprised them. The door was wide open, way back on its hinges. A cupboard was open too, and clothes had been batted aside. What were they looking for that they'd missed the last time they were here? They were looking for Suyin Qu.

"The wound needs stitching," said Laura, when I entered the kitchen. "Charing Cross, A and E. Let's go."

I would have expected to be writing that six hours later we returned from Accident and Emergency after a night spent in the company of belligerent drunks, injured boy racers and the occasional genuine emergency. It wasn't six hours, it was two and a half, thanks to Laura intimidating the young registrar on duty who was summoned to look at Bill Grogan's wound. Stitching it was a matter of priority, she told him with an air of absolute authority.

As we left I asked the triage nurse, on the off chance, if she had dealt with a man with a bullet in his right buttock that evening. Nobody answering that description had presented.

Back at Elwyn Road, Jaikie and Jodie had waited up, although his top half was draped over the kitchen table, a position also much favoured by his younger sister after smoking too much weed.

"He's in shock, I think," said Jodie.

"No, he's acting…" I replied.

He looked up, not pleased. "Dad! Two blokes broke into the house…? Bill, how is it?"

Grogan batted the air aside. "It's a scratch, I kept telling…"

"A scratch that needed twelve stitches," said Laura.

"Same two blokes as last time?" I asked Jaikie.

"Same masks, same boiler suits. How did they get in… I mean, the code at the door…?"

I shrugged. "I don't know, but what's your birthday?"

"Well, if you don't know… 5th July, why?"

"5.7.88. It's all over Wikipedia. I told you to change it…"

He returned to slumping across the table. Bill Grogan sat down beside him in 'his chair'.

"I've let you down," he whispered, then looked up at me. "You still think it's a good idea moving her here?"

"I think it's an even better idea now. Those two bastards are hardly likely to return here. They've been, they've seen and you've shot one of 'em in the arse."

I almost felt the draft as Jaikie and Jodie's ears began to flap.

"Move who?" she asked.

"Suyin. I've found her."

"Dad! I knew you could do it…"

I went over to the cleaver, still sitting on the drainer where I'd left it.

"There's no peep from these buggers for two weeks, while I'm in China. I come back and off they go again. Jodie, get us a plastic bag, will you?"

She took one from a drawer and handed it to me, and I eased the cleaver inside it before placing it in the fridge. "I'll get Gadsden to pick it up. Odds-on chance it's the murder weapon, right? If so it'll have prints on it, maybe even his DNA."

"Proves again they're amateurs," said Grogan. "A pro would've ditched it ten minutes after using it."

"And a pro would not have nicked that bloody bonsai tree." I tapped my head in irritation. "Which I still have not found a home for… up here."

Jodie set down the coffee she'd promised me three hours ago. I took a sip and scalded my lip.

"Who knew I was back from China?" I asked, and then answered my own question. "Quite a few people, but John Smith knew the very *day* I returned. How come? His Chinese 'tour guide' Chao Lin told him. He's also told him Suyin wasn't in China, she was here." I looked round at them as if they might have the answer to my next question. "So, has he started looking for her again?"

"Is he the bloke driving the car?" asked Grogan.

"When I see him, I'll ask him."

***

The following night I collected Suyin from Ventnor Road and moved her into a room at the back of Elwyn. There was a great deal of loose emotion flying around as the three of them were reunited, interspersed with some effusive apologies –– Suyin to Jaikie and Jodie.

Grogan visibly squirmed at the display, but when all the hugging and nose-blowing was over he took her aside and said, simply, "Rules are these. Don't leave the house without me. Don't go to the windows. Don't tell anyone you're here. You understand?"

"My father?" she said.

Grogan looked at me.

"I'll let him know you're safe," I said.

She bowed to me. It seemed such an olde-worlde gesture, but I found myself bowing back.

I crashed in the lounge on a futon, ahead of an early start the next day.

The early start rescheduled itself, due to a long chinwag with Suyin over breakfast. Smalltalk and China. The latter unsettled me, for much as she wanted to be here in England, much as she loved Taylor Mandrake, her heart was still in the place where she'd grown up. You can take the girl out of Leshan but not Leshan out of the girl, it seemed…

There was a bit of Indian summer going on as I drove over to Ravenscourt Park mid morning, and it appeared to have affected people's mood. At Chiswick roundabout there was less of a scrum than usual, even some good manners, and at one point the driver of a Discovery the same colour as mine smiled at me. I smiled back, but hoped it wasn't the forerunner of things to come. I shuddered at the idea of belonging to an unofficial car club celebrating the Discovery marque.

I parked outside John Smith's house and walked up the front path, and as I approached the door a teacherly voice called out to me from his neighbour's front porch.

"Mr Hawk! Lovely to see you again. It *is* Mr Hawk, isn't it?"

I stopped and turned to it. "Yes, Mrs Fournier. Hallo."

"He's not in." She beckoned me anxiously, as if to impart a secret. "He's gone for cat food, should be back in half an hour." She smiled. "I'm doing one of his favourites for lunch?"

I smiled. "Which is?"

"Devilled kidneys on toast. John and Nicky love them. My husband, Nick."

"They're better men than I am. Thanks, I'll find a café and wait."

"No, no, come in and have a coffee." She seemed to falter for a moment, and then softened. "I'd like a word, anyway. If you've time."

It was a fuddy-duddy house, my mother would have said, and I would've agreed. It sounds rich coming from someone who lives in a 350-year-old pile, but whereas Beech Tree has a timeless feel to it, 25 Ravenscourt Lane was Victorian and nothing but. It reminded me of my paternal grandparents' place, which was small but crammed with big furniture, including an oak table my grandmother claimed to have danced on. I liked her. She gave me cake every time I visited and before I went home she would put her forefinger to her lips and slip me a shilling. I digress…

"Nick, my darling, we've company. Mr Hawk."

Nick Fournier looked up from a wicker armchair beside the kitchen range. He'd been holding down a copy of *The Times* as he tried to read it, and now he folded it and stretched out a shaky hand.

"Did she tell you he's gone for cat food?"

"She did. How are you, Mr Fournier?"

"Not so bad. Yourself?"

It's difficult to tell an obviously sick man that you feel as fit as a butcher's dog. I said I was bearing up. Grace signalled to me. Did I want sugar in my coffee? I didn't. She moved an ancient kettle to a back hob on the range and it began to hiss.

And old boss of mine who had a biblical turn of mind once said to me, "By their family photos shall ye know them." I thought it a bit pretentious at the time, but I grew to understand what he meant. There were a few photos dotted around. No children. No newborn babies. No parents in evidence. In pride of place was their wedding photo, with Grace all in white and her husband standing straight in army uniform. Others in the picture formed a loose guard of honour.

"Which regiment?" I asked.

"1st Battalion, Cheshire. That was taken at Aldershot. I'd just come back from a tour in Ulster and… thought we should make it legal."

"We're worried about John," said Grace, suddenly.

"Oh, yes?"

"You're a friend, I know, so we can confide…"

"I wouldn't say friend. More a business acquaintance."

She was surprised. "He speaks as if you were more than that, but never mind. Kindred spirit, then. You both lost wives to the same horror. I've no idea how you've fared since, but you have children, I believe. Johnny has no one. Siblings, parents, other relatives all gone. Bothers me."

"You think he's still grieving for Sophia?"

I was ten years younger than her so she gave me a smile acknowledging my… immaturity. "To lose a loved one at such a young age, well, does the pain ever go away?"

"No, but you get used to it. I meant does he often behave as if she died yesterday, as opposed to seven years ago?"

"Is it really seven? Good heavens. Yes, I'm afraid he does."

"Girlfriend?"

"There've been one or two, but unsuitable."

Nick chuckled. "What she means is that she saw them off. Pity about the last one, though. Drop-dead gorgeous. Amanda."

Grace sniffed. "Maybe I'm a fool for worrying but…" She raised a forefinger. "Just heard his car pull up. Would you care to stay for lunch?" She smiled. "Other dishes are available besides kidneys. There's a ham in the fridge the size of Laurence Olivier. Poached eggs with it?"

I stood up and headed for the door. "Thanks, but I'll just talk over with him what I came for and… leave you to it."

"You've been away, John told us," said Nick. "Abroad somewhere. Anywhere exciting?"

I nodded. "Just a few days. Nice seeing you again."

Outside, John Smith was wrestling boxes of cat food from the boot of his car onto the wall. He saw me approach and smiled.

"The wanderer returns," he said. "Good to see you. Would you mind?"

He handed me a box of cat food, locked his car and gestured me to follow him into the house. We dumped the boxes on the kitchen table and a second later Kublai Khan entered from nowhere, looked at us critically, then jumped on the table to make a point to Smith, who showed him a tin.

"Chicken and tuna chunks. Satisfactory?"

He took a clean bowl from the drainer and filled it. The cat dived on it, rumbling with pleasure.

"You've got devilled kidneys," I said.

He was less than enthusiastic about the prospect. "Really?"

"Grace told me they were your favourite."

"Why the hell I've never put her right is anyone's guess. Drink?"

I glanced at my watch, instinctively, but it didn't deter either of us. He poured me a scotch with ice and opened a beer for himself, then led me through to the living room. It had been cleaned and straightened since the last time I was there. The layer of dust had been removed and the pile of dirty clothes transformed into a neat pile of fresh laundry.

"You have a Jenny Tindall?"

"I share one with the Fourniers. Grace insisted."

"Bit of a mother hen, eh? Meals, cleaner… matchmaking?" He looked at me. "Amanda?"

He flicked back the errant lock of hair and lowered his voice. "For a moment I thought she might be the one. A confidante, like Sophia." He chuckled. "I told Soph most things, stuff I shouldn't have. Kept me sane. The nearest I have now are Nick and Grace."

"How long have you lived here, John?"

"Nine years. A colleague at the office said friends of his were selling. Those friends were the Fourniers. They owned both and needed the money. Six weeks later we moved in."

"Maybe it's time to move on? I've a feeling Sophia would agree."

"Probably." He slumped into the sofa. "So. China. And all things related."

"I found White Crane. Suyin Qu's father owns it, runs it and has no intention whatsoever of building a port in Norfolk."

"So why spend all that money?"

"It was Suyin's idea. She bought into Tricks Farm because the tree-hugger she's fallen in love with asked her to. His name's Taylor Mandrake, old friend of the Bennetts…"

"Are we saying the only person to gain from your trip down the Silk Road is you? There's no Chinese skulduggery for me to wow my section head with? Which I badly need to do if I'm to hang on to my job."

"What exactly have I gained, John?"

"A Land Rover Discovery." He closed his eyes. "Thank God it wasn't a brand new one, I would never have lived it down. Oh, by the way… kudos on finding the tracking device. I had a complaint from a colleague that one of his people had ended up following a consignment of portable lavatories."

"Lucky him. You never know when you'll be caught short."

"You say you spoke to the father. What about Suyin? Have you found her?"

"Oh, yes."

"So where is she? China or England?"

"You know the answer to that, John. Your friend Chao Lin will have told you. Question is, have you started looking for her again?"

He stared at me for a moment, pissholes in the snow again. "What the hell are you saying?"

"You're the only person who hasn't been visited by the meat-cleaver men looking for her. Is that because they're working for you?"

He sat bolt upright, more terrified than offended, I thought. "Good grief, man! You think I killed that immigration officer?"

"You weren't the one to bifurcate his head, no. Nor did you throw a meat cleaver at a friend of mine, night before last. But did you drive the people who did?"

"What?!"

We sat for a moment or two, each waiting for the other to blink first. Literally.

Finally I said, quietly, "You do a nice line in… believability, John. Butter wouldn't melt, eh? But it's the first thing they teach you. How to lie." I glanced up at the photo of his wife. "The second is how to gain sympathy."

He stood up and tried to restore his image, shrugging his jacket into place and buttoning it. Then he attended to the forelock.

"I think it's time you left, Mr Hawk."

***

I was halfway home when Gadsden rang my mobile and gave me a chance to try out the Discovery's in-car phone system, or whatever it was called. I prodded the button on the steering wheel with a picture of a phone on it and his voice came through loud, but not exactly clear.

"You in the shower, guvnor? Sounds like it."

"No, I'm on the A40. What can I do for you?"

"Update. Thanks to the meat cleaver, we reckon we know who killed Opinder Pandeshi. Talk about stupid! Kill someone, keep the weapon, throw it at a bloke like your Grogan. What's his story, by the way? He gave a statement all in half sentences…"

"It's his style, Tom."

"Opinder's DNA's on the cleaver. There are fingerprints too, belonging to Anthony James Devanney, twenty-seven, ex-army. Rap sheet nothing to write home about. GBH from a pub fight, burglary. Five years, did half."

"D'you bring him in?"

He sighed. "We went to his last known and he wasn't there. Hasn't been seen for three weeks."

"Is there a Devanney Senior in the system?"

"Allan Devanney. Age 61. Same address. He hasn't been seen either." He paused. "There's a BOLO out, but I reckon we can go whistle."

"So you know who fired the gun but you still don't know who loaded it."

"Eh?"

"The third person, the one driving the car. These Devanneys of yours are working for him, count on it."

"Yeah, well, Parfitt reckons that Suyin Qu's the driver…"

"What's wrong with him? She can't bloody drive!"

"Don't worry, he's getting on my nerves too. That said, if you fancied poking around the Devanneys' house, we wouldn't complain."

"Don't you have a squad…?"

"We could fit 'em all into a phone box and they'd still have room to fight. What do you say?"

"Send me descriptions, previous and the address."

"Will do."

I pulled off at the exit for Ruislip and waited in a lay-by. Just three minutes later, which I took to be a sign of Parfitt and Gadsden's desperation, the phone pinged with a pile of info. The address was Finchley. I programmed it into the satnav, another first, and headed down the route it gave me.

The Devanneys' house was ex-council, redbrick and foursquare, but the street it was on had a middle-class lacquer to it it. The gardens were neat and showy, parked cars were a cut above average and the recycling bins, though not the Devanneys', were lined up for tomorrow's collection. I reckoned the houses were privately owned, sold to tenants in the eighties for a song and now worth hundreds of thousands.

It's odd how you can tell when a house has been empty, even for a few weeks. It isn't the obvious stuff, like there being no lights on, no sound or even that the post is bulging out of the letterbox. It's more subtle, as if a house is a living thing and, left to itself, goes into hibernation.

There was no police presence, as far as I could tell, and no signs of life up and down the road. I tried the wooden side gate, only to find it was bolted from the inside. Via a retaining wall I struggled, rather than slithered, over the gate and dropped down the other side.

The back garden was downright plain. The lawn was closely cut and a single flowerbed was freshly dug, with a few perennials hunkering down for winter. On what passed for a patio there was a cast-iron round table and four chairs. Nothing else. I peered in through the French windows. The living room was tidy to the point of sterility and there was no feminine touch. No colour, no frill, not even a family photo on the mantlepiece. The kitchen too was spick and span: no dirty pots in the sink, no shopping that needed putting away, not even a chair slightly skewed at the table. The Devanneys were well and truly not at home.

More to the point, there were no bonsai trees, either in the house or outside, nothing to explain why they had taken the juniper from Jaikie's kitchen drainer. I could only think the Devanneys knew it was worth the three grand Suyin had paid for it and they'd taken it to sell. In that case, why leave

Suyin's computer, iPad, her jewellery… and the White Crane and his bellyful of money?

I exited the garden the same way I'd entered, only through the gate this time, not over it. As I headed back to the Discovery a woman in her fifties was wheeling a pushbike through the front gate of the house next door. The basket was spilling over with late vegetables and she herself was dressed for gardening. Muddy wellingtons, old trousers, stiff leather gloves.

"They're away," she called out to me.

I went over to her. "You don't happen to know where?"

She shook her head. "Worrying, really, because he usually drops a note in." She gestured to the vegetables. "I've done what I can to their plot but I know Allan likes to dig it over before winter sets in. I can't do that…"

"Plot? As in allotment?" She nodded. "Where exactly?"

"East Finchley Allotments." She smiled. "We're neighbours there too. Al's E37, I'm 38."

I thanked her for her help. She wasn't aware that she'd given me any.

***

East Finchley Allotments occupied a vast stretch of land, so much so that a visitor could almost believe he or she was in the countryside, not five miles from Piccadilly Circus. The effect was only mildly disturbed by the rattling of Northern Line tube trains somewhere beyond the woodland that appeared to surround the place. E37 was a fair walk from where I'd parked and had a similar neatness to the back garden of the Devanneys' house. Like most other plots, it was fenced off and the runner-bean trellises were still up. In one corner the obligatory sunflowers were nodding down at a few rows of winter veg. Of greater interest to me, however, was the shed at the far end. A table and chairs stood outside it and a sun umbrella was furled in waiting.

Rainwater from the shed roof ran into a water butt. There was even a metal fire pit. It was a place you could live in, at a pinch. As I opened the gate and walked towards it a man in his eighties called out to me.

"Haven't seen him, have you?" he asked.

"'Fraid not. I'm beginning to worry."

He shook his head. "Knows how to take care of himself."

He was sitting in a canvas director's chair on a patch of grass in number 19. As I approached, he took a thermos flask from his pushbike's pannier and proceeded to pour himself a see-through coffee.

"I'd offer you some but there's only one cup. Good man is Allan. Well-liked round here."

"Why's that, do you reckon?"

"Thanks to him, people don't nick produce in this part 'cos they know what'll happen. And there's no more dogging."

"Well, that's… good."

He beckoned me to get closer and lowered his voice. "You know who's got an allotment here, two hundred yards that way?" I shook my head. "Yes, you do, you must've seen the pictures of him on the telly. That M.P. Yeah?"

"Oh… yes, him."

"People were going onto his plot at night. Doing it in his shed, just to say they had. Al caught 'em once and wham! End of."

"How's his son these days?"

He sighed. "Allan used to bring him down weekends, but he never took to fruit and veg. Kids don't, do they?"

"Joined the army, I heard."

The old boy nodded. "Like father, like son. Marines. Allan was in Iraq. Major."

Allan Devanney certainly had kudos in this corner of the world, though it was largely of his own making, I thought. I settled into my role of a long-time-no-see acquaintance.

"What happened to his wife, do you know?"

He laughed. "Must be five, six years now. She buggered off with N42." He pointed up the slight hill. "I saw it coming. He kept bringing her bags of fruit, bunches of flowers and then one day, they both disappeared. Canada, Allan said."

I couldn't help wondering if Canada was a euphemism for a more compelling disappearance. "When d'you last talk to him?"

"Four weeks ago." He touched the side of his nose. "I reckon he's off working."

I smiled. "Same old, same old?"

"Works for the government now. Home Office."

The spiders were back, not the whole platoon but one or two squaddies. "Home Office, eh? Doing what?"

"I don't like to ask but it's… security. There, I've said it. I shouldn't have done."

I dismissed his concern. "Between ourselves." I nodded towards the shed. "I'm just going to have a look."

"He's not there…"

"Yeah, but you never know. Clues."

His manner changed. "Clues? You a copper?"

"No, no," I said, horrified. "Old friend. Concerned."

"It's locked. You'll have to look through the windows." His suspicion that I might be a copper hand taken hold. "And then bugger off, if I were you."

***

I knew from the info Gadsden had texted me that Allan Devanney's wife hadn't left him for the stakeholder at N32, she had divorced him after one too many slaps. By the same token, he hadn't been a major in the Marines but a sergeant in the Royal Corps of Signals. And he'd never set foot in Iraq. There was no mention of him working for the government, and certainly not the Home Office, but given that every exaggeration starts life as a small truth I needed to follow it up. Mention of Home Office and Security had triggered my interest. Alessandro's partner in visa crime worked at the Home Office. A man called Dirk. Were the Devanneys his murderous factotums?

I let myself into Elwyn Road and called out, "Hallo, it's me. Dad, Nathan!"

Grogan came to the dining-room door, his hand stroking the holstered Glock. Assured that it really was me, he waved and hurried back to what he'd been doing. I peered in through the doorway to where he and Suyin were playing Jenga, the game where each player by turn removes a wooden block from a tower and whoever brings down the edifice is the loser. With extreme delicacy Suyin withdrew a block without mishap. Grogan scowled as she stood back and punched the air in victory. He approached the table, reached out and took his turn. The structure remained and it was Suyin's turn to scowl.

"You have to watch her," he called to me. "She cheats."

Suyin was horrified. "I do not cheat! You cheat."

"You jogged the table, Suyin!" he said, referring to an earlier ploy, I imagine. Having considered her strategy, she moved in to take her turn.

I went through to the kitchen, where Jaikie and Jodie were being as old-fashioned as you please. They were reading newspapers. He rose from the table as I jerked a thumb back towards the dining room.

"Amazing, isn't it?" Jaikie said. "Chalk and cheese, and yet… instant mates."

"I need Alessandro Scutari's home address."

Jodie reached for her phone. "How's it going?"

"I'm getting nearer by the day. Everyone says that, I know, but I really am. But don't ask."

She laughed. My phone pinged and I looked at it. An address in Streatham.

"I'm making dinner in a minute," she said. "Shall I include you?"

"No, I'm…" I glanced out through the window. It was dark. "Yeah, Alessandro can wait till tomorrow. Can I kip in the attic room?"

From the dining room came the sound of wooden blocks tumbling into a heap followed by triumphant squeals from Suyin. And a low rumble from Grogan.

***

There was one small curlicue to the events of the day and it served to remind me that, for all her wealth, Suyin was just a girl. Someone's only child. A beloved daughter. It seemed a bit of a stretch, even as I processed the thought, but when I switched out the light in the attic room a host of stars lit up on the ceiling. They had been arranged in the outline shape of a crane. It would've been the last thing she saw before closing her eyes.

Brooking Court was a run of flats above a fading department store on Streatham High Road, an edifice with a big pillared entrance, revolving doors and a constant 'Sale' sign. Access to the apartments above was from the rear, first left and left again. I parked by the iron staircase, which gave this corner of London a cut-down feel of New York. I climbed the metal stairs to number 17 and knocked on the door.

Alessandro Scutari was surprised to see me, though he made a great show of not being so. He stood barring the way, biceps and tattoos rampant and the T-shirt moving over his pecs in time with his breathing. He wasn't keen to admit me, possibly because he had female company. It was early morning and I could smell toast burning.

"Press the button," he called over his shoulder. "What can I do for you, Mr Hawk?"

"Quite a bit. Only not out here."

He stifled a sigh and stepped aside, closing the door behind me.

The flat was of a grand design, in keeping with the shop beneath it, with high ceilings, tall windows and ornate mouldings. The plasterwork had suffered over recent years from the weight of passing traffic shaking it to bits. The walls had last been decorated forty years previously, judging by the dark beige of the era, and the gloss mahogany woodwork was scuffed and peeling. He pointed me towards the kitchen, itself a memorial to the eighties.

I was right, he did have female company. Two girls aged about twelve or thirteen looked up at me, reserved rather than suspicious.

"My daughters," he said. "Liliana, Chiara, this is Mr Hawk."

They said hi and carried on with their breakfast. He threw his hands up in the air, Italian style.

"Quick as you can, girls. Homework first, then we go."

"Somewhere good?" I asked.

"Pizza Hut for lunch. An insult to our Sicilian heritage, but who am I to argue? Then the ski slope at Chatham. Take your toast to your room, *cari*. *Sprigati! Sprigati!*"

They left the kitchen and he made a space at the table for me.

"Kids!" he said, in a tone everyone recognises. "My weekend."

"Are you divorced?"

He shook his head and fingered the gold crucifix hanging round his neck by way of explanation. I sat down and shrugged with my hands.

"I came here to threaten you, Alessandro, to give you the full treatment: sound effects, body language, long stares. I was looking forward to it because I knew you were dodgy the moment I laid eyes on you. Liliana and Chiara have put paid to that."

"Sorry about that." He leaned back against one of the units and folded his arms. "Threaten me with what, exactly?"

I put a smile in my voice. "Telling the world what an exploiter of human misery you are. How you con naive old souls like Ken and Barbara Blake into paying fifteen grand apiece for a visa! Shame on you."

"You've got a fucking nerve, coming here accusing me of…"

"As far as I'm concerned you can keep the scam. Yes, really. However… you remember the two blokes who visited Jaikie and Jodie looking for Suyin? They went to Abiding Earth, Taylor Mandrake's gallery, Tricks Farm, Opinder Pandeshi's… they even turned your office over."

"Same people, you think?"

"Yeah, only they didn't go to your office, did they? You staged all that. Obvious reason was to make yourself look like another victim, not a perpetrator." The smile in my voice broke through to my face. "Is that because you're the man police should be looking for? Are you running two thugs around London, trying to find Suyin in order to screw millions out of her father?"

He dropped his arms to his side. "You what?"

"What's the Italian for *moi*?"

"Have you got any proof of all…"

"None, but that's never stopped me in the past. I mean, there's a couple of Taking and Driving Aways against you…"

He groaned. "Ancient history."

"Yeah, I know, reformed character. But you can play the loving father to the hilt, show me as many daughters as you like, but I've seen family men murder their way out of debt, hardship, relationships, anything that gets in the way. So, did you hire the two blokes to split Opinder Pandeshi's head open? If you did, you're as guilty as they are."

"Why not ask them?"

"Because no one can find them."

He re-folded his arms and smiled. "Bit of a problem, then."

"Not for the cops. They reckon Suyin's behind it, even though she can't drive. And she'd need a stepladder to have reached his head." He laughed. "Easy option for them, you see. Chinese bogey-woman."

"So, are you planning to march me off to the local nick?"

"Not yet. I want to know about your contact at the Home Office. Dirk."

He stared at me as he tried to fashion a response that didn't involve too much truth. What he came up with wasn't bad given the time constraint.

"I know as much about him as I do about… quantum mechanics."

"He hasn't had a visit from the meat-cleaver men either."

He shook his head. "Blind alley, mate. Dirk wouldn't get his hands that dirty."

"I thought you just said you knew nothing about him. Start with his surname?"

"Lindberg. Sir Dirk Lindberg."

"You say that as if it absolves him of everything. He's your partner in crime, Sandro. He's a scumbag, just like you. What's the gong for? Long service, good conduct?"

"No idea. We met in the legal department. He was brought in to shake it up."

"Instead of which he began to shake down the customers? With you as his factotum? Whose idea was it to set up in business, shafting people?"

He raised his voice a little. "If you think I'm going down that road…"

I put a finger to my lips. "All I want to know is where he lives, then I'll leave you in pizza. Word of warning. When I walk out the door do not get in touch with him or I'll blow you both out the water. Address."

-35-

My first task on getting back to the Discovery was to straighten my face, to rid it of the smile I'd deployed in order not to frighten Alessandro's daughters. Second task was to enter Dirk Lindberg's address into the satnav, a job which involved a trawl through the Discovery's dedicated handbook. Instruction manuals have changed so radically in the recent past so as to become unreadable. Words which once had meaning, such as 'time', 'radio', and 'heaters' don't figure in the index anymore. They've been replaced by 'status', 'in-car entertainment' and 'climate control'… I feel a digression welling up so I'll simply admit that I turned to a battered copy of *The R.A.C Book of the Road* and worked out the best route to Wimbledon.

My visit to Alessandro had pitched me into a mild depression and I wasn't entirely sure why … or indeed that he was responsible for it. My vain hope was that meeting Dirk Lindberg would dispel it. He lived at the end of a tree dominated cul-de-sac from where, no doubt, he would claim to hear the gasps of the crowd and the zing of tennis balls going at 140 miles an hour. I parked away from the house and walked the final stretch.

The Cedars was 1920s in style, with rendered white walls and curved metal windows. A chest- high box hedge added to an institutional feel, that of a clinic or care home, perhaps. The curse had been taken off it by a Virginia creeper working its way along the front and up over the roof. Overshadowing the whole place was an enormous cedar tree, dusty, dark and vaguely sinister.

A woman in her mid-fifties was working beneath it, raking dead foliage into a pile. She was slim and well-cared for, expensively anoraked and wearing unnecessary wellingtons.

I called out to her. "Good morning!"

It caught her off guard and she straightened, fluttering a hand at her chest.

"Sorry, sorry. Miles away. Are you lost?"

"I don't think so. This is The Cedars, right? Plural. There's only one."

She laughed politely. "The other came down in the London storm, 1987. Long before our time."

"You must be Lady Lindberg. If so, I'm looking for your husband."

"Ah, yes, well, he's around somewhere. Who are you, may I ask?"

"My name is Hawk."

I entered through the front gate before she had chance to suggest otherwise. She looked me up and down and, at a rough guess, liked what she saw.

"At the back, doing the patio," she said, propping the rake against the tree. "I'll take you round. Are you a colleague from the office?"

I denied it immediately, a moment before Dirk Lindberg appeared round the side of the house.

"Morning," he said, cheerily.

He was a slightly built man with an angular, lopsided stance and pale eyes that were too big for his face. The mass of hair was almost white and seemed to have a life of its own.

"I'd like to talk visas," I said.

My use of the word didn't faze him. "What a boring subject, Mr…"

"Nathan Hawk."

"Who gave you my address, may I ask?"

"I found you through a mutual acquaintance, Professor Kenneth Blake."

He thought for a moment. "No one of that name springs to mind. No matter."

He beckoned me to follow him into the back garden, which was a good deal larger than I'd expected with a perfect lawn winding fifty yards away from us between tall oaks and beeches. On the patio stood an array of stone tubs and urns, not concrete aggregates but the real McCoy. Before I'd arrived he'd been weeding them and chucking the result into a wheelbarrow. His wife now wondered if I'd care for coffee. I thanked her and she led us to the kitchen door where she and Dirk helped each other off with their wellingtons, giggling all the way like flirty teenagers. I wiped my feet on the mat.

"Sweetie, why don't you take Mr Hawk through to the study?" said Lady Lindberg when they'd finished. "I'll bring it into you."

Sweetie wasn't dead keen on the suggestion but agreed to it. "Splendid. This way, Mr, er… Hawk."

It wasn't that he had difficulty remembering the name; he was trawling his memory to see if it rang any bells. He guided me across the front hall, past artefacts on the walls that would have been more at home in a Scottish hunting lodge. Decapitations of various wild animals abounded, including the obligatory coat-hanger deer head. The pictures, the framed photos, were variously of a Scottish retreat with Dirk and his wife standing beside a loch, he with a hunting rifle broken over his arm, she with a knapsack and an indulgent smile. There were two oil-on-canvas portraits bang opposite the front door, a boy and girl in late teens, presumably the Lindberg children.

We reached a door that was locked. He took a key from his pocket, opened it and immediately I was aware of a sound from within, redolent of cicadas chirruping in the heat of the day. As I entered I saw that it came from a large collection of antique clocks, dotted around the room. I glanced at him.

"My passion," he said.

He gestured me to a leather sofa as we tried to sum each other up in smalltalk – the weather, the traffic and where I had parked. He settled behind a desk and shifted a few papers from one side to the other and then back again.

"Kenneth Blake," he said, eventually. "Help me out if you would…"

"He's a client of a business associate of yours. Alessandro Scutari."

He smiled. "Business associate? I'm a civil servant, Mr Hawk…"

I waved his nitpicking aside. "You granted two long-stay visas to a couple from Uzbekistan, biologists whom the Blakes needed in their research establishment. Fifteen thousand pounds apiece."

I'd meant the fact that I knew his prices, and that he was probably running a racket, to be a killer blow, but he didn't flinch. However, he certainly knew at that point, or thought he knew, why I'd come to visit him.

"You need a visa for someone?" he said, quietly. I nodded. "Would you mind awfully if I… patted you down? Old army habits die hard."

I stared at him as he came towards me and gestured for me to stand up. I obliged and he did a brief skim, legs and all.

"And your mobile," he said. "Just set it down on the desk, if you would. Thank you."

He finished feeling me up and returned to the foxhole of his desk.

"Business usually works like this," he said, "Scutari suggests various clients, I then check that they're bona fide and we go from there."

"Bona fide?"

"That they aren't genocidal maniacs or fundamentalist hotheads and the like." He paused. "Back to you again, Mr Hawk."

"I have a friend. A businessman with resources."

"Wanted by his government?"

"Not so far."

"An insurgent?"

"One man's insurgent is another man's…"

He frowned, cabaret style. "Spare me. Just him? No wife, family?"

"He has a daughter. She's already here."

Lady Lindberg called from the other side of the door and her husband went over to open it. She entered with a full tray and set it down on his desk. There were three cups on it, indicating that she intended to take coffee with us. Her husband had other ideas.

"How do you take it, Mr Hawk? White?"

"Please. No sugar."

She poured and handed me the cup and saucer, then served her husband. He smiled and began to nudge her back towards the door, like a sheepdog detaching a ewe from the flock and driving it to a pen. She went unwillingly, making a departing statement by pouring herself a coffee and exiting haughtily with it. Dirk closed the door behind her and picked up the conversation from exactly where we'd left it.

"I shall need details about your friend. The name he wishes to use, for example, a passport in said name, his age and place of birth, his occupation, some reason for being here. All in good time." He smiled. "What's his current name?"

"Kueng Qu."

It was my second attempt at a killer blow but had as much effect as my first. Our conversation wasn't going the way I'd intended. I had at least expected him to sweat a little. Instead he stared at me with the ice-cube eyes and eventually said, "Well I never. Do go on."

"I think you know roughly why I'm here but it bears repeating. The visa scam you and Alessandro Scutari are running has spun out of control. One of you discovered how wealthy Kueng Qu is and set about kidnapping his daughter to hold her to ransom."

He waited for more, just as I waited for his reaction. Eventually he smiled. "So how far have we got with this… insane project?"

"You've hired two ex-army malcontents, guys who couldn't make it back to Civvy Street. Name of Devanney. Father and son. Either you or Scutari has driven them round the country looking for the daughter. Maybe you take the driving in turns, though Sandro reckons you wouldn't get your hands that dirty…"

He shrugged. "So we haven't found her yet?"

"No, but along the way Devanney Junior murdered a friend of hers and left his DNA behind to prove it."

"Oh, dear. I hope the full force of the law has descended on him."

"It hasn't, but still they've kept on looking for the girl. That makes whoever's running them a unique kind of psychopath. As well as having no morality, they're stupid. I mean police are now involved, MI6 are involved…"

"May I ask why *you* are?"

I smiled. "Once a copper…"

He nodded. "Old habits? Nothing better to do?" He gestured round at the clocks. "You should get yourself a hobby."

And as if on cue, every clock in the room began to strike the hour. They weren't all agreed on the exact time, some lagged a few seconds behind others, but by and large they agreed that it was round about midday. Twelve displays of *tempus fugit*. Lindberg had transferred his attention away from me and onto the clocks as if stepping into another world. He held up a hand, cocked his head and listened. He was one short, and eventually a pendulum clock in a recess whirred and tinged. He smiled and went over to it. With great care and delicacy he opened the case, reached in and raised the pendulum by half a turn of a screw at the bottom. He set the clock ticking again and beckoned me to join him.

"Joseph Knibb. Temperamental. 1675. Quite a youngster compared to some of the others." He pointed across the room. "I believe the iron case over there is 1590. Point is, they're all still working, all keeping relatively good time, and yet when most of them were made men still believed the earth was flat."

"You mean it isn't?"

He chuckled. I followed him round the room, partly out of interest in the clocks themselves, but mainly to log away their makers' names in order to price them later. They were, I imagined, one of the reasons he needed a second income stream. Visas.

"In my father's opinion a man with one clock always knows the time," I said. "A man with two is never sure."

He smiled. "And a man with a large collection?"

"He's so rich he doesn't need to know the time."

"I see where you're going. You really do think I'm your villain, Mr Hawk?"

"You're high on my list of suspects."

"And what did you expect to happen today? To saunter in and have me tell you it's a fair cop?" He shook his head. "Why not share your evidence, if you have any? And why aren't the police beating a path to my door?" He paused. "Because you *have* no evidence. French," he said of a three-piece affair I'd paused at. "1755. The candleholders either side of the clock are gilded bronze, the figures Meissen, the flowers…"

I wrapped my fingers round the clock's feet. He watched, apparently without skipping a heartbeat.

"I can see the headline now," I said. "Time Called on Home Office Grandee's Bent Visa Scam."

He chuckled. "A bit wordy…"

"Time Runs Out for Dirty Dirk?"

"Better."

I'd accepted that the conversation wasn't going the way I'd intended and it would need a boost in my favour. I lifted the clock with both hands and turned to him. He blinked slowly and carried on gazing at me.

"If you're trying to threaten me, it won't work. None of my clients will turn on me for fear of being sent back home, many to their deaths. Should you be foolish enough to believe that Alessandro Scutari will blow the whistle… well, I have enough on him to send him away for twenty years." I weighed the clock in my hands. "And the bottom line is I had nothing to do with your murder. Just so there's no hard feelings, I'll arrange Kueng Qu's visa at a knockdown price. Originally it was sixty for him, thirty for the daughter."

Which amounted to what I'd found in the stuffed white crane.

***

The mild depression I'd felt after leaving Alessandro Scutari had transmogrified into angry resentment. When I reached the Discovery I kicked the front tyre, much to the alarm of a man walking his dog on the opposite pavement.

I climbed into the driving seat and waited for the pain in my foot to wear off. I couldn't tell for sure if Dirk Lindberg was the sort of man who, even after his involvement in a brutal murder, would still follow the money. I suspected that he was, but then again so might any of the people I'd met since

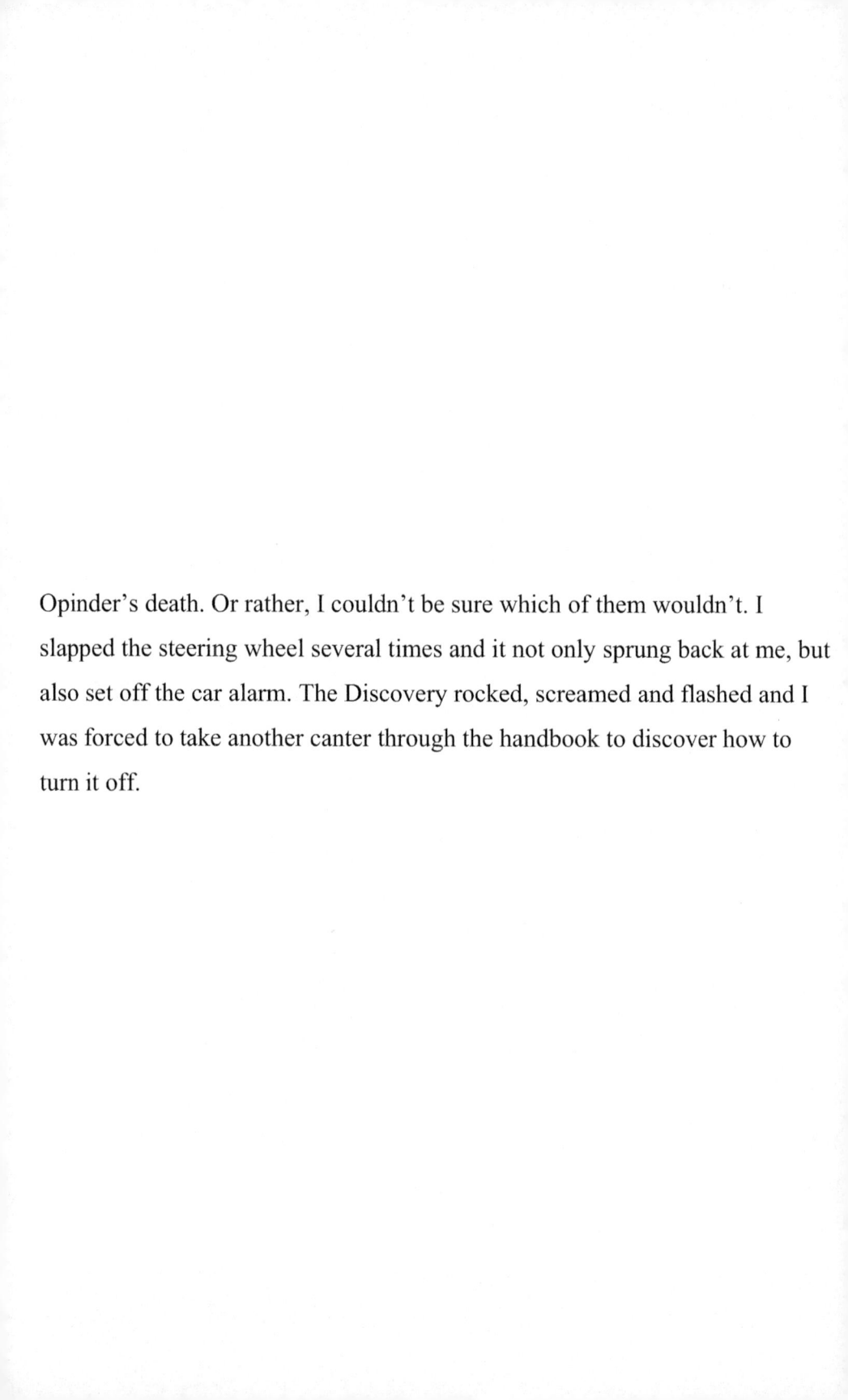

Opinder's death. Or rather, I couldn't be sure which of them wouldn't. I slapped the steering wheel several times and it not only sprung back at me, but also set off the car alarm. The Discovery rocked, screamed and flashed and I was forced to take another canter through the handbook to discover how to turn it off.

When I reached home I was glad there was no one waiting to ask how my day had gone. I picked through some leftovers in the fridge before getting gently pissed and wound up falling asleep on the living-room sofa, head back, mouth open, no doubt looking ten years older and snoring like a pig. I was woken at about four in the morning by my mobile ringing. I thought it was a dream to begin with because it rang off, only to ring again. It said International, or something equally fuzzy on the screen, and I naturally believed it was someone in Mumbai trying to scam me over my electricity bill. It was a chance to vent my spleen.

"What?" I said in a dead voice.

"Dad?" said the other end.

"Who's that?"

"Two guesses," said the caller. "Voice female, implying by use of the word 'Dad' that you're their father."

"Ellie, what the hell…?" I struggled to a sitting position. "It's four in the morning here."

"It's coffee time here."

"Where are you?"

"Pokhara, in Nepal, Dad."

"Christ, you sound like you're in the next room."

It's a generational thing. Along with a zillion others I believe that phone calls from four and a half thousand miles away should be barely audible. I raised my voice and began to enunciate in order to be heard on the other side of the world.

"How are you?" I asked.

"Fine," she said. "I'm coming home for Christmas."

"Really?"

"Via Zurich and Stockholm. I plan to relieve some multinationals of dosh for the orphanage." I laughed. "I'm phoning rather than messaging because I didn't want to go through the usual rigmarole with Fee, 'Why, what's wrong? Have you broken up with Rick? Have you caught bubonic plague? Are you in prison?'"

"I know what you mean." I paused. "Even so, you are alright?" There was silence. I thought she'd been cut off. "Ellie?"

"Yeah, I'm here, Dad. I'm bringing Rick with me. He isn't well."

"What's wrong with him?"

"Basically his guts. He's lost weight. Exhausted all the time. And he's frightened… as am I."

"Are there no doctors in Nepal? Or shouldn't he be going back to his parents? Los Angeles?"

"Dad, his parents are… pretty basic. Sturdy, simple folk. God, that's the worst thing I've said all week."

"I understand."

"I'll be happier if Laura's there to give advice as well. I take it you're back together again, so nearer the day I'll email with flight numbers and stuff. Okay?"

"Before you go, love, you haven't heard from Con, have you?"

"No. Worries me, but I've had other things on my mind."

"Sure, sure…"

"However, I do have an idea…"

***

I spent the next three days writing the message which Ellie had suggested to The Others. It was only four lines long, but the downright lie at its core was a problem.

"Hi, all!" it eventually began. "Ivan Johnson was my mother's second cousin. He died back in August, 94 years old. For some reason he left me money – not a fortune, I'm told, but not to be sniffed at either. His will stated that it should be shared between my children. So more soonest, as they say. Dad x."

Fee was first out of the blocks from New York with her usual scepticism. "Mum never mentioned the name. Are you sure they've got the right Nathan Hawk?"

"There is only one Nathan Hawk," I responded drily.

"Depending on how how much we're talking about, I'd keep it for yourself, Dad," said Jaikie, all the way from Chiswick. "How much is it, by the way?"

"No idea, yet."

Ellie chipped in from Nepal to add authenticity. "You jammy sod, Dad! Money out of the blue? Gimme, gimme."

"Steady on, girl," I answered.

Fee had had time to think. "Dad, are you sure it isn't some scam? Have they asked for your bank details? Where does the news come from? Nigeria?"

"No, from Penzance."

"Still sounds dodgy,"

"If you don't want your share just say so. End of discussion. Love Dad."

I left it there, but conspicuous by its absence was any response from Con.

"Give him time," said Laura Peterson, the evening of the day I pressed the send button. "I mean you lot jump on your messages every day, on WhatsApp every minute! Some of us don't."

"Some of us have a girl at the surgery doing it for you." I took a sip of the wine she'd just poured and noted that the glasses were new and half the size of her old set. "Con's been short of money all his adult life. I dangle some in front of him and he doesn't grab at it. I'm more worried now than I was two weeks ago."

"Your default position."

I had gone round to Chestnut Cottage to put Laura in the loop about Ellie and Terrific Rick's impending visit. The first thing she did was voice sympathy for Ellie even though she wasn't the one who was ill. The strain of watching a partner waste away must be unbearable, she said. Her maternal instincts, once removed, had kicked in and there was no gainsaying them. Jaikie was her favourite and Ellie was a close second. The other two were joint third.

I brought the matter up again over dinner, itself a novel addition to her culinary repertoire. Baked beans on toast followed by two kiwi fruits.

"What does it sound like to you? Weight loss? Fatigue?"

She shook her head. "It could be one of fifty things, but she's right to bring him to London." She smiled. "You know, some people would describe your concern over Con and Terrific Rick as displacement activity. Would they be right?"

I groaned and slid farther down in the chair. "I've missed you."

"Yes, you said the other day."

"Three weeks ago, actually. This Opinder… business isn't going well."

I referred to it as a business rather than a brutal murder to lessen the misery of not having caught his killer.

"So you're thoroughly depressed?" she asked.

"The best chance of catching Opinder's killer is the DNA on Devanney Junior's weapon of choice. It's useless at the moment because the meat-cleaver men have gone to ground. Apart from that there's no description of a possible suspect, no prints, no forensics and, even if the Devanneys are found, will they name the guy running the show? I shouldn't think so."

Laura frowned. "Why?"

"I imagine they're terrified of him. He's taken a coldblooded murder in his stride and kept on following the money, even though the police are now involved, I'm involved, MI6 is involved. That's ruthless, mad, psychopathic, desperate... you name it."

I looked at her to ask if she had a sensible contribution to make.

"Does that description match anyone you've... met in the last month or so?"

"It matches everyone. And no one. You won't understand..."

"Don't get chippy!" she snapped. "I understand perfectly!"

I nodded to the wine bottle for a refill and she obliged, though only up to the halfway mark.

"There's another problem," I said. "Suyin can't stay hidden at Elwyn Road forever. Sooner or later she'll be spotted, apart from which, Bill Grogan has to return to his bloody cactuses sometime."

"Cacti," she corrected.

"I know she can afford an army of bodyguards, but it's no way to live... and all it takes is one chink in the armour. Did I just say chink in relation to a Chinese woman? God, you have to be on your toes these days..." Laura smiled. "As for the motive, can I really swear to it being money? Certainly where there's money there are people lining up to to take it, and if someone gets killed along the way, too bad. But... but... the only place I can prove that the meat-cleaver men visited, apart from Opinder's house, is Elwyn Road. The rest is hearsay. Tricks Farm, Abiding Earth, Taylor Mandrake's gallery. All I have is their word or my speculation. And in Alessandro Scutari's case a fabrication."

She began to clear the table and stack whatever we'd used in the dishwasher. Her method of doing that had always irritated me. She places the knives in one corner of the cutlery tray, forks in another, spoons in another.

"Why not just bung them in anywhere? Why handle them dirty? Far better to handle them when they're clean…"

She said I was giving way to yet more displacement activity. "Take the one you can prove," she added. "Elwyn Road. What were they after?"

I shrugged. "Her money, or simply to kill her. If the latter, why? I mean I've even tried a Chinese connection, hoping that a triad connection or something equally daft would emerge. It hasn't. I simply joined in the current sport of demonising China, only to find I was dealing with a father and daughter who wanted to be together."

She refilled her own glass, then pushed the cork back into the bottle as far as she could. "I think you enjoy the downs of your inquiries as much as the ups. There must be troughs for there to be peaks. Isn't that your thinking?"

"You're doing a Drusilla Ford on me."

"Now there's a thought. So, who exactly *are* the people you've… spoken to?"

The very first had been Francis Stevens, aka Charles Beaumont. Suyin had turned her affections from him to Taylor Mandrake. Had Frank's ego been bruised enough to make him seek revenge? When I first met him I could only see a frightened kid, but that's easy enough to fake. Could he have been one of the two meat-cleaver men? And Taylor Mandrake himself. He knew there was money – lots of it – so had he already siphoned off some in the shape of European art? Did he want more? What about Richard Bennett and his snitty wife? Was there some reason they'd like to be rid of Suyin? To wipe out their debt? Should I go and have another word with him?"

"I thought your favourites were Alessandro Scutari and his partner at the Home Office?" said Laura.

"Kidnap? Ransom? Either or both of them? I can't see it. What I can see is them wanting her dead in case she blows the whistle on their visa scam. Then there's John Smith. From the name onwards he's a dodgy bastard. Does he really work for MI6? I've taken his word, but I've never been to his office, met the head of his section. Maybe he's both spook and killer. He wouldn't be the first."

"You haven't mentioned Abiding Earth."

"I know. I mean their brand of barminess has always been a good cover, but would Ken and Barbie set about kidnapping Suyin Qu? They can't even rig up a decent booby trap."

"There's other people working there, you said. The Uzbeks, the housekeeper, the New Yorkers…"

I sighed. "I should've dug deeper. But my squad is even smaller than Parfitt's. It amounts to me, Bill Grogan… and you as consultant."

"I'm going up in the world. From dog handler to consultant."

I nodded at the wine bottle. "Not very strong, this wine. I mean…"

She slid it across the table and I reached for it. In doing so my sleeve mopped up some of the overspill from dinner. Laura rose and fetched a dishcloth to wipe the table, then paused and thought for a moment.

"I wonder if it's time to employ some lateral thinking." She tossed the dishcloth back into the sink. "Like Ellie did with Con. Instead of looking for him, needle in a haystack, she suggested that you get him to come to you."

"Hasn't worked, has it?"

"Not yet, no. Why don't you play the same trick on Opinder's killer? Why don't you make him come to *you*?"

"If I knew how…"

She sat down again, leaned forward and whispered, though God knows who she imagined might be listening to our conversation. "Suyin hasn't been found, or rather that's what you've told everyone. Why don't you suddenly find her? Tell everyone you're keeping her safe. Then… wait for whoever's after her to turn up?"

"Keeping her safe where? My place?"

"I hadn't got that far…"

I was hesitant about Laura's suggestion, but in the absence of a better plan I decided to go for it.

It was fraught with problems. For a start, it depended on my assumption that whoever wanted to kill or kidnap her would stop at nothing. A close second to that was the problem of what to do with Suyin while I waited for their next move. Should I bring her to Beech Tree for safety or leave her in West London with Jaikie and Jodie? Wherever she went, Bill Grogan would have to go as well and for a moment I collapsed inwardly at the thought of Grogan living in my house… indefinitely. I picked myself up again quickly.

Casting a shadow over all of that was the police investigation. The case was still live, certainly, even if not much progress was being made. However, if Parfitt suddenly heard that I was shielding Suyin he would step in, interview her, maybe even arrest her, and that would be it.

***

I called Gadsden later that same evening to get an update on the police inquiry. He was pleased to hear from me, mainly I think because it was someone to talk to. I got the impression that Mrs Gadsden had thrown in the towel long ago, and if there were any children their father had never mentioned them. He was eating fish and chips, he told me to explain the muffle on the line, and was watching a film that he was happy to pause. I heard the snap of a tag on a beer can and the resultant glug as he poured it into a glass.

"How's your lovely doctor?" he asked. "You're a lucky man."

"She's fine, Tom. The Opinder Pandeshi case…"

"Bugger it! Do we have to?"

"'Fraid so."

"Same as before. The girl's nowhere to be found and the Devanneys have gone AWOL..." He was hacked off enough to allow himself a criticism of his boss. "We're following the army connection now. Have the Devanneys hooked up with old regimental pals? What was their service record like? Et cetera." I heard his teeth clink on the rim of the glass as he drank from it. "The people you've spoken to about Suyin, any of them have army connections? Is the old boy at Abiding Earth a member of Dad's Army? Is Richard Bennett in the T.A?"

"No one springs to mind."

"Anyway, is that all you phoned about... to see how it's going?"

"No. Favour. It's a big ask this, Tom. If I told you that I knew where Suyin Qu was, would you be able to keep it to yourself for, say, three weeks?"

He paused and I heard the beer glass go down on a hard surface.

"Christ, I was enjoying this film till you rang," he said, eventually. "Why would I need to keep it to myself?"

"I wouldn't want Parfitt screeching up to... where she is, all blue lights and siren, and God forbid, arresting her."

"What are you up to, guvnor? No! No, I don't want to know..." He must have picked up the glass again, taken a few mouthfuls. They calmed him down a little. "So far, all you've done is phone me and asked how it's going. I've been evasive. You've left it at that. Agreed?"

"Thanks. Enjoy the rest of the film..."

"Hang on. One condition. Update me. Regular basis."

"Sure. Can that be mutual?"

"Let's make it every day," he said. "How is Carla Natalie McKinnon, by the way?"

"She looks like Winston Churchill, but they all do for the first year."

He chuckled. "Say hi to her for me. And to the doc. Keep in touch."

***

To decide on what to do with Suyin, Laura tossed a coin and I called heads for bringing Suyin to Beech Tree. Had it been tails, a decision to leave her at Elwyn, I would have demanded the best of three.

The only condition Suyin made when we discussed the move was that Bill Grogan should join us. It had been the plan all along, I told her. Theirs was an unlikely friendship, which I was at a loss to explain. Laura described it as one of mutual reserve. In Grogan's case, his close-to-the-chest manner was the habit of a lifetime, Suyin's was a national characteristic. The odd result was that, throughout the days that followed, I would catch them whispering, and sometimes giggling, over shared confidences.

We moved her into Beech Tree at two in the morning, which she considered to be an adventure. Grogan and I thought it a necessary break in our sleep patterns. I assigned him Con's old room, right at the top of the house, where he wouldn't have to stoop, at least not if he kept to the centre of it. Beech Tree creaks at the best of times, sometimes of its own volition, but with a man of Grogan's size walking around it it positively groans. I noticed during the next few days that every time he took a step, a fine dust, the very fabric of the house, would descend from between the beams and the lathe and plaster. I installed Suyin in Fee's old room, directly under him. It gave her a bathroom of her own, which she quickly feminised and spent many hours in.

That first evening I made the mistake of cooking dinner and served up my speciality, grilled salmon with three veg. Such had been Grogan's *à la carte* diet during his time at Elwyn that he paused before starting on it, more in regret than distaste.

"Jodie does this salmon en croute thing with a lattice of pastry, does it to a turn. Right, Su?"

Su, eh? She nodded and he carried on with the praise.

"And a lemony sauce, which is just about the most... I mean, this is nice, only it's not... well, Jodie has time to..."

I ran through the basics with Suyin and her expression ranged from palpable fear to admirable courage. Secrecy concerning her whereabouts was essential, I said. No one must be told. I hammered the point until she closed her eyes to protest that she'd understood the first time. I was just as unsubtle about what to do *when*... not *if and when*, but when, when whoever was after her showed their face. She was to hurry to her room, lock the door, switch off the lights and hunker down in the walk-in loft above the kitchen. She asked about spiders. No spiders, I said. She took my word for it and I went on to say the three of us would spend our evenings in the house, not necessarily together, but with the curtains drawn. The back door would remain unlocked...

"So, if someone comes when we sleep?" she asked, nervously.

I pointed down at Dogge. "She'll let us know."

"Superdog, huh? Nose, ears?" She paused. "How will they know to come here in the first place?"

I smiled. "How does anyone know anything these days? Social media. Even as we speak, Jaikie is broadcasting the fact that his clever father's found you. He won't say where you are, but it doesn't take a genius to work it out..."

I reached into the kitchen drawer and took out the rape alarm that I'd bought for Ellie three years previously and she had never used.

"I want you to carry this. Have it with you at all times. If anything... anything frightens you pull it. It screams like hell..."

"Rape?" she whispered.

I shook my head. "More a personal alarm."

"For rape."

"How long before we can expect…?" Grogan asked.

"I say ten days, max. Ten days and it's all over." He wasn't so sure. "Let's have a tenner on it."

He turned away, dug deep and found a leather pouch with money in it. He took out a ten-pound note, I matched it with mine and placed them both on the dresser beneath a photo of Maggie holding Fee and Con.

Suyin smiled. "I write you a note. An IOU."

"Winner takes all." Anxious to lift the mood even further, I said, "Bill, you should nip over to Headington, see Viv. Take Suyin, show her the cacti, say hallo for me to that big round bugger with fixed bayonets on it."

"*Echinocactus grusonii.*"

He glanced round and asked if there was anything for dessert. I shook my head and they exchanged a dissatisfied glance.

After the fourth day of our routine I worried that we were forgetting the dark purpose of the exercise. I would return to it with a jolt, recalling afresh that someone, someone I probably knew, wanted Suyin's money and possibly her life. I would hurry to check her exact whereabouts and, when I glimpsed her in the garden fussing Dogge, or playing a board game with Grogan, or heard her splashing about in the bath, I would remember that she was somebody's daughter and that he was depending on me to keep her safe.

One evening, day five I believe, I strolled round to Jenny Tindall's to brief her about Suyin. I knew I could count on her discretion. After all, she had 'straightened up' Beech Tree on a weekly basis when Laura was living with me. Not once had she raised an eyebrow or sighed disapprovingly, nor had she made a comment when Laura moved out again. In a village where most people thrive on gossip, Jenny was the exception, but given that her next visit to my house was scheduled for the following day I thought it only right to warn her of Grogan and Suyin's presence. She took the news in her stride, raising a forefinger to her lips as a way of reassuring me.

I'd only been gone half an hour, but in that strange way of realising that something isn't… quite right, I paused halfway down Morton Lane. Beech Tree looked the same as when I'd left it and I was about to dismiss my concern as rogue extrasensory perception when I re-pictured the half-mile stroll to Jenny's house. Tucked in the gateway to a field, closer to her house than mine, had been a small Mercedes I didn't recognise. Sad to say that I know most of the cars, if not all, that belong in Winchendon. This one was new. Normally I would have assumed that it belonged to a visitor to one of the cottages close by. Now, for some reason, it worried me.

It was a clear night so I kept to the shadows as I continued to the house and, instead of walking up the gravel drive, I approached over the grass beside it. Even so, Dogge must have sensed my presence and she barked. I stopped and so did she. As I rounded the house I had a clear view into the kitchen, where the lights were full on. Grogan and Suyin stood facing each other, leaning over something or someone that from their intensity bothered them. I went closer and peered in through the windows.

Taylor Mandrake was seated on a kitchen chair and Suyin was dabbing at his face with the contents of a china bowl. Cotton wool and water. The side of his face had a cut on it from temple to jawbone and he winced each time she touched it. Grogan broke off to fetch more cotton wool from what I laughingly call my first-aid basket. I called out and entered.

"What the fuck…?" I asked. As one does.

Apart from the cut and blood all over his face, his left eye was bruised and starting to swell. More painful to him, I imagined, was the ponytail. In whatever fracas he'd been in someone had hacked off at least ten inches of it and what was left hung round his face in a straggly bob.

"You have nothing, Nathan, nothing first aid! A few plasters, two rolls of cotton wool. Iodine, ten years old…"

"Sorry."

"I'm okay," said Taylor. "Really I am…"

"No, you are not. This cut will need sewing…"

"What happened?" I asked.

"When I closed the gallery, two men came up behind, dragged me to a parked van. They wanted to know where Suyin was."

"Men in masks? Work overalls?"

He nodded. "I told them over and over that I didn't know. Eventually they believed me, threw me out onto the pavement and drove away."

"Not before beating you and giving you a haircut, huh?"

"I drove straight here. To warn you."

"They didn't follow you?"

He shook his head and I went over to my mobile on the dresser.

"Who you phone?" asked Suyin.

"Doctor friend. She's very good with A and E departments and you're right, he needs… sewing." Before I pressed Laura's number, I said, "How did you know Suyin was here, Taylor? Facebook?"

"No, no…"

I looked at Suyin. "You told him where you were. After me asking you to say nothing, you told him."

She looked at me, all doe eyes. "I'm sorry."

"You think we should report it…"

"Police? No, they'll be all over you." I nodded at the two tenners and the IOU note on the dresser. "Come to Daddy."

***

The following night I phoned Tom Gadsden to confide a niggling detail. My intention was more to show willing than anything, to reassure him that I was abiding by our agreement to share.

"Anything to report?" he said.

"Wish I had, Tom."

"So nothing like… you've found her?"

"Suyin? What makes you say that?"

"Your son has three quarters of a million followers on Twitter. I'm one of 'em. Is it true? You found her?"

Every time I'm asked a straight yes or no question my mind rockets back to Roy Pullman, the man who bequeathed me The Map. He once said to me, 'Yes, no, what's the difference?' I'd carried the dodgy logic with me ever since and used it now.

"No."

Gadsden took a few moments to absorb that. "I have to say up front that if I'm not the first to hear about any progress you make, I'll stop being the cuddly cop who's about to retire and become a bastard, right?"

"Absolutely. Listen, you and Parfitt are looking for army connections to the Devanneys, right? I said I didn't know of any."

"You've changed your mind."

"It's tenuous, but John Smith bought the house he lives in from a man called Nicholas Fournier. Major Nicholas Fournier, 1st Battalion, Cheshire Regiment, served in Northern Ireland."

"Devanney was Royal Corps of Signals."

"Chances of them meeting are minimal, I agree. And you'll tell me that Fournier's got Parkinson's anyway, but run him through the mangle, eh?"

***

Notwithstanding Suyin breaking the rules by telling her boyfriend where she was, the rest of the stakeout went smoothly. There was booze to hand, we took turns to make tea and I put on a few ounces as I worked through the store of potato crisps. Laura dropped in occasionally, once with a chicken casserole that Grogan, now a food critic *manqué,* was very complimentary about. She stayed to help us eat it, after which the four of us played Monopoly. It's not a game of skill, by any means, but three hours later the others folded one by one. Suyin was last and groused about it.

As I switched on the dishwasher and let Dogge out for a pee my phone pinged with a text from Tom Gadsden.

"Phone me tomorrow, re army connection. Urgent. Fournier."

It just about made sense. I called him first thing the following morning and asked what the panic was about.

"No panic," he said. "But I think you'll like this…"
I did.

On day eight, Grogan and I sat down to watch a few episodes of a French police series we'd become hooked on. After the first few episodes I'd noticed that, unlike me, Grogan wasn't reading the subtitles. Uncharitably, I assumed he was just watching the pictures until I realised that he understood the original dialogue.

I paused the playback and said, "You speak French, Bill?" He nodded. "How come?"

"Picked it up here and there." He nodded at the screen, irritably. "Your man there's just about to go off the rails. Please." I shrugged to get an answer to my question. "My mother was French."

I nodded and pressed play. "That'll explain your Gallic charm."

The following evening Grogan and I binged on the series again, and just after midnight we decided to watch just one more episode. It soon had us on the edge of our seats and was so gripping that when Dogge, who was sprawled out asleep in front of us, suddenly raised her head and growled, I growled back at her to be quiet. She sat up and looked at me in such a way that I was forced to defer.

"What is it, girl?"

She barked just once. In the gap between the top of the curtains and the beam they were hung from I saw what I took to be the beam from a torch. It flicked across the ceiling and was gone. I turned the television volume down.

"Talk about bloody timing," said Grogan, reaching out to a side table for his Glock and holstering it.

I went to the curtain, twitched it and saw movement out in the lane. Two figures, I thought. They had killed the torch and were now climbing over the five-bar gate. I texted Suyin with instructions to lock the door and go into the loft. When I glanced out again the intruders had disappeared from sight but

Dogge picked them up again when they hit a layer of beech husks. She began to bark for real and they paused.

"Thank you! Quiet, girl!" I whispered.

The visitors glanced at each other. One gestured that they should continue towards the front door.

"How many?" Grogan asked.

"Two."

As we'd discussed on several occasions, he went through to the kitchen to cover the back door while I waited in the hall beside the front door, hinge side. After what seemed like a full two minutes but could only have been ten seconds I saw, in such light as there was, the glint of the front door handle as it turned. In Father and Son's place I would have paused if I'd found the front door unlocked. I would have checked things like windows, lights and sounds from within. Father and Son didn't bother. Nor were they fussed that they'd triggered the porch light. Army veterans though they were, they were also the rank amateurs we had first thought.

The door opened and the top hinge beside me whined as it reached a certain angle. Dogge barked again and ran to the door. She stood watching as the two men entered, then backed away as they encroached farther on to her territory.

"Good dog, good dog," said the older man. A raspy, smoker's voice.

I sidestepped and slammed the door, and they turned to it. I switched on the light and, for one of those moments which gets seared into your memory, we looked at each other. They were dressed in their uniform of B and Q overalls, one piece, dark grey, zipped up at the front, identical work boots. Identical ski masks. The younger of the two unzipped his onesie overall and took out a machete, which had been tucked into his waistband.

"Come at us with that, son, and we'll wrap it round your head."

The older man chuckled. "Who's we? You and your Japanese fighting dog?"

"Me and my silverback." I nodded at Grogan, who had entered from the kitchen to stand behind them.

As they turned to him he took one head in each hand and smashed them together. They seemed to stand for a moment, absolutely still, and then without a sound they dropped where they stood. Machete Boy had taken more of the force than his father and, as he slithered down the wall, he toppled to one side, barely conscious and with blood seeping through his mask. The father began to protest but the pain of doing so cut him short.

"Kitchen," I said.

Grogan hauled the father by the scruff of his overall; I took the son's legs and pulled him along the floor.

While they were still groggy from the collision, we patted them down for more weapons, gaffer-taped their wrists and ankles, then sat them in chairs, back to back in the middle of the floor. We pulled off their identical trainers and then unveiled them, pulling the masks from the top. The father winced as the fabric tore away from two parallel lacerations running from his temple to his jawline and the blood began to run down onto his chest until it found its way to the floor. To this day you can see where it landed. You never quite get bloodstains out of stone. He raised his head and peered at me from a rapidly closing eye. He whispered that I was a bastard.

They weren't recognisable as father and son. The younger man had a squarish, leathery face, pitted with the scars of a youthful skin disease. Unlike his father, the hair was a bloody mop and now straggled at all angles across his head and face. His nose was that of a boxer, flattened and broken, and the blood came from there and his mouth. It looked worse than it probably felt, but he hadn't winced when the mask had been pulled away. He had screamed.

"Devanney, father and son, right?" I said to the older man. "If the boy's Anthony, who are you?"

"Piss off."

I stamped on his foot.

"Allan!" the son yelled.

Any more information we needed was clearly going to come from the son.

I took a Waitrose food bag from the dresser and went into the hall to retrieve the machete. I dangled it in front of Anthony.

"You've gone up in the world. You killed Opinder Pandeshi with a humble meat cleaver. Machete? Who else d'you plan on hacking to death?"

"What you talking about?" he said through bloodied teeth.

"Are you saying you don't know where you are? You're just a pair of wandering house-breakers, all the way from London for the rich pickings? I say you're looking for a Chinese woman called Suyin Qu."

"Dunno what you're…"

"You going to say you've never seen me before?" asked Grogan as he lifted the front of his fisherman's knit to reveal the Glock. "Seen *this* before?"

"No, I bloody…"

"On your feet, son!"

Grogan hauled him to a standing position, turned him a hundred and eighty degrees, grabbed the overalls with both hands and ripped them from neck to crotch.

"What the fuck…?" the father protested.

Given that his ankles were taped together he couldn't step out of the boiler suit. I went to the dresser for the kitchen scissors and finished the job for him. When I'd finished Grogan took the waistband of his jeans and yanked them down. Then the underpants.

"Turn round and bend over," he whispered.

Anthony stared at us in terror. "What?"

"I said turn round and bend over."

"What the fuck do…"

Grogan spun him and folded him in half. He pointed to Anthony's left buttock.

"What's that look like to you, guvnor?"

"Looks to me like he's caught a bullet recently. Whoever's patched it up has done a lousy job. Might need amputating. Sit down."

Bare-arsed and still in some discomfort from where Grogan had shot him outside Elwyn Road, he eased himself onto a wooden chair. I reached down to the jeans and took his mobile phone from the back pocket. I showed it to Anthony's face and the Face ID didn't like what it saw.

"Code?" I asked.

"Fuck off."

I took a breath and fetched the wooden salt mill from the table. Grogan stood over Allan and I held the mill next to the gashes on the father's face. I gave it one turn and a beat later Anthony screamed.

"5312!"

I entered it and ran through the list of WhatsApp contacts until I reached the name I'd expected to find.

"Your driver, your… boss?" I asked, showing it to the father. "Parked at the end of the lane, maybe, round the corner? Waiting for you to say come and get us?" I typed a message and read it out to the Devanneys. "All well. Need a bit of help. She's being difficult."

I added a smiley face and sent it.

I signalled to Grogan that we should tape their mouths and he tore off two strips of gaffer tape.

"My father never went anywhere without two things," he said to Allan. "Gaffer tape to hold things together, WD40 to take 'em apart."

"Wise man," I said. "Turn out the kitchen light, will you? Where's the dog?"

"She went through to the utility when the violence started."

I smiled. "Shut the door on her. I'd rather she didn't hear all this."

It was one of the most satisfying minutes I've lived through. I just wish it had gone on for longer. Headlights swung into Morton Lane and were then switched off. Running lights only. Whoever was behind the wheel was being careful as they crawled down to the house. They did a three-point turn on the grass patch at the very end of the lane and pulled up the other side of the five-bar. A car door opened and closed. Dogge rumbled from the utility and I asked her to be quiet. She'd heard footsteps on the gravel, approaching the front door. The visitor triggered the porch light and the door swung open, groaning when it reached the usual angle. Footsteps approached the kitchen and a voice hissed, "Where are you?"

"Come in, Mrs Fournier," I called as she appeared at the doorway. "Join the bloodbath."

I rose, not so much out of politeness as to prevent her from turning and running. I closed the door behind her and switched on the light. It blinded her for a moment or two as she took in the scene before her. She looked quite different to the busybody neighbour who had been so concerned about John Smith's welfare. Her hair was screwed back in a row of clips, which stretched the skin on her face and gave it a bloodless hue. Her manner was ice cold and unafraid.

"She's not here," I said.

"Who isn't?"

"Suyin Qu."

"And who might she be? And who are these two men?"

Grogan pulled out a chair and gestured for her to sit down in it. I waited for her to settle.

"You've disappointed me, Mrs Fournier. A man gets murdered and I take three months out of my life, I travel 12,000 miles, thinking I'll unravel some plot by the Chinese to build an outpost of empire on the Norfolk coast. What do I find instead? The person responsible is someone's next-door bloody neighbour."

She smiled, honing the razor-blade lips to a fine edge. "I don't know who you think I am…"

I laughed. "I hate nosey neighbours. And by God we've got our share of 'em here in this village. They're never in it for the good of other people. Only for themselves."

She smiled with those razor lips. A fan of wrinkles appeared either side of her mouth. "I don't know who you think I am, and I certainly have no idea who you and your friend…"

I held up a hand. "I don't know nuffink, m'lud? This man here, these two ruffians, I mean, all I did was break down outside his house, which just happens to be at the end of a no through road. I was a poor frightened woman who'd lost her way. Bill, take Allan's tape off his mouth."

Grogan reached out and yanked it hard and fast.

"I meant to say gently. Listen to me, Allan. Gracie here's about to drop you and your boy right in it…"

Fournier looked at Allan. "My advice to you, whoever you are, is to say nothing."

"And she starts by denying that she knows you. Get her to say your name."

Allan thought for a moment, then asked, "Who am I, Sergeant?"

"I beg your pardon?"

"My name!"

She shrugged. "Allan. He just said."

"Surname?"

She laughed. "Well, if you don't know that…"

I smiled at him. "See what I mean? Her mind's going nineteen to the dozen, working on the story she'll spin when the three of you are done for murder, your boy for committing it, you two for joint enterprise…"

"I have never clapped eyes on either of these men," said Grace.

"Then let me introduce you. Grace, this is Allan Devanney: Al, Sergeant Grace Fournier." I stooped down to within a foot of Grace's face. "That photo of you and your husband, wedding day, taken where? Aldershot? Him in uniform, you in white, and taped to the silver frame the Queen's Commendation Medal for Bravery. Being male I thought it was his. It wasn't. It was yours, Sergeant." I turned to Grogan. "She isn't your average nosey neighbour, Bill. She was one of us. Copper. Royal Military Police."

She stared at me and began to clap slowly in mock applause.

"That's how you met Allan here. When he was in the Signals you questioned him about nicking an officer's car. Outcome was some other poor bastard took the rap and after that, Allan was yours. And he's put his carjacking skills to good use. Fresh car for you to drive every time you hit the road? In your search for Suyin Qu?"

"Who is this… woman?"

"Don't waste your breath. You teased it out of John Smith when you took over from his wife as a shoulder to cry on. A confidante. To a trained investigator like you he was a pushover, gave you every detail you needed about this wealthy young woman and didn't even realise he was doing it. Why did you need the money? End-of-life lottery win? Some weird and wonderful cure for your husband's illness? Or was it the challenge of it all?"

"I still have no idea what you're talking about."

"I bet Allan and Tony here know, and for a shorter stay at Her Majesty's pleasure they'll stuff you like a turkey. Would you like to meet her?

Suyin? No? I bet she'd like to meet you. Tape her up, Bill. Oh, before I forget… your husband doesn't have a bonsai collection, does he?"

She glanced at me with contempt, looking away as Grogan fastened her to the chair by her wrists and ankles. When he'd finished I asked him to nip upstairs and ask Suyin to come and join us. He took the stairs three at a time in his rush and on reaching the landing he called out, "Su, come on down! It's over!"

I heard her shift in her hiding place, then her footsteps as she picked her way to the loft door.

"Come and meet the three people who tried to kidnap you," I heard him say. "I mean, you don't have to but seeing them… well, puts 'em in perspective."

"What is… perspective?"

"Lets you see them for what they really are. Scum. You know what scum is? Course, course…"

He entered the kitchen ahead of her and took her over to Grace and the Devanneys.

"Not much to look at, are they? The young one killed Opinder, by the way, but all three are guilty of murder."

Allan was the only one of them who seemed interested. Suyin puzzled him, dressed as she was in torn jeans and sneakers, a sweater of Jaikie's, God knows how many sizes too big for her. She adjusted her glasses.

"You mean she's a… billionaire?" Allan asked me, quietly.

"Oh, yes. Anything you want to say, Suyin?"

She nodded and scowled at the three of them and eventually spat out, "In China you would die!"

"Here it's worse," said Grogan. "They get to live in a slum prison, all expenses paid. I'll put the kettle on."

I took my mobile from the dresser, stopped the recording I'd made, and phoned Gadsden. He told me that he and Parfitt would be there in an hour. They arrived 53 minutes later.

There's no more to say, really. The trials were due the following March and in the meantime the Devanneys were remanded in custody. So too was Grace Fournier, in spite of weeping and gnashing about her husband's condition. The judge reckoned that anyone who might have brushed a murder under the carpet would be a flight risk.

Suyin Qu came out of hiding and Taylor Mandrake asked her to marry him. She said yes. Neither Bill Grogan nor I think he's right for her... but then we're not marrying him. I just hope I can keep my lip buttoned between now and the wedding.

Laura and I had mixed feelings about Ellie coming home for Christmas. It would be great to see her but that was overshadowed by whatever might be wrong with Terrific Rick.

Yes, I kept the money from the stuffed crane. I thought of it as payment. I mean, it's not as if Suyin needed it. She didn't even remember it was there. If you sense I'm feeling guilty about it, you'd be right, even though I've only spent ten grand of it. Not on me. On Suyin. The rest of it's in the safe. The white crane lives in the corner of the living room. I've grown quite fond of it.

***

I drove to Wimbledon on the first Friday in December, and so did every other human being. London was heaving with that pre-Christmas orgy of spending, the forced jollity of works parties and decorated buildings. And it was cold and wet.

I parked outside the Lindbergs' house. The rain had stopped and the first thing I noticed was their cars. Gleaming white and bright black. The Discovery was more mottled beige, thanks to the country lanes around Beech

Tree. Sir Dirk and his wife were in the front garden: he was up a ladder propped against a branch of the cedar tree, stringing up a set of lights across the boughs, she was footing the ladder. They had both turned to me as I'd drawn up but, having replaced the suit with leather jacket and jeans, they took a moment or so to recall me.

"Ah, Mr… Hawk," said Dirk from on high. "I was wondering where you'd got to."

He descended the ladder and shook my hand with cautious *bonhomie*.

"Are you here for lunch, Mr Hawk?" his wife asked.

"Thank you, but no."

"Right, well… we've had coffee but I could always rustle one up."

"I won't be staying long."

Lindberg smiled at me. "Come on into the house. We'll finish the lights later, my love."

Once in the front hall, Lady Lindberg veered off to the kitchen and her husband led me over to his sanctum. As he unlocked the door the ticking and tocking reached me, but at least I'd timed my visit to five minutes past twelve. There would be no clock-chiming choir doing its stuff for at least another fifty minutes.

"Have a seat," said Lindberg.

"No, thanks."

I took an A3 envelope from my inside pocket and set it down on his desk.

"Details of a friend for whom I'd like you to provide all the necessary…"

He laughed. "Oh, would you?"

I whispered, pantomime style. "If you don't, bang goes your little sideline. The gentleman whose details are in the envelope requires passport, visa, NHS number… well, you're the expert, you tell me what else he needs."

He opened the envelope, took out the A4 sheet and photo I'd provided and reached for his reading glasses.

"A Mr Kueng Qu, by the look of it. Does he plan to use that name?"

"Oh, yes. Unlike the Russians, the Chinese don't send people here to murder their dissidents."

Lindberg thought for a moment and then nodded, prior to giving me one last tug, "The price for my work… let's say twenty thousand?"

"Let's not. Let's say five, on delivery. To me. My address is there…"

He turned, quite distracted, as one of the clocks struck the quarter with an olde-worlde jingle. He checked his watch. Another on the other side of the room joined in. Then another. I hadn't banked on more music.

"I'll leave you to it," I said.

"Sorry, sorry. Yes, nice to see you again, Mr…"

"Hawk."

Somewhere between Wimbledon and Chiswick I broke a lifelong rule that I'd established soon after buying my first car. I took the Discovery through a carwash and returned it to its original colour.

***

Back in Winchendon I parked well away from the big beech and its flock of roosting pigeons. I even toyed with the idea of throwing a tarpaulin over the Discovery to protect my investment, the twenty quid it had cost to clean it. I hadn't noticed the skinny, pasty-looking man sitting on the ground beside the front door. He had blended in with the stonework. His clothes were gray and old, yet refusing to fall apart. He wore a woollen beanie, also grey. He stood up with what appeared to be some difficulty, smiled and came towards me. When I recognised him I expected his first words to be something like, "About this money we've inherited from Ivan, then." Instead he came right up close and said, "Hallo, Dad, how's it going?"

End

Postscript

This serves to remind me that it's unwise to go chasing red herrings, however much they cry out for attention.

The bonsai juniper had nagged at me throughout this case. I believed the Devanneys had stolen it from Jaikie's kitchen drainer to give to whoever they worked for. As a sop, maybe, for failing to deliver the goods. Part of me expected to find it among a collection belonging to Alessandro Scutari, Dirk Lindgard, Nick Fournier... even Professor Ken Blake. It never turned up.

I was partly right. They had stolen it as a present.

I attended the bail hearing for Grace Fournier and I was delighted when the judge remanded her in custody, along with the Devanneys. There was a face in the courtroom that I recognised, that of a middle-aged woman, smartly dressed, hair specially done for the occasion, but in the absence of her pushbike and front basket of vegetables I took a few moments to place her. I still don't know her name, but she was the Devanneys' next-door neighbour. After the hearing she told me in wide-eyed disbelief that two such lovely men as Allan and Tony could not have committed such a vile murder. As an example of their 'loveliness' she cited an example of Devanney Senior's thoughtfulness. He had bought her a present, just five or six weeks ago, to thank her for looking after his allotment. It was a bonsai juniper to add to her collection. It was at least a hundred and fifty years old and must have cost a fortune. Knowing Suyin, I didn't doubt it.

Printed in Great Britain
by Amazon